The Naked Queen

The Naked Queen

A Tangential Arthurian Legend

Discovered, translated, and edited by
Alan R. Hall

To Mary,
My Beautiful Wife,
who will always be
My Queen

To order additional copies of this book, contact:
Xlibris
1-888-795-4274
www.Xlibris.com
Orders@Xlibris.com
783499

CONTENTS

PART IV
THE FREEING OF THE KING, AND THE QUEST OF DARIEN

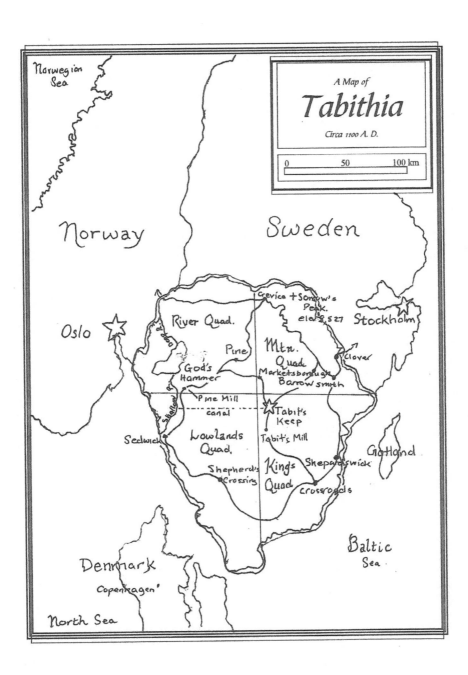

PROLOGUE

In the days preceding Camelot, before Arthur was as we remember him; when his youth and lack of seasoning were still a source of vexation to his ministers; it is said that, early in his reign, just after the sun had brought a bright but chilly Spring morning, the guardian of the gate came and reported that the king did have a visitor. The king asked the guardian the name of this man, and 'twas nought he knew; but the guardian told his liege that this man was a gentleman, who said he brought news to King Arthur from the court of the far-away king, Ballizar, who did rule the kingdom of Tabithia.

Arthur knew neither king nor kingdom, and, his curiosity piqued, he gave the man audience. Immediately upon entry to the walled garden, where Arthur was practicing his falconry, the messenger entreated the king for privacy, as the words he had to tell were for Arthur's ears alone. Perplexed but intrigued, the king sent the servants from the garden, and bade the gentleman deliver his message with dispatch.

"What news, then, of King Ballizar?"

"Your Majesty, the king is dead." The messenger, still on one knee, made his words plain. Artur grew impatient.

"We know of no Ballizar, King or no. What good or ill is his death to us?"

"Sire, my name is Darien. I come to thee to bring the tale of the king's rule, of how he and the queen he chose both ruled, and died. From their wedding to the king's death, 'twas a span of twenty-seven years. I have traveled far, but have found none who could tell me what it means. Then, as I traveled in your country, between the blue and the green mountains, as I walked along a lake, I heard a voice command me to seek thee out, and I found the words wise, for thy name even now is known in lands far from England's shores."

"Her name thou wouldst not recognize, but she is known as the Lady in the Lake. We, too, have heard that voice, and obeyed. Thy telling of it gives thee entry here, and we would have the tale of this King Ballizar."

"'Tis a tale both benevolent and wicked, for the telling begins with sin most evil. I bring my tale to thee in the belief that thou may profit from it, and learn the wisdom buried within. I do so, for I have been burdened with this tale for many a year, and, now 'tis done, I must unburden myself, and leave this heavy mystery with one who may understand it better. Though I am a gentleman of the King's Court, I know not the ways of a king, for surely Ballizar was not like any other. Yet there is something in me that tells me ye are the man I seek. I have come, therefore, many kingdoms cross'd, to present thee with it, a tale I still cannot fathom. It will take minds far more keen than mine to decipher it."

"And how much of this king's reign wouldst thou relate?" asked the king. "For we would hear this tale, but we have yet to break our fast, and would dine. We invite thee to sit here and join us, and tell thy tale; if nothing else it would have earned thee a decent meal."

"Your Majesty is most gracious, I do thank thee. I know my tale might seem a mere folly to a man such as yourself; yet I would tell thee all, though it may take the better part of the morning."

"Should it take the day, we would have it, for thou hast intrigued us greatly. We would hear thy tale as thou wouldst tell it, so pray begin, and we will have our breakfast and thy words together."

"'Tis a tale that has filled many a soul in Tabithia with wonder and fear, for it begins with sin most foul and wicked. I pray that ye shall hear it all, nonetheless, for good doth rise from it.

"I ask thee, Sire, hast heard tale of the Naked Queen?"

"Many a tale, and most wondrous and strange that I thought them tales alone."

"Many a tale be but pure fantasy, brought to light by some knave's wicked imagination. Most of these tales are as false as they are fantastic. But I know the true tale, and it is that which I do bring for thy wisdom."

"'Tis this queen ye wish to speak of?"

"Aye, Sire. It is the tale of Syrenya I have brought thee, and how she did overcome and cease the king's most wicked sins, and teach him belevolence. But tis a tale that begins most wickedly…"

PART I

King Ballizar, First Night,
And the Coming of Syrenya

Chapter 1

The Black Sins of Ballizar

He who would be known, after his passing, as Ballizar the Benevolent, did begin his rule in a most wicked and terrible manner. For several years after he ascended the throne, twas said he would be the Bachelor King, for his queen's throne sat vacant beside him at court. Those rumors would enrage him, for he sought a lady to be his queen most keenly. But those poor women who would vie to be his queen would, on the first night of their stay, flee the castle in pain and fear, never to return.

Those at court did steadfastly conceal this secret, for it was full of shame. Even among those women within the castle, nought could endure the king's prowess and fortitude. 'Twas soon known that even those lusty wenches he commanded take to his bed, could not endure his unslakable desires. The women would appear to the physician, bruised and battered, and yea, torn inside. None would ever speak of their trial, but only hang their heads, and weep most bitterly. The king would not come out of his chambers, and indeed, twas thought a boon, for even through the thick walls, he could be heard raging, bellowing, in such a way as to fright the entire court.

Soon after his sixth anniversary on the throne did pass, the king did bring a blackness to Tabithia, for his desires did o'ertake him, and he began a horrid ritual. Knights had he, brawny men who would do whatever his bidding. Those he would send out to scour the kingdom, and the news they brought back would spell the doom for some wretched woman. From their offerings, the king would select some woman, and this poor damsel would be set to trial, made naked and ashamed, and raped. Yet that was not the least of it. This he did in the full view of his court, who must not only view it, but stay through the entire filthy enterprise.

The maiden—be she wench, lady, wife or no—would be brought to the castle on the first night of each full moon. First Night, the king called it, but twas far too benevolent a name for these black horrors. Stripped she would be, and made to stand before all in her shame. He would command she face him, and would ask questions of her. These were questions no maid should be forced to answer, yet answer she must give, and never softly, but in a voice to be heard 'round the chamber, or it would be painful for her.

He would keep the wretch standing before the court, naked, her head hung down, and her poor body shivering frightfully. Use of these vile questions would at length cause the king to find some dire fault with the woman, and she would straightaway be sentenced, by decree, to endure a trial so severe as to separate her from her sanity; indeed, it did go that way for some. For others, woe and shame would follow, for if a woman were to survive this evil deed sane, she would most likely become heavy with child, a bastard of the terrible knights the king used in his ritual.

Sentence having been passed, the king would put the woman to test at once, her poor and bitter peadings unheard. A feather mattress was brought before the court—so warm and innocent a thing to be put to such wicked use. For the trial was always the same. The woman must bear the weight of twelve men, one immediately after the other. This affliction was presented there, for all to see, even though we could not guess the king's black motives for such a cruelty. Most of those so sentenced could scarce endure half that number, and would be removed, screaming or unconscious, from the court. The bed would be withdrawn, the court dismissed, and the king would settle into a black and sordid musing.

But the test of endurance wrought upon the poor victims of First Night was not even then complete. For twas necessary that these women first endure the evil touch of other women, two wenches who were fair, but born of Lesbos. Their duty it was to try and enflame the woman, and thus prepare her for her trial, but most often the poor maid was so repulsed that it had the opposite effect. Yet never once did the king intervene or bank his lust; he would have the woman destroyed before the court. There were plottings, most coming immediately after First Night, to murder him, so vile a presentation did he command. These mutterings were, however, either never taken up, or squelched by the knights who served the blackened Ballizar.

His ministers and priests did plead with him to stop this bloody ritual, or at least to say its meaning. These entreaties brought forth the king's wrath, and he would rail at them, thus:

"Know thou full well that we do nothing without reason. Our reasons are our own, and we will not be accosted by the likes of thee for explanation!" A black woe did fall upon the castle and the court. The king was greatly feared by all, father, mother, son and daughter. But most by the wretched daughter who was summoned to court, for twas believed from that first summons, that the life of the poor girl was ended.

Arthur slammed his glass on the table in rage.

"By God, thou art a villain, to speak to me thus. This creature ye call Ballizar is no man at all, but a monster! This passes all reason! Varlet, thy tone must change, or we'll have ye thrown from the ballustrade! 'Tis evil ye bring within our walls, and we shall thrash thee for it!"

"Wise king, thou speakest truly," whispered the man, lowering his head. "I did tell thee that this was a tale that began most wickedly, but the worst has passed. The dark night of evil that was upon the reign of Ballizar was deep, but its passing did bring joy and peace to the kingdom, for it brought to our land Ballizar's confessor, forgiver, and the gentle wisdom of the mysterious lady who was soon exalted. Tis this vile First Night that brought to Tabithia the Naked Queen."

CHAPTER 2

Syrenya

Twas near the end of the king's eighth year of reign, and the second of this First Night. The court was assembled and again forced to view yet another, but this night, all would be changed. The king had scarce begun, the poor wretch trembling before him, when a voice did ring from across the chamber, bringing him up short. A woman's voice it was, and all who turned to see her gasped, for this beauteous lady did enter the chamber completely unclad, as naked as the poor child who stood before the king. And in truth, her stunning beauty did lend truth to the words she spoke.

"King Ballizar, I charge thee, to cease this mad ritual and release the child. And if thou would not, I charge thee still, to take me in her place. By any event, this child must be set free."

"By God, but thou art a saucy wench," bellowed the king. "and who might ye be, to speak thus to King Ballizar?"

"My name is Syrenya, born of serenity, reared to love peace. There be no peace in thy kingdom now. Add not to thy sin. I tell thee I shall take this child's place, and ye may have thy way with me. I know what thou wouldst have me do, and this I shall do, but ye must send the child home."

"Tis fair enough." agreed the king. He did wave his hand, and the young woman did grab her stolen cloak and flee, and was forgot soon after her parting. For the entire court did now stare at this raven-tressed stranger, and many did ask, who is she, how came she here, how could she know this place? Those there were who called her witch, or sorceress, others who prayed that she could do as she said, and put a halt to this madness.

Syrenya was a woman most fair, one whom the sculptors would feign have as a model; she did, with no exaggeration, rival Helena in her beauty. She was, too, unknown to all at court; twas certain she had never crossed this chamber before. As the child ran past her, she did advance on the king, and though she was observed by all, she had eyes only for him. Twas easy to see the flame she did ignite in the king, for his eyes burned with unholy light, his body aching for this woman—this could be seen, yea, from across the room.

She stopped scarce an arm's length from the king, and gracefull bowed to one knee; she did bow her head and address the king most respectfully.

"My lord, I come to do thy bidding. Do with me what thou wilt." Even in the speaking of it, she showed no fear, but instead a bearing most poised, and, thought many, of a regal stature. The king demanded that she rise, and she did so, turning her gaze up to meet him, calm as lake water, and she did wait. For a time, neither spoke, each one sizing up the other, until at last, the king broke the silence.

"Whence come ye, woman?"

My lord, tis a place distant, and unknown to thee. To name it would serve thee nought."

"Impertinence! Wilt thou answer us or no? Take care, wench, and trouble me not, or twill go frightful hard for thee!"

"My lord, I would answer. If thou dost like the answer or not, tis the truth."

The two did stare at each other long, the king's face a sea of emotion, hers as calm as a windless day. Then the king did speak again, and his words became familiar to us. He began the ritual.

"Art thou wed, woman?"

"Nay, Sire, I am not. But love I have had, and in abundance."

"What love? Speak of it."

"My lord, three loves have I had, and one within the time of another."

"What, three at once?"

"Nay, Sire, but of a time. None knew of the others."

"So, if loved ye were, as ye say, then ye surely did receive the offer of marriage?"

"My lord speaks true. I did, of each one."

"And yet, thou art still unwed. Thou wouldst break three hearts in thy pride."

"Nay, milord. I broke no hearts. I merely took no husband. Well I was loved, and I sent none away, but kept all. Twas a blessing thrice renewed."

"Say, then, woman, the reason thou dids't refuse. Tis pride, or I am much mistaken."

"Milord, thou art. I had reason enow, and did give it. First, I was not in love. Each of my suitors was dear to me, but not so much as that. Second, there was not one of which could satisfy me. This second reason, I kept to myself. But I did, one day, contrive to have all three, at different times of the day. By the end, I still was not satisfied."

"Then, by God, we shall see what it takes! Where are my wenches?"

At his question, both the nudes, always at court, did rise.

"Here we are…"

"My lord." Twas their way, always to speak on top of each other.

"Take this woman to thy chamber, use thy skills upon her, cloak her as prescribed, and bring her back here to me. Satisfy me, and I will give her up to thee forthwith." This drew a gasp from the court, for the king had never spoken thus before. The two did as the king commanded, and she did go with them; twas thought by some, almost willingly. But though she did follow, twas with a backward gait, for she left the room with her eyes still upon the king, and his, still upon her. Upon the instant she departed the chamber, she did deliver to him a most seductive smile.

CHAPTER 3

Alissa and Ariadne

"Lady, I can see well how thou doest taunt him. I prithee do not. The king is proud, and taunts gone too long on are cruelly punished." This gentle entreaty was spoken by Alissa, fair of skin and hair. Her flesh was so white as to rival alabaster, and her golden hair nearly as white, as well. This she did say to Syrenya immediately they stepped from court, and her blue eyes showed the fear she felt.

"Child, I fear him not. All that he would do, I would have him do. Thy charge is to bring me back to him as prescribed. Pray lead me there, and back again, for speed is of the essence. If I do not return forthwith, I fear the king shall fall on some other poor child, and I will have to win my battle all o'er again. Please, let us make haste!"

"Lady, I would tell thee truly, from the moment thou didst arrive, the king has had eyes for nought but thee. Pray, put your fears to rest." This was spoke by Ariadne, as full fair as her mate, but in different manner. Auburn-haired, green-eyed, with billowing tresses that covered her shoulders, she was in tone of a luscious cinnamon color, as if the sun had touched her often. And indeed, it had touched everywhere; her creamy skin was all of one hue.

"Children, I charge thee, take me back to that chamber as soon as ye can; for what the king would have befall me, I know full well. I know, too, what the next step would be, even though none before me has made it from the first trial to the second."

"Lady, ye speak in riddles," said Ariadne, but she did quickly return to her task. The three walked briskly down the hall and came to the wenches' door. They ushered Syrenya in, and closed and barred the door. Only then did they turn and begin their preparations.

"What has the king commanded thee to do, Alissa?"

"Lady, thou shall be taken, again and yet again. Tis our duty to use our skills to make the coming pain easier, so thee may stand more of it. Ariadne and I are skilled at massage, and have giv'n many a poor wretch ease of the pain." She looked down at the floor, then up again. "Though he hast given us our lives, still it sickens me to see what he hath done to these poor women." The two aided her onto the bed, and began their massages.

"The king has given thee thy lives? How so?"

"Lady, we have both grown here within the kingdom of Tabithia; when we did learn of our desire for each other, twas careful planning required, for were we caught in embrace, we would certainly be cast out, or worse. We did contrive to act as sisters, so we could share a house; that worked for awhile, but soon the miserable populace, that which is dumped at the bottom of the heap, they did grow suspicious of us. Overtures were made that we would be tarred and feathered, if ever there came proof of our union. The trouble would have reached a head if not for the king's knights. Though they saw it as sport, twas our lives they saved. They took us from the village, and we were ridden to the castle, I caught round the middle by one giant arm, Allisa by another, as they drove on. I could see that Alissa did think as I did, that they harmed us not, though if they had plundered us, right before the rabble, those people would have screamed taunts at the doing of it. So we held tight, and prayed, and, it seems, our prayers were answered. That is, after a fashion."

"Upon arrival at the castle, we were stripped; it did put the fear within us all again. We were put before the king thus, naked as babes." Alissa had taken up the tale. "He listened to the knight that brought us in, nodded his head, and sent the man away. He stared at us both with expression scarce to be read, and we, who knew not what came next, did but stare back at him. Presently, after he did examine us all o'er with his eyes, he sat back in his chair and began to speak.

"So, ye two are lovers." We spoke not, and twas wise, for it was not a question that required answering. He merely kept on. "Hast either of ye ever known a man?" At this, we did but shake our heads. He settled into a study, but of what we knew not. When he spoke, his words did make us wide-eyed at our good fortune.

"The pair of thee will join our court," spake he, "and ye shall do so as ye are now. We would have ye show some of the prigs hereabouts that there is more on earth that they have dreamt. Ye shall be taunted and cursed, no doubt, but the court shall hear us, and harm ye not. When ye do go about, outside the castle, ye shall cover thyselves, of course. Thou wilt find clothes enough in thy chambers. Pray follow this child and she will lead thee."

Our thanks and relief, however, fell on deaf ears, for he cut us short.

"Think not thy king has gone soft, ye saucy wenches, for though ye shall have thy lives and each other, know ye that whatever we command thee to do, ye must do it, and with dispatch, and make no bones about it. Is that clear?" Silent nods were sufficient. "All right, then. Be in court this afternoon at three. Between our chambers, and thine, and the court, ye shall not need thy closet. Remember now, we would present thee at court. Fail us not."

Lady, we knew not at all what the king did have in store for us. But we kept our word, and did come to court at three. When we entered, twas a terrible and hateful noise did erupt.

"Sire," screamed one woman, "They are unholy. Wilt thou cast them out?"

"Nay, woman, we will not. These young whelps are here at our command. For 'tis the likes of thee that they are here. Twill teach thee tolerance, or at least the appearance of it, for each and every one of ye shall know, they are now a part of this court. Wenches, attend me."

We did but slowly ascend the throne, but he did grasp our hands and pull us up. He turned us around, and we did stand there, naked, and there was a hiss that rippled through the court.

"Take care, o proud king, for thou dost trifle with God's law." This from one of the priests.

"What does thou know of God's law? Ye know that ye are as ignornat of it as we. These two lasses are fair. They are obedient, like good children. And they are pleasant for mine eye to look upon. All the rest is of no matter.

Tis set: those of this court will accept these two as a part of our court, and do it straightaway. We'll have no harm befall them. If thou shouldst try, thy screams will rend the night, truly. Dost know our mind on this?" Tis a question he asked them often, in a loud and ringing voice, and there was but one answer, a hearty, "Aye my lord!" But though they did respond with the words, twas clear their hearts were not in it. Standing on either side of the king, even there, the weight of the eyes of the court fell upon us. 'Twould be many a fortnight before we could rest our fears."

"And so, thou hast been with the king how long?"

"Five…"

"Nay, six years, Lady."

"Why dost thou call me Lady?" Surprise was their reaction.

"Lady, art thou not?"

"Aye, I am, in mine own country. But I have no such credentials here. 'Twould do me no good, if I had. And that is not why I have come. But no matter. I would know thy ages."

"Lady, I am five-and-twenty. Alissa is twenty-six."

"Then tis clear I must stop referring to thee as children. Very well then: thou art Alissa and Ariadne. I shall remember it. And I thank thee for the work of thy hands. 'Tis a gentle art that ye lend. Now, quickly, what of this cloaking?"

"Lady, the woman must appear before the king, and he shall command that ye undress thyself. Only one has refused. The worms must have eaten her bones by this time. Augh! Twas a foul business…"

"Alissa, dost thou not consider it odd that the king would have me dressed, just to have me undress again? That strikes me as a bit daft."

"Yea, Lady, methinks thou hast the way of it," said the fair one, her voice shaking with damped laughter. "But let it not be heard so. The king is a frightful man when he is crossed."

Twas prescribed by the king, that after these nudes had massaged the night's victim, that she be put into a gauze coverlet; and though it did cover her body, it did cling like skin, and twas so thin that the poor child would feel as naked in it as out. Over this gauze went a black cloak. When brought before the king again, at midnight, she would be commanded to disrobe. Twas hard enough for her to give up the cloak; it were harder still for her to remove the gauze, for it was her only protection, and it was no easy thing to remove. By the time she was done, the poor woman would be weeping.

Ariadne and Alissa dressed this regal woman, gauze first, cloak second, and then checked their handiwork. Alissa pronounced their duty at an end.

"There thou art, Lady, but I must confess this business makes no sense for thee, who doth arrive the way he would have thee, already."

"Very well, then, Ladies, I charge thee: return me to the king." But though she spoke plainly, the two women did not move. She comprehended immediately. "There is more to tell. Pray, then, let's have it." Alissa spoke.

"Milady, immediately before thy trial—and how thou wouldst know what it is is passing strange to me—we two shall be commanded to pleasure thee, again, as a means of preparing thee for the trial. But it is certain that our ministrations have served more to repulse, than to excite. We thought we should prepare thee for it."

"Tis wise of thee, and I thank thee for the news. Fear ye not; for I do enjoy a woman's touch as much as a man's. Ye shall see a sight far different than any poor wetch hast given thee to date. Methinks ye two shall fall upon each other for pleasure before I am done this night. Now, dispatch: let us return to the court."

CHAPTER 4

The Ritual

Syrenya strode boldly into the chamber, followed behind by the two women, as if already they were a part of her train. Tis possible the king did sense this, for he questioned them brusquely. "Thou didst do as we commanded? Hast used thy skills?" But it was the lady who spoke.

"Sire, they did, and twas most comforting, for I have traveled far to be here, and the rest was pleasant. But, Sire, I have come to thee for a purpose, and I would have that purpose begun. Look on me, and command me what I am to do, for I am ready."

"Then, wench, hear us well." The king had pushed himself forward, sitting on the edge of his throne, so that he could see her better. She was nought two feet beyond his reach. "We do command thee first, if thou art an obedient woman, to doff thy cloak, and face us full."

The lady did then perform such a stunt as did almost wring laughter from the court; twas only the king's stern countenance that did prevent it. She loosed the bow at her throat, caught the cloak at its top corners, and did swirl it around herself twice, before letting it fly—directly into the seat of the empty throne beside the king. It did make him growl, but though he picked it up and shook it, he did place it there again.

"Wench, thou art too full of impertinence. We trow we will teach thee some manners this night. Now, woman, before our court, remove thy gauze, and feel their eyes upon thy shame."

She actually laughed, a low chuckle that was pleasing, though by no means to the king.

"My lord, I do but return to the state in which I came. Tis as natural for me as clothes are to thyself. But I will do as thou hast commanded, for I have a point in't." She slowly, at that range, indeed seductively, unwrapt herself from the fabric, and when twas done, she did gather it up in her hands and, thrusting it forward with her head bowed, laid it on the king's lap. All did jump in surprise; twas known throughout the court, nay, any court, that rash touching of the king was forbidden. It did, indeed, cause the king himself to jerk back, as if that lacy thing were a viper or the kind. But the lady dropped it reverently into his lap, touching him not. But with it, she did speak this most mysterious thing.

"My lord, I do as thy will commands. And I return this wrap to thee, for tis yours and will be yours, aye, and all that it has enveloped, as well." Twas clear the king had had enough; he did bellow enough to fright the maids, though she closest to him did ne'er flinch.

"I obey, my lord but in my mind I would feign move directly to part three." Again she had succeeded in silencing him, and yea, all the court, as well, for we know nothing of what she spoke.

Alissa and Ariadne did advance slowly, and came to each side of her. She reached out and took their hands, placing each on one of her breasts. "My sisters, I am yours, and would feel thy pleasuring most greedily. Have me, sisters; for I know twill please the king if ye do press thy affections upon me. Come my sweets, and kiss me." This brought forth a loud but mixed reaction from the crowd. Some saw evil; others, wonder; still others were perplexed by it; and others still, inflamed. Twas a strong man indeed who could watch three lusty wenches pleasure each other, and remain unmoved. At one point, and twas long after they had begun, the lady did reach a hand out toward the throne. "My liege, wouldn't thou join us? T'would please me greatly." This was more than the king could bear.

"Enough!" he bellowed, and frightened, Ariadne and Alissa retreated in fear. "Thou dost think ye can trifle with this court, naked, subservient, bold and impertinent all in one. But we shall hear thy tune change when ye face the twelve. With dispatch, then; here is thy bed, wench. Now, bring in the first man!"

The ritual, now a full two years old, had changed greatly between the start and now. At the beginning, t'would be the duty of the woman to undress the men she must endure. Now, they came forward naked, eager to be done with this business and get away again. 'Twas decided among the men that those who would be last in the previous First Night, and therefore almost assuredly would not be used at all, would have to be first the next time. Thus first came Crandall, a brawny man with a giant red beard, who did advance on her with a weapon that was cocked and ready. But the lady did not shy, but instead, advanced on him. It brought him to a stop. She moved toward him most seductively, and opened her arms to him.

"Sir, I can see thou dost want me. Wouldst join me in my bed this night? Thou dost have the look of skill about thee, and I would wish to give thee a merry romp. Pray come, and have me. For tis decreed, I am yours, and ye may do with me what thou wilt."

This bold, seductive tone perplexed the man; but it did moreover excite him, and he moved quickly to fall upon her, where she waited with open arms and a smile that would flatter any man. He did take her roughly, and she chuckled at it; though the way of it had become 'make swift work of it, and fly,' not this night. For the lady, rather than fight him in vain, did instead pleasure him, and before long they were in a lusty union. She did keep up a patter meant to enflame the man, praising his prowess, urging him to work faster, and faster still. Then she said loudly, as if she meant for all to hear, "Yes, good sir, lead me again up thy mighty mountain, from the top of which I may fly, and fly again!"

This baffled the king, but did prick up the ears of the wenches, who moved forward, and to either side of the lovebed.

"My lord, thou didst charge us early on, that we should count those pleasurable explosions that are a woman's gift for pleasuring her man. Until now, there have been nought to count. But now, we have already counted three. Woulds't have us count them all?"

"Yes dammit, count! I do demand it!"

"Yes, my ladies, do; for if I leave the counting to thee then I may concentrate more on this most excellent man!" Then she did match word to deed, and enflame him once more with her lips and her fingers. She was intent upon having him receive his pleasure, as well. But while they did enflame each other, the woman whispered something to the man, and as a result, he rewarded her with a powerful kiss. She had pitched it to be for his ears alone, but Ariadne, who was close on that side, did hear it, as well.

"Sir, I do thank thee, thou are a pleasing romp. Pray tell thy fellows to come to me unafraid, for I will give them all I did give to thee. Speak truly, for thee, thy mates, and I shall put a stop to this First Night, here and now. After tonight we shall see no more of it."

Shortly thereafter, Crandall left the chamber, but it was too long a moment before the next arrived. The king nearly burst forth in wrath; the man's entrance came with no time to spare. He went immediately to work, for he feared to look at the king. But Syrenya welcomed him, and what ensued was much the same as Crandall had been, before. No screams, no piteous struggle, but a true and lusty union she did make of them, as if they were completely alone upon their marriage bed. And the prophesy she did put to the two woman earlier did come to pass; indeed, twas not only the wenches who did fall upon one another with desire, so enflaming was the spectacle that this astounded court did witness.

By habit, the king did start First Night upon the stroke of midnight; usually, twas over in less than two hours, though long and hated hours they be. This night, the men came and went, and twas the tenth, the eleventh, and finally the twelfth that came to take this woman. And from start to finish she did welcome them, please them, and by all accounts, be the happier for it. All the court was silenced when the last man left her bed, and some did say, regretfully. But now, for the first time, the ritual had been completed; and now we knew not what to expect. The lady lay, spent but smiling, and did hum a tume so soft, it barely reached the people; twas for the king alone she did murmer so.

As for the king, he did not seem so much surprised, as baffled. Twas clear to all that she had come knowing what she must do, and i'faith, she did do it, and to the very end. Now, as the sun was rising, and the first rays of light slanted into the chamber, so too did she rise from her lusty bed, and return again to the king, and gracefully bow down as she had before. Her voice cut through heavy stillness, and still it did have that regal tone.

"My liege, I have done as thou hast commanded. Does it please thee?"

The king said nothing; he did merely stare at her for the longest time. During that time, she never spoke nor moved, and yea, the court did the same. Fully a quarter hour had passed before the king spoke, and when he did, it was in a tone that none had ever associated with this filthy business.

"Thou hast completed the first two parts of the Ritual. Ye are the first to do so. This has earned thee rest, and food, and shelter until the night comes. When it does, we shall send for thee, and thou shalt come. Then ye shall know the third part of this ritual."

"Aye, my lord, I will; and for me, the time will be a very long time, indeed."

As she spoke, the sun burst into the chamber in its entire morning splendor, and, as if told it out loud, we did know that First Night would come no more. Before the crowd dispersed to leave the chamber, there was a hearty cheering, and men did hug their wives, and slap the backs of their fellows, and tears did run aplenty. While this was done, neither the king nor the lady moved. After the crowd had left the chamber, all abuzz about this newly come relief, the king reached out his right hand and touched the top of her head, gently.

"Woman, thou art bold indeed, to know of thy task and to come here nonetheless. Thou must go with these ladies and rest, and let them work their art upon thee, for thou must surely be beyond weariness. Food is being prepared for thee. Woulds't thou have thy cloak?" With this question, he did pick up the garment, but Syrenya, now standing upright again, spoke quickly.

"Nay, my lord, I prithee, leave it where it is. I shall come to claim it anon." With that, she turned, and linked arms with the two who now seemed as if bound to her, and the three did walk slowly, almost regally, from the chamber. But again, as she had done before, she turned and gave the king a smile the like of which would turn most men's knees to water. Then she spoke.

"Until tonight, my liege, when I will attend thee." And then they were gone. The king, now having been shown the end of this blackness, never stirred, but did sit there, tis thought, astounded, for many long moments, before he, too, rose and left the court.

"Methinks, Darien," said Arthur easily, 'thou dost play us for sport. Ye tell this tale as if ye were present at every instant. But thee and we know tis not possible. Judging your age to be not much more than thirty, ye would still be a lad when this Syrenya came to Tabithia; ye would have known nothing of any of this for years yet."

"Sire, thou dost know my mind. I was, indeed, only a child when Syrenya first entered the castle. But for reasons I have never been able to descern, the Queen, Ariadne, and Alissa would tell me these things, over and over, for hours at a time, as if they wanted to be sure I remembered all of it. It is carved in my brain, word for word, as I have told it to thee."

"I had thought as much. But ye know not what the reason be? Surely, they did decide twould be you by some action or event that did single thee out. Is there no such event ye can recall, then?"

"None, Sire, though I have wracked my brain o'er it. But special I must have been, truly, for the queen did come to call me Son. But I shall speak of that anon; it comes later in the tale."

"Have on, then. Perhaps the story, when told to new ears, will yeild up its secrets."

"Milord, were it so, twould be a blessing to me…"

CHAPTER 5

After, and Before

Scarcely had the door swung shut, before both Ariadne and Alissa set up a squealing with their o'erflowing delight. The two did speak at once, and bubbled with excitement so they could scarce be understood. Syrenya had to quiet them before she could make head or tail of their energetic discourse.

"Oh, Lady, what a night thou hath brought to us!" Alissa was breathless with her excitement, and gulped air as she spoke. "Ye have broke the spell, Lady. Ye will be exalted in this kingdom for thy sacrifice, and thy glory!"

"Lady, there are those here who will bless thee for thine actions tonight. Is this the reason ye have come? To fulfill these several parts of the ritual? How couldst thou have known? How could it have reached thine ears, in this country of yours, so far away?"

"My darlings, I will tell thee. I shall tell the king, as well, anon. But pray, keep this news a secret, for full knowledge may stir evil within the court. For we who are the Peacemankers are often mistaken for creatures thine own court would fear, and seek to destroy. Promise me."

"We promise, Lady. But what is this ye speak of? Who are the Peacemakers?"

"The Peacemakers have been taught to use every device they can muster to return peace to lands in fear. We do love peace; it is our commitment to restore it where ever it may be restored. We are not always successful, but we make the attempt, nevertheless. When we were brought word of what was transpiring in this court, and we mulled it over, twas decided that I was the best of us to take it on. I am here in that cause. I plan to stay until I have completed my quest."

"Lady, ye do make my head buzz all 'round with thy riddles," Ariadne said, shaking her head as if to clear it of these words that meant so little to her. "But if thou hast come to bring this land peace, then ye have already done more than anyone has ever done, now that ye have shattered this wicked ritual!"

"The ritual was only the first part of the task, my sweets. Tonight I will know if I can complete my test, or must admit defeat. I will know, and ye, too, shall know, whether I stay, or else defeated, leave this place. If the king has plagued his kingdom with this ritual, it is indeed for a specific reason, though the way he went about it seems deranged, as if he were driven to it. But enough, I beg thee! Until I am with the king tonight, there is nought to do but sleep, and prepare. I would have some of that food the king mentioned, for such a night's work is a hungry business."

Alissa skipped toward her chambers, and pointed. "See, Lady, they do bring it now, to our chamber. Come and eat, and we shall relax thee, and ye shall sleep, safe and well." She turned and impulsively leapt in Syrenya's direction, and gave her a massive embrace. "Thou are like a savior, Lady, and I am so very happy thou hast come!"

"Oh Alissa, he forgot…" Ariadne's words needed no explanation, for Alissa understood immediately. The two giggled together, as if they held a great secret. They turned and grinned at Syrenya like cats in the cream.

"All right, ye saucy wenches, out with it!" she challenged, in mock demand.

"Lady, thou didst provide much sport this night, for the knights obviously, and for the court, as well. But ye were amply rewarded for thy work. Thou didst have—and I cannot believe it still!—thirty-seven orgasms tonight!!"

"Tis so? Well, then, I did better than I thought. I only counted thirty-three." This, and the wry look she gave them, were enough to send Ariadne and Alissa into spasms of laughter. For a long minute, there was nought that could hush them. The only way she could think to stop them was to take each by the arm and propel them all toward chamber, food, and rest.

Once they were inside, Ariadne barred the door again. The action had puzzled their guest the first time; now she had to ask. Alissa sobered almost immediately, though it was clear her mirth had not been fully depleted.

"Oh, Lady, we must; there have been several attempts to enter this chamber by people who meant nought but mischief. Once was a man so besotted by drink, he was convinced he could 'cure' us of our 'affliction.' Together we did bowl him out again. But also there have been the king's holy men, who have beaten on the door and cursed us, when they found their way blocked. Even though we enjoy the protection of the king, methinks there be those about the castle who would willingly suffer his wrath, if only they could relieve themselves of the pair of us. We have told the king as much, and since that time we have noticed that the knights are more visible to us than they once were. I think the king would be sure that those who might do us harm would be better stopped before, rather than after, any attempt. I do confess it; I think he doth love us."

"Alissa!" Ariadne burst out. "Thou hast never told me so!"

"And with good cause, to hear the shock in thy voice, my sweet. But ye know what I say is true. Thou hast commented on the knights being more in view of late."

During this conversation, the three had begun to pick over the ample tray of food that sat on the table. They were gathered 'round it, eating as they talked, and picking out this morsel and that, as they stood.

"To tell thee true, Ariadne," said Syrenya, "I do believe much as doth Alissa. Methinks the king hath loved thee both, and for quite a time. Both of ye know thy place is closest to the king of anyone in court, including the priests."

"Hast never spoke of it," Ariadne returned, petulantly, and it was a question whether she meant the king or her mate. "It might have saved me many a fright. There are times I have full feared his temper. When his troubles do plague him, hast happened more than once that he hath injured some poor member of the court, though he hath been filled with regret after. I fear if he were to take it in his head to do so, he could take me off this earth with the back of his hand."

"Then ye should know he doth love us, for even in his most vile temper, he hast never even threatened thee, nor me, either. But I do know full well of what ye say, sister; I have seen him lay low a man, twere he ever so unfortunate as to be nearby when the king was afflicted."

"Afflicted?" asked the lady. "What is thy meaning? Describe it to me."

"Lady, dost remember what we told thee, uh—twas only last night? That the king could find no woman that could withstand him? His doctors have tried many a means to relieve him of his pain when the desire is upon him. So hot doth it grow in him that he fair rages, as if caught up in a flame."

"How often doth he become so?"

"That is the peculiar thing, Lady," Alissa replied. "It doth come on him all of a sudden, and with no pattern the doctors can predict. Thou hast put a stop to this wicked business, Lady, but if thou wouldst fully appease him, then thy work is far from done."

"Well I do know it. Can we bathe? I am sore in need of a scrubbing." Syrenya wrinkled her nose as she spoke. And if any has cause, twas she. Ariadne nodded, but spoke in a different manner.

"Thou hast a most pleasant scent about thee, Lady. Tis enow to make me wish to return to our affections in court."

"Not," spoke the Naked Queen, "until I am bathed and presentable. Then I would have thee take me to thy bed. Ye have become most sweet to me, and good lovemaking will relax me so I may sleep. I have as much work to do this night as last!"

"Then we shall attend thee, and give thee thy bath. Twill be a lovely preamble..."

Both took an arm, and Alissa and Ariadne led their new lover to the pool that was theirs, within the walled court outside their chamber. To their delight, the servants had provided urns of hot water, and the three did immerse themselves and bathe, though there was not so much the need to scrub as apparent as were the pleasures of the water, and each other's gentle touch.

Great thick and bleached towels were at hand, and the three brusquely dried each other, the act a form of foreplay. By the time the two had put Syrenya to bed in their large and ample four-poster, all were inflamed, and sleep did not come for many a sweet hour. But the afternoon sun found all three curled around each other in blissful and innocent sleep, and there they did stay until nightfall.

Alissa awoke to find their guest absent, and took a start and woke Ariadne. But a moment spent with her head cocked relieved their fears.

"She hath returned to the pool, love. Methinks she doth prepare herself for the king."

"I fear for her, Ariadne. Suppose she meets with the same fate as all the others? Then all shall be in vain, for after last night, the king will be deep in his desires."

"Fear not, my sweet," said Syrenya, returning from the pool as she dried her hair. "I do know what is in store, and if I am right, then I shall have as wild a night tonight as I did last! Fear not, Alissa. I am well prepared; he shall not hurt me. If I am right, he cannot. But even if he can, he will not let any harm befall me."

"How can ye be so certain, Lady?" begged Alissa.

"For the same reason he hath never hurt thee, Alissa. The king doth love me."

"Well," spoke the king, with his head shaking. "We shall be in need of a companion in our bed this night, and no mistake. But thy tale hath reached only the second day, and already the morn is half over. We can imagine what did unfold, for thou hast said Ballizar did make her his queen. Why not proceed to a point beyond the night? I am tested to believe thou dost tell so lusty a tale for the joy of it."

"Sire, I tell it because I am charged to do so. The Queen herself said unto me, 'My son, when thou dost tell this tale, leave out not a syllable, as I have taught it thee. If men are to know of this good fortune, pray they have it all, and let not civility rule thy tongue. Say all.'"

"Well, then, we cannot ignore entreaties of a woman gone on to her reward, can we? Come within, Darien, and we shall discourse in warmer surroundings." For indeed, the day had grown colder, and clouds scudded the sky. The two walked slowly into the castle, and Darien was amazed at the sheer size of it. He did remark that King Ballizar's castle, though it did fit the definition, was nought compared to this.

"It is the English way," answered Arthur, and amusement found its way into his voice. "Though we be reserved by nature in our person, we are grand in our architecture. Let us tarry here awhile," so saying as he turned into a room. "And we shall enjoy the comfort of a fire. Spring it may be, but in England the Winter doth not surrender so easily."

"My lord, thy kindness humbles me. I hope that this lengthy discourse will serve thee well, for thou hast been a most honorable host..."

CHAPTER 6

In the King's Chamber

They heard a knock upon the door, and Alissa inquired who was there. Twas a squire, a servant of the court; he said he had been sent to bring Syrenya to the king. Without another word, Syrenya kissed both her friends, and unbolted the door and stepped out. Her sudden appearance did cause the youth discomfort, for he did blush all scarlet, and lower his head; he would not look at her.

"Lady, pray cloak thyself!" he did beg, for it was obvious that he had never before been in the presence of a naked woman. "I am to bring thee forthwith to the king, but I can scarce look on thee. Thy beauty stings mine eyes."

"Then close them, young squire, and if ye cannot view me, pray hear me, then. Wast thou not in court o'er last night?"

"Nay, Lady, it is forbidden for servants to be in the court during First Night. But I have heard rumor that the woman brought before the king last night did fulfull his commands, and that First Night has reached an end. We were all undone by the news, for we all did believe that the ritual would go on until there were no maids left inside Tabithia."

As she listened to him, Syrenya took his arm and turned him toward the king's chamber. He did not pull away, but he did blush deeply. She spoke to him softly, as if to calm his nervous fears.

"Good youth, I am that woman. And now I am to meet the king in his chambers, and see if I may bring peace to king as well as kingdom."

"Oh, Lady, it doth afright me to hear thee say it!"

"Why so?"

"Lady, we have watched a full torrent of ladies enter that chamber, and all were of a mind they could content him. But there has been nought who could assuage him; indeed, quite the opposite. Women have left his chamber battered and bleeding! I am afraid for thee, Lady, that ye may meet with the same fate as all the others."

"Fear not, my lad. I do know full well what I have been summoned to do, and with luck, I will do it, and all will be well. But thou hast yet to open thine eyes, squire. Woulds't not look on me? Am I not fair?"

"Oh, Lady, truly! But thy beauty doth do me discomfort." And indeed his squirming did prove it. He was full blown by her touch. "I have yet to share the flesh with any woman, though I have longed for it. I have not the skill to bring a wench to my bed. Not even the serving maids take me seriously. I feel the proper fool, and do smart for it." His demeanor had become so downtrodden, that Syrenya stopped their progress. She did look this way and that, but twas known that she was to come to the king, and no one barred their passage at all.

"Fair youth, hear me. Twill be a lesson giv'n in haste, but I will show thee the proper way to make a woman take notice of thee. First, thou must be bold, for it is the duty of a man to ask a maid for kisses. She will not bestow them unless asked."

"I know not how to kiss, milady."

"And that is what I am about to show thee. First, relax this pent up stiffness, and teach thyself to relax. There, that's better. Keep an eye out; there are few women who cannot detect a roving eye. Engage some lass in conversation; compliment her hair, her dress. Though they may mock, few young women can withstand honest flattery. Then take her with thy fingers under her chin, thus, and turn her face up to thee. Pay close attention, for if she would have thee kiss her, twill be thy lips she will watch. Once ye have ascertained it, gently place thy lips against hers, thus..." Syrenya kissed the youth, and gave him full benefit of lips, teeth, and tongue. The youth was near defeated; if she had not held to him, he would have slid to the floor in his rapture.

"Now, then, squire, kiss me, and show me thou hast learned from the lesson."

He did tremble a bit, but made himself bold, and kissed the lady, and did almost deliver to her what she had to him. Syrenya declared him a model student, and that, when next they did meet, she would ask of him if his wooing had begun. His eyes watered, and he took her hand and pressed his forehead to it, and gave her a thousand thanks. Then, seeing that by now they were within sight of the king's chamber, he did pull himself up and race away, before Syrenya could speak again. She smiled after him, then went to meet with her own wooer.

She did not knock; she merely pushed open the door, stepped in, and shut it behind her.

"Lock it," said the king, hoarsely, from across the room. He was standing, cloaked, with his back to her. She did so. Turning back, she could see he was all in shadow, and still did face the wall. When he spoke, twas not the voice of a king, but of man in torment.

"Syrenya, I prithee, fail me not! For if ye are defeated by these demon desires, then I fear I shall be damned." He spoke in what came out as a moan, for all pained was he.

"Sire!" she cried, "Thou art in agony! Let me relieve thee!" She took the few steps that separated them, turned the king, and came upon what was a bane to other women. But she did scarce mark it, before she was on her knees before him, and took the bulbous head between her lips, and stroked it with her tongue, while she did move her hand up and down the shaft in slow rhythm. He went stiff, and his robe fell to the ground. She reached out and drew him nearer, and brought his tormented stiffness a little more into her mouth, and touched the base of the head with her tongue. A few moments more, and twas done. The king looked down on her with something on his face that may have been thanks, may have been wonder, but still within that face did blaze the red coals of his lust. He spoke not, but reached out, possessed her, and swung her into his arms and carried her bodily to the bed. Now, she knew, came the last trial, for in moments she would know if she had succeeded, or failed.

His lips sought hers, and pressed in upon her. She took his head in her arms, and ventured to return the kiss in kind. It broke loose his fires, and he became nought but pasison, and need, and desire. These first few hours, she knew, would tell her if, finally, some woman who could handle him would bring him peace. If she could not slake his desires, then she will have failed, and brought but respite to the people of Tabithia, until the king's unholy desires did again o'ertake him. She caressed him, yeilded her body up to him, and whispered sweetly in his ear.

"Yes, my Liege; come into me, and I will hold thee sweetly. Thou may rest thy fears, Sire. For I have come for no other reason than to release thee from thy torment. Ye may possess me, and make of me thine own, and I shall bring to thee sweet peace. Do it, my Liege, for now is the moment of truth. Have me. Have me, Sire!"

He could no longer withhold, and took her roughly. She had but a second's doubt, but then knew that all was well. He did fit her—snugly, but he fit. And that was all she needed to know. Now all would be as it should be, and this mighty king would win his battle against his darkness, and know peace. And thus, so would his subjects.

Immediately the king possessed her, he felt a cool comfort surround his swollen gland. She did grip him, and move under him, and he was filled with fire. Ride her hard, he did, and scarce was aware of it, for he burned so that he must find release, or be consumed. She did fit her body to him, and match his rhythm, and though it seemed a very long time, he was soon released, and fire flowed from his loins into hers. He was afraid, for a moment, for it was here that most women fled from him, screaming. Not this night. She was here, and she would stay here, and his desires would be routed. Now at rest, he puffed as he lay atop her, and her cool hand stroked his back, and she did smile up at him.

"Art thou still here, milady?" he asked, as if to be sure. "Thou hast not up and fled, like all before thee?"

"Nay, Sire, and never will. I have crossed many lands to find thee, and now I have, ye shall not be rid of me. I shall stay, and be thy concubine, and ye will know peace at last." But his reaction did put a start into her, for he grabbed her wrists forcefully, pinned her to the bed, and growled his disapproval.

"Never! Thou art no concubine. Thou art a Lady, my Lady, and I shall exalt thee. Thou shalt be the King's Consort, and Queen of Tabithia. For I would wed thee straight, and bring to thee thy wedding dress. At first light, it shall be done. By evening, we will be wed. By the following morn, thou shalt sit beside me at court, and there shall be no more talk of this Bachelor King. Behold us here, the King and Queen of the Land!"

Syrenya's eyes did o'erflow, and she did hard embrace him. "Oh, my good lord, speakest thou truly? I shall be thy bride? Tis all I have hoped for, from the time I did set out for this place. Take me, Sire, please again, for thy words heve enflamed me, and I would have thy wondrous size again inside me. Wondrous large thing! It doth fill me, and I do believe I shall at last know satisfaction. Come, my lord, and fill me, and I shall come for thee throughout this, our night of long-sought bliss. Take me, sire, and slake thy thirst, for the more thou doest drink of me, the more there is to give! Oh! Oh, yes. YES! Thou ART my lord! AHH! Press in upon me, for I do fly! Oh, sweet mercy! My lord, give me thy stamina, and press me long beneath thee. For I am thine, truly, and thou mayst have me at thy will! Thou shalt ride me to the dawn, and I thy fiery steed shall be. And thou cans't ride me at a trot, and post upon me. It is a mighty stand! Onward to day, and keep me in want of thee, and we shall know sweet succor."

In this vein did she talk him through the night, and keep him stiff for her, and she did hold him firm, and move for his pleasure. Though it was now somewhat abated, his fiery need was still upon him, and she would have it so, for she did need him just as much.

The night moved into its full darkness. The two did pause, and match their breathing, and give a brief respite. Syrenya again gave out with that seductive low chuckle, and straight the king queried her.

"My lord," she asked, with a trace of the imp in her eyes, "wouldst have me bound? Spread out on this great four-poster, or tied to yon post, and helpless before thy desires? I confess it doth fire my loins to think on't."

"By god, but thou art a game sport! I would have asked many before thee, but most did shy, and, if pressed, flee; but never once did any suggest the course, and desire it! My Queen, the Wench! I shall tie thee, and thou wilst beg me for my mast before I am through with thee. See here!" He reached across to the bedside table, pulled forth the drawer, and brought out a handful of brightly colored fabrics. They were but lengths of ribbon, but their purpose was to some women a fear, and to others a delight. The king pushed himself up, and back off the bed, and then he did playfully pull her by the legs, until she did stand upright against him. He lifted her arms, and had her clasp the heads of the bedposts; then he quickly tied them there. Syrenya felt a rush of passion, and strained to kiss her captor, and his hands did explore and discover and know her well. He did find all her secret places, and give her delirious pleasures. This went on for nigh a half-hour, and Syrenya reveled in her helpless desires. But soon she was at the end of her tether, and she begged the king a boon.

"Sire," she breathed, "Prithee, have me! I am undone from thy favors, and I am all fire! Grant me this boon, Sire. Within, I beg thee!"

He moved behind her, crawled onto and knelt on the bed. Leaning forward, he kissed her naked shoulders, the sweet nape of her neck, as he reached down, took her by the loins, and pulled her body back towards him. She wondered what he was about to do, as he did move her well off the ground, her legs thrust out before her by the bed. With his breath in her ear, he moved her up his thighs until she was in posiiton, and then he possessed her, and she did keen, in high sweet voice, at the pleasure he did give her. He reached around and took her plump breasts in his hands, and did give them a gentle squeezing, that sent her higher. Her hips did grind as of their own volition, and fly she did, and many times, before they were through.

She was fair spent after these ministrations, but he lowered her until her feet again found the floor, and moved around in fromt of her. He took her head in his hands, and began bestowing kisses upon her, but what was at first sweet did turn to lusty flame, for his intent was to have her all o'er with his tongue. She was near crazed by it, and moaned softly between gasps of air. His final kiss he bestowed upon her delta, but he did tarry there long, and brought his lady to many an explosion of passion.

Still aflame, he took her standing, and tied though she was, she did wrap her legs around him, and rock them both. The king was a long time finishing his work, and at the end, the two were, if only for a time, spent.

Lying alongside her delicious body, the king stroked her gently, and something akin to a purr did issue from her lips. He began to tell her of the wedding to come.

"Syrenya, thou shalt be a most wondrous bride! When thou dost see the gown I would have thee wear...I can see thee in it in my mind's eye, and though it be now nearer than ever before, I am filled with wonder at the spectacle!"

"My king, and soon husband, let me query thee. For I would with grateful joy wear for thee my wedding dress; but only that. The robes and gowns of a queen are strange to me, and I would ask thee to grant me a boon. Cover me not, but let me remain as I am, and show this whole country—nay, this whole world—how I do belong to thee."

"Syrenya, I have planned many a year to learn thee, but it will be a most educational time, for thou art fair full of surprises! Woulds't thou truly go about as ye have, with nought to warm thee or shield thee from prying eyes? For prying eyes there will be, truly, after the experience this court had last night. I fear ye would become the source of many a pinch and tickle, and though I think ye might enjoy it a little, it is not the way of a queen to weather such."

"Milord, well I do know it. But thou mayst prevent such with but a word, and none would dare touch me that I would not have do so. But though I have lived in nought but my skin, and would feign continue, there is also another reason for my wish. I would have thee know that, at any time, at any place, when thy desires do strike thee, I will be ready, and willing, to come to thy aid, and we shall battle those dark forces together. Always it will be so, if it is within my power to have it thus. I know full well what I ask, milord, but I do ask it of thee most humbly. Clothe me not, for I would feel imprison'd; I know thou would not do so to me."

"My Queen, I may at some time, years hence perhaps, wonder how thou hast spellbound me. I find that I am helpess to keep from thee anything that thou woulds't wish so heartily. But I do have something for thee that may change thy mind, if only a little." He rose from the bed and moved to his chest, opening the massive lid. It rose silently, for all its weight, and from within he drew a scarlet cloak, bright as new fire and ring'd all 'round with the whitest ermine. He took it up gently and brought it to her.

"This, my queen, is thy badge of office. I have thought that, when at last I did have a queen by my side at court, that she should wear it, and thus prove herself ready to rule. Wilt thou not? It is fair gorgeous a cloak, is it not?"

"My lord, I am struck. Truly, it is a most beautiful garment. Let me say this, and see if thou dost approve. This cloak shall take the place of the one that rests on the throne now—I did tell thee I would return to claim it—and it shall cloak the throne where I will sit. When I do, I shall pull it forward over a shoulder, thus donning this regal office without having to fully do so. For I do, even in the face of this scarlet beauty, eschew clothing. I have done so all my life. If I do as I have described, will it be enough? Methinks I shall fall to stroking it, cloaking me or no, for tis a most wonderous wrap!"

The king pondered this, seriously, for he knew there would need to be some compromise here. As is so with any marriage, regal or not. He decided it would be so, and told her as much. Her delight was instantaneous, and she did bolt into his arms. Before long, they had again taken to their bed, for twas still many hours before dawn, and furious activity, would come to them.

PART II

The Queen of Tabithia

CHAPTER 7

The Wedding Dress

Both Alissa and Ariadne slept little that night, full of all that was happening around them. This woman was a wonder! They did try to imagine what was going on in the king's rooms, and talk of that and how it had come to pass did make the hours fly. Twas already dawn, and though they both wished to hear of how the night had passed, they were heavy with the want of sleep, when suddenly there came a hamering on the door that did roust them rudely from their slumbers. At first the two thought that there was another intruder at hand, but they straight did hear Syrenya's excited voice beg them entry, and they flew from their bed to admit her. Her hair was all disheveled, and she did have that lusty scent of musk that Ariadne had noticed before, but her words were wondrous to the ears of these two, who never dreamt to hear them spoke at all.

"Ladies, Ladies! See my joy! It is done, the king is new and well, and he hath sent me to fetch the pair of thee, for I need thy help, and quickly! Come, and go with me to see my wedding dress! He did tell me straight, that he swore long ago that she who could drive out his demon lusts would straight become his queen, and he hath proposed! Nay, neither, but he did declare it! That I would be Queen of Tabithia, and wed this very day! Oh, my darlings, come in haste! He hath described a gown so wondrous I must rest mine eyes upon it, to tell if it be real. Oh, sisters, I am o'rjoyed! We shall be free of these demonics, and I shall wear a crown! Quickly, then, take me to the tailor's, for he has gone ahead to fetch it, and ye must lead me there. Hurry, darlings, I am in haste! Fly, or I shall outpace thee, and know not where I go."

Though the two would question her at length, there was nought to do but obey, for Syrenya was jubilant, and they were charged to keep up with her. They made two wrong turns before coming to the door of the tailor's, and she suddenly stopped. Taking a deep breath, and brushing out her hair with her fingers, she whisered to them ever so softly.

"Now, my sweets, let me take my breath, and then we shall enter, but with grace, I pray; twould not become a lady to appear too eager, especially when all but the doing of it is settled! Hush! For I hear him within. Now tell me, ladies, how fond of thy naked bodies thou art, for if thee are to be my bridesmaids, gowns there must be for thee. Nay, nay, hold thy questions! There will be time enow, and I wish to tell thee all, but now I must be fit to my wedding gown, and must show my king proper respect, for he is passing proud of it, and wants my reaction. Let us enter peacably, then, and know I will tell thee all anon. Now, then, Ariadne, knock the door. Speak first, Alissa, and tell the king ye have brought me here as he did command. Now, go in."

Alissa's head was all abuzz, but she did with but a small difficulty recite her lines, and the three of them did now bow to their king. He did smile so benevolently, that the two were put in wonder. But he took the hand of their charge, and brought it to his lips, and gently kissed it. Then he moved himself aside, and in the center of the room was a gown that brought gasps from them, so fine a gament it was! Syrenya said nothing, for her eyes said all. Her tears did flow, and she had such a look of bliss upon her counteance, that her king was fair pleased. She reached out for it, and stepped nearer; her other hand covered her mouth, but even so could not cover that smile. When she had reached it, she knelt down on her knees and gathered up the skirt of it, and laid her cheek upon it, and for a few moments felt a sweet rapture; then she turned to her king, and knelt to him on one knee, and her words were soft and loving.

"Oh, my lord, what is this thou hast given me? It feels made from clouds, and sewn in heaven! I would have your eyes upon me as I wear it, and see thy love pour out of them! Oh, my lord! Thou spoke true last night; it is a regal beauty, and I will wear it for thee alone, and no other. Embrace me, Sire! For I am truly happy, and will spend my life as thy bride!"

He picked her up in a single motion and swung her around, held tight in a mighty embrace. A long kiss, and he set her to earth. When he spoke, the two young women heard a sound in his voice that they had never heard before. It was the sound of peaceful serenity, and it did soften his words. But twas as if the bride and groom were alone, for he had eyes for nought but her.

"Our new bride, thou hast pleased us greatly We'll leave thee now, for the seamstress will be thy companion for the next few hours, and there is much we must do, as well. When we see thee next, ye shall join us before a priest, and we will be wed. Hast my wenches agreed to be thy bridesmaids?"

"Aye, Sire!" they chorused, and they did grin most broadly. The king did pause for a moment, as if pondering, and then he said in mock surprise, "I do believe it will be the first time I have seen a gown on any of thee!" The two lovers had the grace to blush; but the bride merely hugged her king's neck and whispered something in his ear. For a reaction, he did slap her bottom, and muttered, "saucy wench!" Then he took up his own wedding garb, and made his exit. Only then did the ladies see that the seamstress was sitting quietly, just beyond the gown.

"Good morrow, mistress," said Syrenya as she recovered herself. "If we are to make this luscious thing cover this well-used carcass as it should, we shall be perhaps all morning of it! I have brought us some help; and, too, they should see their gowns, as well."

The four worked diligently for many an hour, and the morning was near gone by the time all three of the ladies found themselves before the mirror. Ariadne found her voice first, but it was still a whisper.

"Oh, my sisters! How beautiful thou art! Milady, thou looks to be a most beauteous and lovely queen!"

The dress was of creamy silk, almost white; it came off the shoulders, blossomed at Syrenya's bust, and then was tightly fitted to her own curves and dimples. A veil was placed on her head, and it was fastened to a train that formed a lacy arch as it trailed behind her. Alissa, poor child, could do nought but stare, and she knew not where to look: at her new and dazzling queen, her own luscious mate, or the reflection of herself in the mirror. The gowns were almost identical, except that the one accentuated Alissa's platinum hair, and the other deepened the fire that shown from Ariadne's eyes. Syrenya held her hands clasped tightly below her chin, and her lips did rest upon them, and it seemed she was in prayer, so still was she. Then she opened her eyes, and they fair shone.

"If I cannot stop this crying, then I will be a very thirsty bride!" Then she held her arms out to both of them, and the three embraced, and there were yet more happy tears. Then Ariadne, Alissa, and the seamstress began the task of removing the gown in preparation for the wedding, for already it did hug her torso as if it were her skin, and made very bold what was supposed to be, at least, the illusion of demure innocence. Alissa later remembered thinking that there would be very little in this world that could do such a thing to this queen!

Having left the dresses with the seamstress, the three ladies returned to Alissa and Ariadne's chamber. Amazingly, where before eyes were averted when anyone looked upon the nudes, now came very proper bows and curtsies every time they passed someone. They were so shocked at the reaction that it was several moments before they realized that all the castle must know by now, and that they walked in the presence of the Queen. Even so, it was a new and heady experience for the two, who had never in their lives known anything but looks of suspicion and doubt. The seamstress had told Syrneya that her chambers were being made ready, but that she thought it would take the better part of the day. This was excellent excuse for the nudes to ferry Syrenya back to their quarters, and have the story of what had happened to bring on this sudden and extraordinary change in all the castle.

For the first time since Syrenya had arrived, the door to the chamber was left open, for servants and maids were in and out constantly, preparing the queen for her wedding. The first order of business was a bath, and this was the perfect time to tell the story, for none would interrupt the queen at her bath. As Alissa and Ariadne scented the water, and washed and combed out Syrenya's raven locks, she told them of how she had known quickly that she would succeed, for the key was whether she could hold him. It was that one thing that had been a question that had troubled her as she had bathed the second time, just before going to meet her king. Now she told all to her friends, including the scarlet and ermine cloak, and how it would be used. Alissa, who, it was becoming clear to Syrenya, was the more conservative of the pair, queried her queen on the propriety of the Queen of Tabithia eschewing clothing, but while she did explain her response, a thought occurred to Syrenya, and she grew serious for a moment.

"Darlings, while we were with the seamstress, I did note well how pleased ye both were with thy gowns. It makes me ask a question that I had not thought to ask until now. Tell me truly; if ye both did have thy way, woulds't thou prefer thy skins, or feign have gowns upon thee? Know now, they would be as fine as thy bridesmaid's dresses, for thou art ladies of this court. Say now, what would be thy preference?"

"Syrenya," said Alissa, "we were, as ye know, commanded by the king to be nudes; he did grant us clothes were we to leave the castle, but we never dreamed of doing so, so naked we have remained. For my part, never did it occur to me that I may be otherwise. But when thee arrived, and did share our state, and do so freely, I was made aware of two things at once; first, that with thee I felt ever so much more at ease with my skin; and second, that until thee were here, I was not. Twas the command of the king, and I did not think on it further. But to have so beautiful a gown, and to feel its softness upon my skin, I did have a rogue thought that it would be good, if we were allowed to wear such beautiful clothes, and save our naked skin for each other." The queen (for that is already how Alissa did think on her) nodded.

"Ariadne?"

"I was trying to form an answer while Alissa was speaking, Lady—oh, should we call thee that now?"

"It is the name thou gave me upon my arrival; if ye would call me that, or Syrenya, it would please me."

"I was listening to Alissa and I discovered that she feels the very same as I; it was never a choice, and we had accepted it, and ne'er dwelt upon it. And I find that she is even more beautiful to me, after we have been wearing such gowns, than she was while we were always bare. But I cannot see the purpose of thy question."

"I did not miss the fact that the two of thee had hungry eyes for each other in thy gowns. And having always been naked, it is a different thing for me to ask it of the king, as it is when he doth command it of thee. So am I right when I think that, when given the chance, thou wouldst both prefer to be dressed?" Nods from both. "Then I do believe I have a way to arrange it."

The lovers were wide-eyed. The thought, after all these years, of being more like the others at court was something they had not dare dream. Now this wondrous lady would make it come true. Ariadne felt her love grow towards this woman she had only known for three days. Only that, though it seemed she had been here forever; now, she would be.

"If ye were matrons, thou wouldst have the right to dress, for it is the custom that a wife keep herself only for her husband. Is this not true?"

"Yes, Lady, but there be no priest in the land that would consent to marry us."

"Twas not a priest I had in mind. Twas a queen." Complete wonderment.

"Syrenya, cans't thou do such a thing? A queen hath the right to marry her subjects together?"

"I don't know. But I mean to find out."

CHAPTER 8

The Wedding

Syrenya's detailed description of the night she had spent with the king was almost more than the two cound bear; were it not for the wedding that drew ever nearer, they would not have let their charge leave the bath, for they were ferociously in want of her, and each other. But the constant noise of servants coming and going drew their attention to what must be done, and the three emerged, scented and cleansed, and ready for the heady gowns they would be dressed in. The maids did quickly shush the men out the door as they entered, for twas no man to view the queen until she appeared to her husband, and the work ahead was no job for a male. The gowns were taken up, and first the Queen was fitted to her wedding gown, and all the maids did admire and compliment it. One made so bold as to state that she was even more beautiful than before, and Syrenya accepted the compliment as it was intended. The maids would know soon enough that this was the first and last thing (save the scarlet cloak) that she would wear for her entire reign.

Now embraced by her dress, Syrenya saw to the gilding of her maidens. It was a strange and wondrous thing for her, who had grown to womanhood bare, that such gowns coud actually make these two more beautiful. Her mind drifted to her king, and she wondered if he would mark it. For the asking of another boon so soon after her nuptials was perhaps less than prudent, especially since it was asking the king to undo a royal command. But she put the thought aside for later contemplation. Even though there was barely enough time to arrange all that would take place on this day, the mind of the Queen was sore bent on passing that time, and seeing the king as he beheld his dress, and his queen.

As the ladies and their maids left the chamber, they could see and hear that the bustle inside had been but a shadow of the noise that rang the halls, in preparation for the king's wedding. The chapel, kept neat and tidy by the priests but rarely used, was now opened up, and strewn with flowers and garlands. The shutters were opened, and the sunlight streamed in and lit the sanctuary with a brilliant light. Though by six the torches would be lit, this spectacle met the bride with her first steps in, and she was hushed, and reverent. She did stop, and kneel, and cross herself. The two bridesmaids, having not been exposed to such an action ere now, did their best to repeat the move, but managed it only after a fashion. Then the three were rushed into a side chamber near the entry, for the king and his train were heard nearing the front of the sanctuary, where there stood a priest to wed them. The king wore garments he had kept for this moment only, and was a regal spectacle, from boots to crown, in raiments no ordinary man in Tabithia could dream of.

The mighty pipes of the organ were sounded as the chapel began to fill; lords and ladies dressed properly for the event, and Alissa and Ariadne had never seen such rich and sumptuous attire. The entire court was bright and cheerful in a way that, scarcely a week ago, could nought be imagined. Ladies squeezed the hands of their friends through long white gloves, and the men wore the finest black silk, befitting a coronation. Syrenya stopped upon the word; she and the king had discussed no coronation, so preoccupied had they both been with their preparations. No matter, thought the new Queen, it is a thing for the king to decide, and for her to obey, and joyously. She wondered, after such a night as they had last night, what delights would be coming on their wedding night. The thought made her adjust her lovely gown, for even now, she did desire his sheets and his touch, and would the ceremony be swift, and the reception (at least for them) short. Her last fleeting thought, as she made to begin her walk down to meet her king, was the delight of his taking this gown off her.

The king had made his entrance, at the far end of the aisle, and now bowed his head briefly to acknowledge the subdued applause. He took his place in front of Father Benedic, the high priest of the court, and the organ began its splendid sound, the wedding march, and it was sweet in Syrenya's ears. Her eyes seeking his, she began the slow walk to the altar, and did see in her new husband's eyes a look of wonder, and joy, and love. And that look remained, through the long procession, through the ceremony, and most emphatically, when he raised her veil and kissed her. The people of the court erupted, in their joyous approval, to rival the noise they made the morning First Night passed away forever, and they had been freed from darkness.

As befitted a king and queen, Ballizar took the hand of his new queen, and laying it upon his arm, took her at a regal gait down the aisle she had just traversed. Hails were set up to the new Queen Syrenya, of Tabithia, and she felt the joyous tears on her face as she walked, dazzled and dazzling, down the length of the chapel.

The king quickly swept her into the chamber from which they had come, only a moment before the crowd began spilling from the sanctuary. He immediately swung her into his arms, and clasped her firmly to him, and let loose a laugh that was so foreign to the Ballizar she had come to know, that Syrenya was lost in blissful wonder. She wanted immediately to hear that sound, again and again, as she walked through the years of their reign beside him. And then he caught her in a sudden and arduous kiss, and nought was in her mind, or her heart, but the moment, and her king.

The festival hall—a chamber long unused in this castle—had been done up in such a splendor that not one person could recall the rival of it. Food overflowed the long tables, more flowers were on display than any thought were held in the entirety of Tabithia, and the chandeliers and torches burned brilliantly across the vast span of the room. At the far end, a huge fire burned in a royal-sized fireplace, where several pots still bubbled in preperation for this, the most joyous feast in all the land. Just beyond the inner wall of the room, another feast had been laid, for all the subjects who could be notified of the event descended on the castle, and their celebration would be, if not as splendid, at least as boisterous. On a raised dais close by the fire, the king and queen took their seats, and twas many a long moment before anyone turned his attention back to the feast, for cheers and applause, shouts and blessings, were heaped upon the newlyweds. There was not a one of them there that knew not that, had this beautiful lady not come, then this joyous occasion could not even have been conceived. And their joy at the coming of their new queen was real and true, and it would remain thus, throughout her reign. The saga of Queen Syrenya had begun.

"Darien, I know thou art sworn to tell all the story as it has been taught to thee, but we are not going to hear another vivid description of what went on in the king's chambers, are we?" It was not so much a question as it was a declaration that such would not please the king.

"Sire, I cannot know how thee dost know such things, truly. But ye are correct—whatever traspired on their wedding night, neither ever spoke of it; indeed, even after some rather ardent pleading, Ariadne and Alissa could still not wrest it from their queen. All she would say was that it was between herself and the king, and whatever it was, they took it to their graves with them. I could not tell thee if I chose."

"Well, I am glad of that. But it does leave open an interesting point of speculation, does it not? How much was play and how much a vying for position? A king who can refuse his queen nothing is no longer ruler of the land."

"Milord, it has been the speculation on such that did fill many an hour over the years, between myself, Ariadne, and Alissa. But they never again asked, and we will never know. By the end we were no more knowledgeable of the facts than when we started.

"From her very first day at court, Syrenya's influence was felt throughout the land, and, I daresay, beyond its borders, as well. Tales of the Naked Queen spread like wildfire, and there were many a delegation from foreign lands who begged audience of the king, I suspect, for no other reason than to see for themselves if the tales were true.

"But the thing that confused us all at the coronation—for it was hardly that, taking only a few minutes at court the next day—was exactly what the queen had chosen for a crown. While all did know that there was a Queen's Crown awaiting her, what she actually took on was a simple diamond tiara, no small thing in itself, but certainly nothing even close to a crown. It was the only piece of ornamentation she ever wore; it served as crown, wedding band, and jewelry thence. It was indeed a remarkable spectacle…"

PART III

The Reign of King Ballizar And Queen Syrenya of Tabithia

CHAPTER 9

Coronation Day

The next day was still one of festivity, and those at the keep were happy to drop their burdens for a time, and share in the king's good fortune. There had been no announcement of when the queen would be crowned, and as the time for court drew nigh, there was speculation that, perhaps, not all went well during the night. Indeed, when the clock struck three, and the king entered the chamber alone, it did set up a most undignified buzzing within the court. But the king merely took his throne, and announced that the first order of business was a happy event, in that the king would crown his new bride, and the court should then know that the lady known as Syrenya would soon be queen of the realm. There was no small amount of relief in the court's ardent applause.

But the court was now due another shock, for Syrenya entered at her cue the exact same way she had entered the first night she had arrived—no ornamentation of any kind, but merely wearing the same poise and sense of royalty that she had exhibited then. She made her way majestically toward her new throne, and while she did, the king himself took up the duty of removing the dark cloak she had flung there—for it rested there still—and replacing it with the scarlet cloak that had so pleased his bride two nights ago. He draped it so that it rested on the back of the throne, and billowed down around its arms.

Syrenya came to the foot of the dais, knelt there on both knees, and looked up at her king with a most radiant smile. He rose, stepped down to meet her, and took her hands and raised her up. Taking then her right arm, the king brought her to and had her take her seat upon the throne. As she did so, she reached out, took the folds of the scarlet cloak, and pulled them forward so they draped about her shoulders, giving the apearance that she wore it, though it did not even now cover her entirely.

The king went and stood upon her right side, and motioned to the door. It opened, and a lady of the court entered with her young son, a lad of no more than four, who carried with a most stern and responsible countenance a scarlet, velvet pillow, on which did rest a diamond tiara. This brought still more verbal speculation from the crowd, for the queen's crown, which apparently still remained in the royal vaults, was a far richer treasure than this simple ornamentation.

The boy continued his crossing of the vast chamber, and as he approached the throne, the queen made a point of looking down, catching his attention, and smiling sweetly. The child broke into a broad grin, though he did not change his pace. When he arrived at the royal dais, he knelt, and offered up the pillow, raising it high as he could over his head. The king himself stepped down, lifted the tiara as reverently as it had arrived, remounted the dais and, moving behind Syrenya's throne, did place it gently upon her ebony tresses. Having done so, he moved to his own throne and, standing in front of it, he took the queen's left hand and drew her up. The scarlet cloak fell away, so that the new queen stood before all in just the same manner as she had broken the spell upon the keep.

Her eyes were warm and radiant, as they loooked out over the court. Many sat in reverent silence, waiting for her to speak; others whispered behind their hands to their neighbors, wondering if this development were a blessing or a foreboding event. It seemed clear that the queen preferred her nakedness to the robes of a queen; yet there were many—and the ministers and priests were among them—that hoped the queen would choose modesty, and cloak herself after she spoke. Others still gleaned the purpose, and meaning, of her choice, and were anxious to see how it would be put to the people of the court. Syrenya gestured for silence, and the buzzings subsided.

"Lords and ladies of this royal court," she began, "I would have thee know that this honor, that has been bestowed upon me by thy noble king, is a charge that I take on with all the solemnity and grace it doth require. It is my promise to thee, and to all of Tabithia, that I shall be at the king's side whenever he is at court, and indeed beyond the court, when it comes to that. I surmise, however, that the fact that I have taken neither robes nor crown doth trouble some of thee, and I would have thee know the reasons for these choices.

"I was born in a land a great distance from Tabithia, my new home. When I came here for the purpose of releasing the king from his demons, I knew that entering the court that night would have a greater impact if I did so bare; all those who were there know this. But now the work I have come to do is nearly completed, and I have been given this new honor: to serve our Lord, to serve our king, and to serve the people of Tabithia. But I wish to tell thee the reasons for what ye have seen today, lest speculation draw a different conclusion.

"In my lands, we are a simple folk, and due to that and the climate, we have never taken up the habit of clothing ourselves; we have always believed that the body as God made it is a beautiful creation in itself, and needs no gilding. Thus I have grown believing it so, and have eschewed clothing as a matter of course. Thus I find that, even though I now live in a country with different attitudes, I find I must still refrain from donning such, for it would be sore uncomfortable for me. Also, I wish to remain as I was when I came to thee. For this reason, the king and I have agreed that I may do so, and thus give out the word that I am the king's wife, and would have the world know of it. But there is a second reason for my decision, and this ye must hear, for it is the greater reason of the two.

"All of thee do know that the rage which o'ertakes thy king, my Ballizar, and to what extent it can control him. One of the tasks I took on when I arrived was to relieve him of these burdens, and allow him to rule, as he would do, justly and fairly toward all his subjects. To that end, I believe it is my duty to be able to ease his fevers immediately they overtake him; the best way I know to accomplish this is to remain as I am, and thus be able to aid the king as swiftly as possible. Thy king hast suffered gravely during his reign; he is now due release from these fevers, and if I am the one who can do that for him, then I will remain in my naked state until such time as the king is free of his affliction. Therefore I do announce unto thee, and ask thy blessing for, this decision. I would now like to know whether this court doth approve or disapprove of me as thy Naked Queen."

There was much murmering within the crowd; Syrenya could hear that there were many who thought that this was a mark upon the throne, and they would not have it so. But there were others, and the more so, who found Syrenya's words wise, and in keeping with the solemn vow to be an aid to her king. One minister took it upon himself to sort out the feelings of the people, for Queen Syrenya stood before them, awaiting an answer. He with all good speed did poll the court, and stood in front of them, facing the throne, to give her the results of his work.

"Your Grace, Queen Syrenya of Tabithia, it is the opinion of this court that thou hast given ample reason for thy decision, and we do support it. Long Live Queen Syrenya and King Ballizar!" Shouts and cheers did follow quickly upon the minister's proclamation.

"Sire," continued the minister, "when shall we begin planning for the coronation?" The king rose, took the queen by the hand, and made his announcement.

"Tarek, our ministers, and all our court: know ye now that discussion and agreement between thy king and queen hath chosen a simple and elegant coronation, and ye have witnessed it today. Lady Syrenya is now Queen of Tabithia."

Indeed, all the court was stunned, for never in their lives had there been any notion of a queen's coronation done in so simple a fashion; and more than that, that the king himself should crown her, rather than preside over the deed, which was usually performed—said those who knew—by the high priest, thus indicating that this was a crowning sanctified by God. Instead, the high priest who had married them the day before, Father Benedic, did raise his arms from his usual location, and spoke a blessing, thus:

"Be it now known that the ruler of Tabithia, King Ballizar, hath taken to be his bride the lady Syrenya, who now and henceforth shall rule at his side, before this court, and under the eyes of Almighty God. May the blessings of the Lord be upon them. Amen."

While the ears of the court were upon the priest, their eyes were upon the royal couple, who both attended to their own business during this blessing. Ballizar regained his seat, and while he did so, Syrenya bent quietly to the young lad who was still standing there, and whispered to him. He nodded, and turned and pointed to his mother, who was still standing near the door they had entered. A quick motion by the queen asked if the boy might remain upon the dais, and the lady nodded reverently, and curtsied. The queen then pulled again upon her cloak, draping it across her right side, and then did reach out her arms and take up the boy, and sit him upon her knee. The lad grasped her cloak, and leaned upon her, and there he rested for the remainder of the afternoon, watching, and being instructed by the queen on all that took place, while his mother sat and watched with shining eyes and a blissful smile upon her face.

Twas only this, and the coronation was complete. The court was still in stunned silence. It was not until a man who still had his wits about him shouted out, "Long live Queen Syrenya!" that the cry was taken up, and the court began to applaud, reverently at first, and then more boisterously. Soon the chamber near shook with their recognition of this new Queen, who had come, and broken Tabithia's shame, and made of her king a man who smiled often, and was seen as a most benevolent ruler. The remainder of the time left at court this day did prove it so, for the king was most gentle in the questions he asked of those who came to seek his favor. This had not happened at any other time during the king's reign, as far as this court knew. Up until this day, their king had been brusque, somewhat impatient, and also somewhat expidient in his decisions. Though this was obvious to the court and, more so, to those who sought him out, none would ever have complained so, for in those days twas known full well that the king's wrath was far more fearful a thing than any answer he might give; those who suffered for it did so silently. Beginning this day, twould be a far, far different air at King Ballizar's court, for what was once thought of as a most unlikely benevolence came to be the order of the day, and there were many who blessed this naked queen, and the day she arrived in Tabithia.

The king reached out, took his new bride's left hand and placed it upon the right arm of his throne, and rested his own hand upon it. He then nodded to his ministers, and the scribe called the first of the king's petitioners forth. Court was now in session.

The folk who this day brought their grievances before the king, having witnessed this most singular spectacle, came forth with an air of apprehension, knowing not what to expect. The king held sway as was his wont, but with a far more tempered and jucidious air, and all did wonder at this change, and hoped that it would remain so. Court at the castle of Ballizar was a time that had been, before now, something that most simply waited out, impatiently, until the petitioners were none, and court was over.

Twould be a far different audience now and forever hence. The king, many prayed, was now free of those devils that had plagued him, and this marked a new day for this court, and for all the people.

The king sat and listened patiently while each came to present his case. For the most part, he did hear and answer, and did govern as he had done. Only occasionally did he lean to his right, and whisper to his new queen; he then made his decision, and those who had come expecting little help came away both rewarded and amazed at their good fortune. This king was tended toward kindness and affirmation. Many who came to seek his grace did receive it, at least in far greater number than was had before.

Nearing the end of court, as shadows began to stretch across the chamber, the lad who was sitting with the queen yawned, and she lifted him gently, placed him upon the dais in front of her, and pointed the way to his mother. He needed little coaxing, and took to his path with a far quicker gait than he had at first traversed it. The lady scooped him up when he reached her, cradled his head upon her shoulder, and took the child out. Syrenya then returned her hand to the king's throne, and it was again taken up, even as both did listen to their subject's petitions. All proceeded calmly until, even while the last man made his request, a wizened old elder entered the court all in agitation. He went straight to the minister who held the book, and made his request. The minister caught the eye of the king, who nodded; then he wrote down the man's name and bade him sit. He did so, but did chafe at the delay. Twas clear he was not a man used to waiting.

Finally, the petitioner ahead of him thanked the king, bowed, and took his leave. The elder was on his feet in a shot, almost before he was called upon.

"Sire!" he cried, and again, "Sire! I do ask of thee with all humbleness, to hear my plight, for I am sore afflicted with this burden." Ballizar motioned for him to come forward, and continue.

"My name is Alderon; I am the elder in the coastal town of Shepardswick, here in the King's Quadrant. I come with a most aggregious affliction, and ask respectfully that ye do grant me the boon of divorce from my wife." This caused no little stir among the court and especially among the priests, for it was a very rare thing for any man to forsake his wife and find the king open to his request. For the first time that day, Ballizar frowned, and leant toward his queen and whispered quickly. She nodded, and the king bade the man state his case.

"My Liege, I am a man respected in my town and in the quadrant; I have administered thy laws with authority and patience, and few have felt poorly dealt with when I rule. I have within the past three years taken a second wife, my first having died some fifteen years ago. She hast borne me a son, who is now but two years old. But with all this, I am enraged, and would ask thy permission to be rid of her. Her presence in my house hath sore begun to grate upon me."

"And what is it that she has done to offend thee so, elder?" asked the king.

"Sire, I am cuckolded! She has put the horns upon me, and I am engraged. Those who used to hold me in respect now titter behind my back, and my authority is abused. I know it; she knows it; and so doth the entire quadrant know it! I am..." The elder stopped, sputtering, and tried to regain some composure, but with little success. "I am a source of amusement, Sire. I prithee, good Sire, to grant me this boon."

"This is no simple thing that thou hast asked of us, Elder. Thou knowest that divorce is against the law of the land."

"Sire, I am aware of it. It took me great courage to travel here, and I almost made it not with my indecision. But I can stand no more! I am cuckolded, Sire, and not just once, but thrice! And with a different man each time! It is more than a reasonable man can withstand!"

By this time the man was shaking with rage and indignation. The king took to pondering what he had heard, and for awhile he was silent. Then the queen leaned toward him and whispered something, and the king nodded. Then he again addressed the elder.

"Elder Alderon, meet and pay homage to thy new Queen, Syrenya. She has a question or two of thee." The elder looked startled, stared at the queen as if he had only just noticed her, and then suddenly remembered his place, and made a deep bow. "Long live Your Grace," he said.

"I thank thee, sir. Say ye that thou hast been married three years?"

"Almost on, Your Grace. Twould be our third anniversary two months hence, if indeed it comes at all."

"And thou art positive she hast sullied thy bed?"

"Your Grace, she did admit as much to me! Upon the very first day. She was so repentant, and pitiful, that I attempted forgiveness of the deed, for she did say that, while she consented to this man, it was to be rid of him, for he had pestered her for weeks, while I presided in the town. She told me his name, and I had him brought up, and upon his insolent admission, did banish him from my quadrant. I would have had him whipped, twere in my power. But we have seen nought of him again. And now, there are two more, and because of what I did to the first, she will not even reveal their names! It is past all reason, and I am ravaged by shame. I have cast her out, but she pleads so piteously, and I cannot rout her. So unless thy will go my way, I cannot resolve the matter."

"How long ago was the first offence?"

"Eight months and a fortnight, Your Grace."

"That is exceptionally accurate."

"It is not a day I will likely forget, Your Grace."

"I suspect that is true for thy wife, as well. Forgive this next question, but I must know thine answer. Hast the two of thee lain together since that time?" At this, the elder looked down at the floor. His response was almost inaudible.

"Nay, Your Grace. She has come to me once or twice, but I could not receive her."

"Thou didst note clearly that thou didst *try* to forgive her. I perceive that thou hast not been entirely successful."

"It is true, Your Grace, I confess it. But it would not have been so had it not been for the others. I was on my way toward forgiveness when I discovered that there had been two others since that time. It is more than I can bear!"

"Thou hast said she bore thee a son. She is younger than thee, may I say?"

"Yes, Your Grace. Maritha is a young woman, though well into her childbearing years. I remember her age as being 20, give or take."

"And how long was it before she again trespassed upon thee?"

"It were about five months between the first and the second man, Your Grace."

"And the third?"

"Quite near at hand, Your Grace. Not yet a week."

"I see. Hast thou taken her to a priest?"

"Er, no, ah…why, Your Grace?"

"She hath broken a commandment, sir. She is in need of shriving." He stopped, and looked down at his feet.

"I have not the will to do so, Milady."

"I fear ye do her an injustice, Sir. Shriving is more than penance; it is a strong warning not to repeat the sin. She is to be forgiven, if she will be shriven. Would thou not have it so?"

"Forgiven or not, I still wear these horns."

"I see no horns, Sir. It is thee who dost feel the weight of them."

"And I feel them most keenly, Milady."

"It is often the case, when a man takes a bride young enough to be his child. For though ye have had a long and productive life, thy wife is still young. Her own body, Sir, persecutes the woman. She cannot go without thy attentions for such lengthy periods. It is folly to make her do so, for it is obvious that she hast forsaken thee only when it is beyond her ability to keep from doing so. I do ask of thee yet another day before we rule on thy cause, Sir. I would take it as a kindness if thou wouldst return on the morrow, and we shall see thee first. But it is essential that thou must bring thy bride with thee. Wilt thou do as I ask thee?" The old man looked desolate, but said yes, he would return tomorrow, and bring his wife, as the queen requested. But he made it clear that he could not understand the necessity of it. The queen spoke to him gently.

"Sir, if thou wilt, it is possible that we may set things right, and need not split thee from thy bride. For I see that thou dost still dote upon her, despite thy justifiable wrath." At this, tears began to flow down the old man's face.

"Your Grace, I do confess it."

"Then let us see thee both here, at three of the clock tomorrow. We shall bring this unfortunate situation to an end at that time, I do promise thee."

"Your Grace, I shall do as thou hast prescribed. Until the morrow, Milady; Sire."

It was the last case at court. The members were all abuzz with what they had seen today, and asked themselves many questions about many points. They did shake their heads, that they would never learn the ways of royalty. As the king rose, Syrenya did as well, leaned into him, and promised to attend him straight, but that she would speak with Alissa and Ariadne. The two waited for her by the door.

"I think we shall dine soon, my queen. If thou art ready, we shall eat at the king's table. The wenches will dine with us, as well."

"Very well, milord. We shall attend thee at table."

"It shall prove interesting, I do believe, my lovely."

"Twill turn heads, and that is the way of it, milord."

"We shall dine at seven. Will that give thee enough time?"

"I think that should be ample, my husband. We shall see thee anon."

The nudes had spent their day at court as usual, off to the right of the throne, and throughout the day, they had exchanged looks with their queen that meant they were full of questions. Syrenya redraped her cloak on her throne and went to them. The three locked arms, and the questions came immediately. Syrenya laughed.

"Well, ladies, I can see that the new court has changed only a little. What would ye have me say to thee?" Both spake together.

"Where is thy gown..."

"...who is the child, Lady?" This from Alissa.

"Well, you two do have the art of coming right to significant points, I see. Very well. Attend me, and I will show thee thy queen's quarters." This was a welcome topic, for the two were particularly anxious to see these new appointments. They went straight to her rooms, on the far side of the king's own bedchamber. The first thing Ariadne looked for was the door, and indeed, there it was, opening between her chambers and the king's. Ariadne spoke as if her discovery was a proof of some kind.

"Aha! I had thought as much."

"Thou hadst known as much, Wench," said the queen, laughing. "I myself did spy it when I was in the king's chambers, and I had more on my mind at that time than hast either of thee."

"Oh, Syrenya, this is lovely..." Alissa had wonderment in her voice. In the corner of the room, standing nearly as tall as the chamber and with its headboard against the far wall, stood a huge four-poster bed. The mahogany posts supported a canopy, and there were curtains all around it. A velvet coverlet the shade of dark wine was spread across it. "And quite big enough for two, I see."

"Thou wouldst have been surprised if it were not, tease. But come, and see what else we can find." She led the way out of the room though a door at the back, and came upon that she wished to show them: she stood aside and waved an arm in presentation.

"Oh, Lady!" Ariadne marveled at the marble bath, larger than their own, and having two gold knobs in one wall, near the top, and the whole room was surrounded, enclosed, and heated, unlike theirs, which was open at the top. There was a marble vanity, a marble bench, and a chaise. Ariadne turned, put one hand on her hip and waggled a finger of the other at the queen. She gave her a very serious look and said, "Oh, Lady, thou art very wicked. Why, who knows what debauchery may go on in this room." Then, unable to keep up the pose, she burst into laughter.

The queen took each of them by the elbow, and escorted them over to a wall which had against it a large armoire, saying, "Were there time, I would debauch thee both, for thy wicked tongues!" And all three laughed.

But when the queen pulled back the doors to the armoire, all laughter ceased.

"Syrenya! Oh, these are beautiful! Why dids't thou not wear one of these in thy crowning? And come to that, what kind of a coronation do ye call that? No pomp, no glory…no feast, even!" And Ariadne seemed genuinely put out.

"The coronation was discussed between the king and I. I wanted as quiet and as quick a crowning as I could get, and none of the trappings of these royal spectacles. I am the queen, yes, but first and formost I am Ballizar's wife, and that is the more important role. The people may put me on a pedestal, if they choose. But those at court need have no such lofty thoughts of me. I should be a most unique queen, my ladies, were I expected to strut and flutter around in such bolts of cloth. Nay, my sweets, I had these brought here because here ye may dress in private. For ye shall wear thy favorites to dinner this very evening." Both stared at her, eyes wide and mouths agape. "Well, you two, get thee to it! We have but half an hour until dinner! Be quick!"

"But you said…"

"But how did you…"

"Dress, and I will tell thee. I did use a bit of the womanly wiles on him, I fear. It is something I shall have to keep in check, and use most rarely. I do not want him to think, at any time, that I would ever move against his wishes. He is my lord, and he will remain so. But I queried him about thee, and ye were the topics of quite a discussion before court this day!"

"I was cold at court today," Ariadne grumbled. "Even naked, I would like a bench to sit on from time to time. I sometimes feel more like a lioness than a member of the court."

"I have always told thee that thou art special to the king, and more his own than thou art members of court. And there were many a reason the king could give for having thee bare at court. I simply knocked them down, one by one, until he had no reason left to keep thee thus. And I let him think it was his idea that, now that the queen is naked, it woud not do for younger, more comely maids to outshine her at court. So he had me bring the dresses thou hast never used here, so ye could try them on at will. They will be returned to thy closets, by morning."

"But what did he say?"

"He told me that he did think of thee as lionesses, brave and bold though all men about would harm thee. He was impressed at thy bravery. He also admitted that he could rest his eyes upon thee from time to time, and court would be a little less tedious, as a result. I don't know that ye have noticed, fair ones, that there is not a wench, nor maid, nor lady that can rival thy natural beauties. Hast they shown no jealouy toward thee?"

"Nay, Lady, they thought, to a man, that we were bare as a means of punishment for our wicked ways. Twas never thought a boon by any at court."

"More thought it a boon than ye might think, precious. I have queried some of the men about and they all said twas easy for their eyes to rest upon thee, as well. Thou dost have quite a following now, thy seventh year at court. More so than not, I do believe, mostly because thou hast carried thyselves with grace and without shame. There are more than a few who think that ye are courageous, and are fair impressed with thee."

"Lady!" breathed Alissa. "Sayest thou truly? It seems that it would scarce be so. In the eyes of the priests, we are evil, pure and simple. And in the eyes of many of the matrons about, as well. They are fair done in with trying to explain our purpose to their children's questions."

"Precisely what I told the king. Having won half the court with thy bravery, why not let them win the rest of the court with their piety? 'Woulds't thou not say,' I queried him, 'that there are any at court who are as gentle, and loving, and as monogamous, as those two?' And he did confess he could not. So I gave him my last reason, and all came down. I told him that if I were the Naked Queen, as many have begun to call me even after a mere twenty-four hours, it would not do to have one of his wenches mistaken for his queen. And he did laugh heartily, and we spoke no more of it. Thou art now fully-deemed Ladies of this Court. And I would have thee behave that way, young ladies, lest my ardent speech for thee go to nought." It sounded very seriously spoken, but Syrenya could not keep it so. She laughed, and both did laugh with her. Now they did see to their dresses. But the two still had questions, and while they worked, the conversation continued.

"Thou hast worn thy wedding dress, Lady, why not wear a coronation gown? These here are sumptuously made, and rich in texture and color. I am myself overcome with the notion that we may dress like the other ladies of the court." Alissa still spoke in the whisper she took on when things were beginning to be too much for her.

"Alissa, my child, thou art a sweet thing, and thy questions do thee honor; but having lived my whole life this way, I am not used to the trappings of clothing. I wore that wedding dress only so long as it took for the king to get me out of it, and believe me, I was most appreciative." Ariadne has a retort to that, but she decided against it. Instead she asked her another question.

"Lady, who was the child thou didst keep at court? He is not a child I have seen before."

"Twas his court debut," replied Syrenya, smiling at the thought. "He is a precious child, and one we shall need to keep aware of. His father was killed in the border skirmish, ye would remember, two years ago with that band of rogues. Now, his mother is gravely ill, and I am in deep sympathy for her and her son. I have promised her he will be well cared for, and grow to be a gentleman of the court. I charge thee that ye will help me to keep that promise."

"Is it Lady Berniece?" asked Ariadne, as if she knew already but wanted to be wrong.

"Yes, it is. Her boy's name is Darius."

"We must also see to her, Lady, and help her in her last days. What is her illness?"

"It is one that the physicians cannot stop. Her body has gone wild, and grows more inside her than it should. The more it grows, the closer to death she becomes. The doctors have estimated only another six months of life for her."

"Syrenya, that's horrible!"

"Yes, it is indeed. But Lady Berniece is of strong stock, and she told me that such an illness has struck in her family before. She always knew the possibility that she would develop it, as well. Now she prays that it will not strike down her son, for he is all she has left, to comfort her in the months ahead. I have promised that we shall always be available to her, and I am glad to hear thee promise it. But this sad intercourse is marring the occasion! Dress, Ladies, for we meet the king at table at seven. Quickly, now."

Ariadne chose a gown of purple velvet, with a lavender jacket. The gown was high at the neck, and gave space between it and Ariadne's neck for the long tresses of her hair. She pinched them back and hung them straight down her back before Syrenya helped her on with her jacket.

"When was the last time either of thee wore shoes?"

"Shoes!" they chorused. Alissa continued, "We have had nought but slippers all our days, even before we were brought to the castle."

"Well, slippers it must be, then. But note that these gowns are meant to brush the floor, not sweep it as this one does now. Shoes are a woman's friend; they raise her in height, and thus in stature. I think that ye should well consider the advantages of this, and practice until thou art comfortable wearing them at court. We will not push it," she continued, "but it should be a goal toward which we shall work. I want thee to have every advantage at court, for I do have grand ideas for both of thee. Now, quickly, Alissa, and we shall go. The king and I do have a surprise for thee at court."

Alissa chose a royal blue gown, split below the bodice so that it was pleated in the middle, and swept out behind her as she walked. She also chose a very handsome bonnet, which covered most of her platinum hair.

"I do suspect that the two ladies who join me at the king's table shall be the discussion of all the court. Thou shalt not be recognized at all in these disguises. Ye both do look the proper ladies, and I am pleased to bring thee to the king. He looks forward to the reaction ye shall get from the rest of the dining hall."

At the hall, all eyes turned when the queen entered, followed by the two ladies. All three advanced to the king's table, where he sat at the one end and Father Benedic sat at the other. Those one or two guests at the king's table usually sat to his right. The queen now took up her rightful place there. This arrangement gave the room the best view of the king, queen and their guests, and as the three were given their seats, the general noise in the room increased. Father Benedic gave the ladies a solicitious smile, and asked if the queen would make the introductions. She graciously complied.

"These are my new ladies-in-waiting, Father Benedic." This caused a wide-eyed reaction from the two. "But thou hast seen them at court before; surely if thou dids't think upon it, ye would recognize them." Alissa dropped her head and blushed, as if she could do such a thing on cue; Ariadne gave the father a full face, with but a small smile upon her lips. The father studied them carefully, and then confessed that he knew them not. To this Syrenya replied, "But, Father, of course ye do. Thou cannot have forgotten Alissa and Ariadne, surely."

Slowly, it dawned upon the father that these were the nudes, and his face went bright scarlet. "Why…why, yes of…of course, I do recognize thee. Well! Thou art very comely in thy new gowns…"

"I thank thee, Father," said Aridane in her best lady's voice, as if the comment were but her due. Alissa blushed again, and the queen did marvel at how she seemed to accomplish it as if on command. The two together completely undid the poor priest, and he sat with his mouth half open, as if he had something to say, but not the wherewithal to say it.

"Thou must get used to them, Father," said the queen sweetly, "for I am undone without my train. I promised them a place at table if they would consent to be my ladies. I am heartily pleased that they have honored me with their acquiescence." Ariadne and Alissa, fortunately, spoke not. The Father, however, seemed to have a great deal to say, for it all came out at once, and stymied his reply. When he found his tongue, it was not to the ladies that he spoke.

"My lord, I have just remembered; I have not gotten for thee the answer to thy question in court two days ago. I am remiss; I will see to it straightaway.'" Then, excusing himself, he abruptly rose and left the table and, a moment later, the hall. As soon as the door had shut behind him, the king gave out with a hearty roar of laughter, and it was so foreign a sound to the people that everyone suddenly went silent. Having started, the king found it difficult to stop, and the queen queried him. Between fits of laughter, he explained to the queen and her ladies that he had asked no question of Benedic two days ago. With this, he roared again, and tears streamed down his face, and his companions, though ladies enough to cover their mouths, did have a merry time of it all 'round, both from the Father, and the good king as well. He had not laughed as wildly as this at all, since the wenches had come to court seven years ago. One of the men below stood and called to the king.

"My lord, thou art well amused. Pray share the joke with us all."

"There is no joke!" bellowed the king merrily. "These two ladies are the queen's new ladies-in-waiting. They have come from this noble court, sir; cans't thou identify them?" The man looked confused, stared at the table, and then gave his head a slow shake.

"Nay, Sire, I cannot."

"Neither could Father Benedic! And that is the joke!" The king was consumed by another fit of merriment, as the man slowly regained his seat. It was several moments before the king could control himself, but even so, he chuckled throughout the meal, and even went so far as to wink at the two, whose bright smiles and deep blushes revealed their own confusion.

CHAPTER 9A

Maritha's Story

Many of those present during the last hour of court yesterday were eager for court to resume this afternoon, for they wished to hear the results of the tale of Alderon and his Maritha. Several had come early to obtain their favorite seat, and when they did, they stopped in their tracks. Something new had been added since last evening. A crushed velvet couch sat beyond the queen's throne, directly upon the floor that the nudes had taken up, traditionally now, for the last seven years. There came the speculation that the queen had supplanted them with ladies more to her liking, but those who had eyes said she would never do such. Nevertheless, when the two ladies, who had sat with the king and queen at dinner the night before, came in and claimed their seats, some were smug in their opining, and others were just as much confused.

It was hard on three when the king arrived, with his queen on his arm, and mounted the dais. Syrenya took her place before her throne as Ballizar did his. But before they sat, Syrenya made a loud and clear announcement to the room.

"Lords and Ladies, if thou wouldst attend me," she said, and all grew silent. "I wish to introduce to thee two ladies who have graciously agreed to be my ladies-in-waiting. Ladies, if thou wilt…" The pair rose. "She closest to me is the Lady Alissa, and beyond her, the Lady Ariadne. Please join me in welcoming them to their new station."

Some began to applaud automatically and politely, until someone said in a voice louder than she intended, "The Nudes!" and pandemonium erupted. The priests stood horrified, and many of the men took to a loud and boisterous applause—and some of the ladies, as well. Others of their sex were tight-lipped and silent, and had they been given their way, they would have left the court immediately. To all this reaction the queen stood, and smiled, and the two of her ladies, too, did smile; and soon, all was calmer. To Alissa and Ariadne, who had been silently dreading this moment, it was clear that the atmosphere in the chamber was a good deal lighter than it had been only moments before, and they had to admit that the queen had been right in her view that they had friends at court. If nothing else, this gave them a proper gauge of who was and who wasn't. Father Benedic, to his credit, led the applause with a smile upon his face. It was a step in the right direction, he thought to himself; if they cannot be converted, at least now they may be clothed.

The king waited until the din began to quiet, and then he called to his minister, "we shall see the first petitioner," and court was in session.

As he had promised his queen the day before, Alderon had returned, and brought with him his young wife, who was laden with their infant son. She seemed afraid; it was clear that she feared being in this place. She stared in amazement at the Naked Queen, and did her best to appear humble before a court that was, by the telling yesterday, already inclined to condemn her. At a motion from the queen, she stepped forward tentatively, and came to the foot of the throne.

"Tell me, child, what is thy name?" asked the queen gently.

"Maritha, your ladi…Your Grace," she stammered.

"And thine age?"

"I have only just reached two decades, M'um."

"And is this the child I heard tell of, yesterday? What is his name?"

"Brindel, Your Grace, after my husband's father."

"May I?" asked the queen, and Maritha offered up the child, whom Syrenya held deftly but gently. "He is a strapping youth, Maritha, and he doth favor thee, about the eyes. And, too, he is a happy child, from all I may see."

"He is my joy, Your Grace. I humbly beg of thee, please do not take him from me!"

"Why, child, where did ye get such a notion? I have no desire to split thee from thy child, nor from thy husband, either, if he, and ye also, will obey me."

"Tell me what I am to do, Your Grace," Maritha replied. Alderon, for his part, remained silent. Before she answered, the queen walked with the child over to Ariadne and Alissa, and gave the child to Alissa to hold. She bent and whispered, and the two rose, and stood behind their couch, which the queen then sat upon. "Come here, Maritha, and sit beside me."

She patted the cushion beside her. All the court was in stunned silence. Alderon could not believe his ears, and even the king looked on in interest, to see what his queen was about. Maritha slowly did as she was told, and lowered herself onto the sofa.

"Now, then, child," spoke the queen gently. "Three seasons ago, thou didst have a terrible time of it, didst thee not?"

"Aye, Your Grace, I did." Maritha seemed astonished. She could neither believe her ears; was she really going to be able to tell her side of things? She rushed on when the queen bade her continue. "Twas in the fall of last year, Your Grace. I was putting out the laundry when this youth came bounding into my yard. He was a pretty youth, but boisterous and loud, and he did fright Brindel, who set up a wailing. I scooped up my child, told the boy to leave immediately, and fled into the house. I did hardly get the door shut and bolted, before he came abanging on't.

"'Oh, Maritha,' he did say, 'I cannot leave, not until I have tasted thy sweet lips.' He did anger me with his impertinece, and I told him to get out, or my husband would deal with him. He said, 'Thy husband is too old for thee, gentle Maritha. Take instead this sturdy youth, and I will give thee all thy satisfaction.'

'No! Never,' I screamed, and went into the back room of the house and slammed the door behind me. It set poor Brindel to weeping again, but it did, apparently, cause this scoundrel to leave my house. I saw him not again that day.

"But to my mounting fear, he did return unto the house, again and again. He did tell me insolent and terrible things, of what he wanted to do to me, and how he would make me leave my husband after but one time with him. Each time I did abuse him, and tell him I would tell my husband, and that this youth would smart for his insolence. It worried him not a whit. He said, 'Why, Maritha, why wouldst thou do such a thing? I have harmed thee nought. I have not even touched thee, though I do ache for it. And what wouldst thou say to thy husband, that old man? That ye do fear a common youth? He would take it as flirting, Maritha, make no mistake. Twould be on thy head that came his wrath.'

"He was a liar!" cried Alderon, who could not contain himself. "Thou should have told me, Maritha." But the queen held up her hand, and bade Maritha continue.

"His words did frighten me, Your Grace. I believed he could make it appear so, so silver was his wicked tongue. He would come every day, and never at the same time, so that I might lay a trap for him, with my husband or an official. He was clever, Milady, and I was all nerves before long. He did harrass me for a full three weeks, and each day to a worse degree than the day before. Finally I did ask of him, 'If I should give thee what ye ask, would ye leave this place, and trouble me no further?' I made him swear it, Your Grace. And then I let him in. He took me right there, my queen, on the floor! I lay motionless and let him do what he wished. It seemed an eternity, but after a lengthy time, it was over. 'Remember thy pledge, rascal, and trouble me no further!' I screamed at him. But he just grinned that maddening grin, and sauntered away like a Cock-o-the-walk. I wept most bitterly, Your Grace, and I knew that I could not hide my shame from Alderon. We have had never a secret between us, and I knew I must tell him all."

"Dear Maritha," spoke the queen gently, "dost thou not know? Ye were raped, child. Thy tiny consent weakens not the case. This man must be fair glad he got only what he did, and not been brought before this court for hanging!" The queen was livid, and all the room was silent. "Hast thou heard thy wife, Alderon? Do I not speak truly? Thee of all must know best the law that governs here."

"Your Grace, thou dost speak truly. Maritha, my child, why dids't thou not tell me this? The rogue did badger thee, and weaken thee. There was no shame in thee, and hadst ye told me what I hear today, the man would have been hanged, and no mistake!" To which Maritha replied, very softly, "I know this, milord my husband. But though he did put me in a dreadful place, with all his wooing, he was only a young fool, and may have deserved the thrashing thou didst wish to give him. But even now, I cannot be responsible for a man's death. I prayed he would stay away, and that prayer was answered. I also prayed that my lord would forgive me, but that, I fear, is not to be."

"Maritha," whispered Alderon, "My child..." But the queen held up her hand, and Alderon fell silent.

"But the story does not end there, does it, Maritha. Thou hast more to tell."

"Aye, and it shames me to the quick to think on't. After what I had hoped was a proper interval, I did go to my husband and seek his warmth, and the solace of his bed. But he would not give it. He wanted to forgive me, I knew, but he could not. And it was that way for five long months, Milady. I was near distracted by his turning away! I did need him so..."

"What happened, Maritha?"

"Twas a young man I knew in the village; we did play together when we were small. He had no bride, though elder than I; when I could stand it no longer, I went to him. I begged him release me, and he consented. Twas that, Your Grace, and no more. And I swore before him that it would never happen again. And he did kiss my forehead, and tell me that he knew it would not, and all would be well; my husband would soon forgive me. I prayed that he was right, and I ran home, to be there when Alderon arrived."

"I did tell thee as much, did I not, Sir?"

"Aye," was all the old man could muster.

"But there is still more, Maritha. Unburden thyself; tell all."

"My Queen, I am full of shame! Twas even less time than before that my body did betray me. I hungered, and was fair undone. I could not return to my old friend; we had sworn it would be thus no more. So I found a comely youth, and did steal him away, and let him have me in the wood. He was all fire and passion, for I do believe he had not been so blessed as to have a wench as eager as was I. 'Remember now,' I told him. 'Our time is over. But know ye now, ye may seek thine own girl, and thou shouldst please her well. Say it will be so.' He was all teary-eyed, but he did say so, and I gathered myself together and walked a ways back to town with him.

'I left him at the stone wall and hurried home, so as to compose myself before Alderon arrived home. But the moment he did lay eyes on me, he could see my guilt. Oh, it was terrible, Your Grace! He did upbraid me most awfully, and I could do nought for it. He made me tell all, of both, and then he sent me to tend the child. But he was livid, and that day and next were fair horrors for me. He would not look, he would not speak to me, and I knew better than to come to him at night. I could not bear it, and pled with him to forgive me, that it was hunger and no more. He was about casting me out forever, so towering was his rage. I was prostrate with grief, and begged most pitiously, and he did relent. But there have been no more than two words at a time between us, Your Grace, and I would fair wish to die than to shame him further!" This deep emotion brought Maritha to tears.

After a stern and lengthy look at Alderon, who for his part had the grace to lower his head, the queen spoke gently to her charge.

"Maritha, I can see clearly why ye have done what ye did. And the first man was ne'er thy fault; thou hadst been waylaid. I myself could not have thought of another course than the one ye took—and he did, at least, keep his word, and stay away after, though I do believe thy husband's heavy hand upon him did put the fear of God into him.

"After so long a period of chastity afterwards didst thou suffer, that ye must do something. That is plain. And to seek out a trusted friend was wise. But, Maritha, thy third transgression cannot be so easily laid aside. I do know that thou wast less than lucid, but to steal away a boy and set him on the road to manhood early, might just as easily cause him harm as good. I am sorry to say it, but before all this can be put right, thou must be shriven. Know ye this? Do I not speak truly?" Maritha continued to weep.

"Yes, Your Grace, I do know it. Yet I do fear it so; others in the town who have suffered it do tell me horrible stories! It doth fright me to the quick. But if thou dost say so, then I will stand up under it. If it restores me to my husband and my child, I will do anything!"

"Only what God and the Church do ask, child, and no more. But I must see it done, so that I may know this mediation of mine hath proved true. Hold a moment." With this, she rose and spoke softly to her ladies, both of whom nodded gravely. Alissa returned the child to her, and she walked over and gave the babe to Alderon, and was most brusque with him.

"Thou dost see now, Alderon, how thine own folly did add to hers. She goes now to be shriven, and then we will return her to thee. But if she doth bear up under it, and willingly return to thee, thou must forgive her all, and clasp her to thy breast. All that she has done is either for thee, or because of thee. If thou wilt still find fault in her after shriving, and her absolution, then it is thee who art the guilty one. Dost thou know this to be true?" The man had been weeping, and was fair contrite, and did fear for his wife.

"Your Grace, I have already forgiven her all, and know my part in't. Can she not escape this shriving? I myself have heard of it, and it seems unnecessary to subject her to it now."

"Thy words do thee well, Alderon; but make no mistake. This is a deed that must be done, not only to keep her faithful, but to save her immortal soul. It must be done. But it is a penance that is soon ended. Take thy child, and wait for thy wife in the courtyard. She will be returned to thee anon." She then turned to the king, and spoke for all to hear.

"My Liege, I must go and tend to this child, and bring her back to the righteous path. I beg that ye do continue court without me. I shall not be overlong."

"As ye wish, my queen. Do what is just."

"Aye, Milord." And with that, she took the young wife, and her two ladies, and left the chamber. Once beyond its walls, however, a great change came over her, and she did speak conspiratorily, and move them all toward Alissa and Ariadne's chamber.

"What wilt thou do to me, Your Grace?" stammered the girl, still very much afright.

"Why, my child, I will do not a whit to thee. Thou hast confessed, and in the presence of a priest. All that we need do now is wait for him. He shall come anon, and thou shalt have absolution." Maritha was wide-eyed, and some color did return to her cheek. "I did let thy husband believe that ye were to suffer for thy indiscretions, for knowing that thou didst go to them willingly so that ye could remain with him is strong medicine."

"But what of the penance, Your Grace? Need I not suffer for my penance?"

"My dear child, thou hast suffered enough! It is so in many lands, that shriving doth carry with it a usually stiff 'penance,' which in point of fact is punishment, disguised as grace. But the true meaning of the word 'shrive' or 'shriving' means nothing more than to confess thy sins, and be absolved of them. No penance for thee, my child; thou art now free of thy sins, for I see Father Benedic approaching. Come in, Good Father, and pray absolve this child of her guilt, and return her to her rightful husband."

"If ye and thy ladies will leave us alone for a moment, Your Grace, it shall be done."

In response, the queen turned away, gathered up her ladies, and left the chamber. Moments later, Father Benedic came out with his arm about

Maritha, who was weeping, not from fear or pain, but from relief, and from the joy of being reunited with her husband.

"I feared this morning that I would be torn from my family, and cast out! But thou hast returned me to my husband and my son. Oh, Your Grace! May God smile upon thee for thy wise and tempered counsel. No more dalliances, verily."

"Be certain, too, that Alderon upholds his end of the contract. He has duties, too, both to thee and to thy child."

"I think we need not be concerned with that, Your Grace," spoke Father Benedic. "I walked with him to his wagon, and he was dreadful afraid for his wife. He loves thee sorely, Maritha."

"And I him, Father, with all my heart. Blessings on all of thee, for righting this terrible wrong. I must now find my husband, for I have missed him sorely. Blessings on thee, Father!"

"And on thee, my child. Go with God."

"Father, please return to court, and inform the king that we will wait upon him shortly. I must have a word with my maidens. Only a moment, no longer. My thanks, Father." Syrenya waited until the priest had left their sight, and then turned to Alissa, who twas clear was on the verge of tears. "What is it, my sweet?" she asked, in deep concern.

"Even with all her sins, the Father did happily absolve her of them. The most he hath ever done for Ariadne or me is to try and hide his monstrous indignation. He hath never spoken a single word to either of us, except in rebuke. How can he hate us so?" And the tears came. Ariadne went to her side, and held her in her arms, and she did weep. But it was Syrenya who gave her peace with her words.

"Alissa, my sweet, thou must not concern thyself with the Father! He has been bred into his calling. He dost know that the teachings say that the two of thee, and all like thee, are not allowed to be members of the Roman Catholic Church, even though it is yet another of the stupid laws that men, and mark me, I said men, who are long since dead, wrote down. His learning is of the strictest sort, all obedience and worship, and devil take those who would not do so. It is the way with every priest, precious, and not only in this land. He hath his brain chocked full of such drivel, to the point that it is second nature to him. He knows not what to do with thee, for he sees that thou art good, obedient, caring, loving human beings whose love for each other makes thee happily monogamous. But even with all that, he stumbles over the one thing about thee that is different. He is incapable of understanding thy loving attachment to each other.

"See, then, Alissa, how this doth color his mind. He was pleased and proud to be a part of something that he reads as the very essence of his calling: the reuniting of a man and a woman within the bonds of holy matrimony, made even greater a deed in that here was a child also to be considered. But he has seen thy ways, and found them faultless, and he knows not what to make of thee. Thou didst note his countenance at table last night, surely. And this afternoon at court, he did stand and lead the applause for the pair of thee. Thy innate goodness, Alissa, must understand his plight; he has been taught that thy ways are wicked, and he sees clearly that they are not. Allow him some more time; I am sure he will come around. But please do not cry over it, precious. To see thy tears cuts me to the core. Here, now, kiss thy mate; and me. There now. Shall we return to court?"

Alissa had ceased her weeping, and now there was a faintness of a smile to her face.

"Yes Syrenya," she said. "Let us return to court."

Upon their entry, the court and the king stood, and gave their naked queen polite but heartfelt applause at her very judicius handling of this plight. The queen smiled, climbed the dais, and grasped her husband's outstretched hand. She bowed solemnly, then gracefully resumed her throne and again, brought the cloak over her shoulder. The king, still clutching her left hand, leaned over to her and whispered, "thou art a marvel, my darling. We had not the slightest idea how to bring this tangle of raw emotion to a satisfactory end. Yet thou didst know instantly where the trouble lay. We will tell thee straight, milove, that ye continue to amaze us."

"And hope that I always will, my liege. Twould be a folly for a woman to give up all her secrets at once, and leave nothing to be discovered later."

At that the king chuckled, and returned his attention to the masses.

"Well, Darien, thy queen is unique, to say the least," spoke King Arthur. "But hold a moment; let us go back to this 'coronation' that ye spoke of. Could that not have been thee, who did bring the queen's tiara? It would easily explain why she would choose thee for her historian, later. Is it not so?"

"Sire, I thought that it must be. But I am told otherwise, and I myself have no memory of it. It did seem the logical answer, but it was not. So the simplest answer, unfortunately, was not the correct one. I have bruised my brain, trying to see if I could recall any of the tale except what was told to me, but it is not there. So apparently the youth Darius and I are not the same person."

"Pity," spoke the king, ruminating again on the scene. Then another thought struck him. "Didst thou know the Lady Berniece?"

"Nay, Sire, I did not. Alissa told me that she passed on before I was but five years old. The queen told me that Darius was sent off for schooling, and long after, when I asked of him again, she told me he had left the court, to make his way in the world. So the only part of him I was to know was the part he took in the coronation."

"Then what of thy parents? Hast thou consulted them on this?"

"My parents died of cholora before I ever laid eyes on their faces, Sire. From my birth I have been cared for by the nurses of the king's court."

"Well, then, Darien, my good fellow. Thy tale seems only just started, and already it is noontime. How much more dost thou have for us?"

"I am afraid, Sire, that ye hit upon it when ye thought it might take the day. But after a few notable incidents of their rule, the story moves to how the king and queen died. It is this conclusion, as much as any other part of the tale, that hast left me so baffled. Woulds't thou prefer that we stop?"

"Great heavens, no, Darien. We must have it all now, for this is truly an intriguing tale. It is simply that it is time for luncheon. Surely after such a long telling of this tale, thou art parched, to say the least." The king reached out and pulled a bellpull, and a moment later a boy appeared. The king told the boy his wants, and the lad bowed, and left.

"Now, Sir, please continue."

"SIRE!" came a call from down the hallway. "Sire, we have been seeking thee everywhere. Hast thou forgotten the many tasks that need thy royal approval this day? Thou hast promised to keep a more careful eye upon thy docket, Sire. Pray come away, for there is much ye must be consulted on."

"Darien," spoke the king, with a bit of aggravation, "please meet Callister, my chief minister. The man is a taskmaster."

"How do you do, Sir?" said Calister, a bit put out with the interruption. "We will attempt to keep thee amused while the king is at his duties, Sir. But, Sire, ye must come away at once."

"Callister, how may times have I told thee that there is no 'must' where the king is concerned? These duties, as ye call them, are exactly why we have such capable people as thyself to take care of them. We have invited our guest to join us at luncheon, and until he hath completed his most interesting tale, the king 'must' remain here. There is no matter so grave before this court that thou art unable to handle it, Callister. We look to thee to do so."

"Yes, Your Majesty." Callister gave a slight bow, turned, and retreated the way he came, casting his eyes to heaven as he did so. The king let go with a sound that seemed part laugh, and part snort.

"He only calls us that when he is put out with us. The man means well, God knows, but sometimes he can be perfectly insufferable. Now, Darien, continue."

Chapter 10

Father Benedic

After court that day, Father Benedic returned to his rooms, and made a long and detailed entry in his journal about Alderon and his wife. But having completed the tellng of it, he laid down his quill and pondered over the last three days. It had been literally an overnight courtship, which began with the breaking of the wickedness of First Night; for that alone, this woman must be praised, for she did accomplish it with such grace that none could but admire her for it.

And the change in the king! Gracious heavens, but the man was transformed! One of his ministers had come late this past evening and told him of the merry time the king had at his expense, but he was glad of any mirth that the king should have, whether it be at his expense or no. Never before had the king been in so benevolent a mood; why, the things that had happened in court these past two days were astonishing, when compared to the court the king gave before she had arrived here.

And she! How didst she divine the crux of the matter with old Alderon? He himself would have been blinded by Alderon's rage, for it was righteously told. He would, in all honesty, have taken that wife and sent her packing, according to the law of the land. And his years with the king told him that Ballizar would have done the same. And yet, it would have been a terrible mistake, for it would have caused the misery of three people, and the destruction of a family. This new queen was indeed a marvel.

How she had talked Ballizar into letting those poor women dress was beyond his imagining. Only the Lord knows how he had tried. Now, at least, there would be the semblance of order at court, without the strange and questioning looks that were thrown his way whenever the king welcomed representatives from the surrounding countries. To find two lovely young women apart and bare, and looking more like cats than people, was a terrible affront to some of these gentlemen; and it was sore a temptation to others. He had actually been asked about them by one rouguish foreigner, who was deeply disturbed when the father had told him of their predeliction; "what a waste," said the man, shaking his head and looking down at his feet. Father Benedic, of course, agreed with him immediately, but he suspected that the man had a different meaning in mind when he spoke.

What is to be done about them, though? The queen finally cloaks them from all the eyes at court, only to remain as she came, completely unclad, and more comfortable for it than if she were wearing a queen's gown! Surely she has not covered them out of jealousy, so they are no longer nude with her—nay, from what he could see, all three were the happier for it. It seemed the arrival at this keep of the Lady Syrenya was a God-given gift, even with her stupifying practice of eschewing garb. He believed he would have a conference about it with her, once she had been here awhile, and seen the difference in our culture when compared to hers.

God only knows, he ruminated, what happened in the king's chambers these last three nights. He was just as happy not to know the details, but it was obvious that the king was a new man because of it. It had now been over 72 hours, and if the king's wicked desires had manifested themselves in that time, he was not aware of it. So she hath brought peace to his marriage bed, as well. Whence came she? She had even refused to answer the king's own question when he asked her about her origins; and as far as most of the people at court knew, she had not yet revealed that information to anyone, including her new ladies-in-waiting.

Lady Ariadne and Lady Alissa; the phrase sounded somehow strange to him. He was being forced to come to grips with the fact that, even though the king had long ago made them members of the court, they had become in the father's eyes more like the king's mascots than anything else. Except for court they kept to themselves; to see them upon the dais of the king's table startled him so, that he was as yet unable to completely assimilate this drastic change in protocol. But on this point, he told himself, having them dressed and a part of the court was a good deal easier for him to deal with than their naked bodies had been these seven years. But the thought of the pair again brought him up short; what was it he had seen this very night upon their hands at dinner? He made no inquiry, but it looked entirely to him as if they wore new jewelry: *wedding bands?!* Rings of gold and diamonds, no less, and worn on the ring finger of the left hand...this was something he felt the queen had a hand in. This was beyond bending the rules; the union of members of the same sex in marriage was a sin strictly forbidden in the Church, and he was sure that Queen Syrenya knew it. But he would find out soon enough.

Alone in his room with his own thoughts, the father was finally able to admit to himself that their naked beauty did sometimes give him an uncomfortable turn. The fact that any contact with them would violate both their preferences, and the Church's, kept him from giving in to the temptation, fortunately; but now, given their new wardroabe, it would be hard for the uninformed individual to distinguish these two from any other ladies at court. On this point, he was not quite ready to simply let it go. Surely all the teachings of the Church have not been lost upon them. These two new ladies were models of proper behavior, even he had to admit that. If only he could find a way to release them of their periloous desire for each other! It was a thorn in his side that they should be under such a wicked spell. In all else, they would be model Catholics, and suitable material for a queen's train. But he was determined to speak to her about their sin, and maybe would be able to obtain her help in counseling them. Her way with Maritha proved her an able counselor.

Well, getting them dressed was not a bad beginning; perhaps there was hope for their souls yet. If only the queen could persuade them against their damning desires—and if he could only persuade the queen to take to the sumptuous wardrobe that was already hers. If he was able to achieve these two ends, then when his time came to return to heaven, he could feel justly proud of the work he had accomplished here on earth.

He was about to snuff his candle and turn in when a short rapping on his door drew his attention. He opened the door to a page; what was the problem now? But the page only handed him a short note, and waited for the father to give him a reply.

"Yes, my lad. Tell her I will be there straight." Then he placed the open note upon his desk and redonned his robe. In an impeccable hand, the note read, "I desire that ye should wait upon me at ten this evening in the courtroom antechamber. There are matters we must discuss." It was signed only with a large, scripted "S." It was hard upon ten now; he wondered if she was there already. It would never do to keep the queen waiting.

Having just reached the antechamber, he could see light coming from the small window set in the door. He composed himself and, taking a deep breath, knocked twice.

"Pray come in, Father," was the response. Benedic entered and shut the door behind him.

"Good evening, Your Grace," he said easily. He was greatly relieved to find that she had donned her scarlet cloak; he would not, at least, be forced to stare at those magnificent breasts all through the conference. Then, taking in the room, he noticed that the candle on the table illuminated a large bible, open before her on the table.

"Ah, Your Grace, I am pleased to see that ye keep up with thy bible. I thought it might be so, after seeing thy Solomon-like handling of the elder and his bride."

"Thank thee, Father," she said simply, and let it hang there. He was not certain whether she was thanking him for his approval of her bible studies, or for his referral to Solomon in reference to her success. She remained seated, with the table between them; there was no other chair. "I have donned this cloak in honor of thy station, Father. I know that my naked body gives thee discomfort." Another double meaning. Was he in trouble here?

"Father, before we begin on weightier matters, I would have thee know that ye left the Lady Alissa in tears when ye bore my message back to the king this afternoon."

"I am sorry to hear it, Your Grace. Dost thou know the cause?"

"Oh, yes, I know it. I wonder if thou dost."

"I can think of nothing I could have done to upset her, Your Grace; I doubt I even spoke to her, so concerned was I for—"

"That is quite the point, Father. You never even spoke to her." She then was silent, leaving the poor father feeling rather the worse for missing something the queen obviously felt was important. He could not for the life of him figure out what it was. When she did speak again, it did nothing to relieve his discomfort.

"She believes ye do hate them, Father, her and Ariadne."

"Beg pardon, Your Grace?"

"She told me this afternoon that she feels ye do hate them."

"Why on earth would she…"

"She noted the joy and alacrity with which ye absolved Maritha, despite the fact that she had, justly or not, committed three acts of adultery. That is rather a steep sin, is it not, Father?"

"It is, indeed, Your Grace. But ye saw for thyself that Maritha did confess her sin, and be heartily sorry for it. I would be remiss in my duties if I did not absolve her. That is pretty much what I do. Your Grace."

"That is the second time in two days ye have used that term, Father. 'Remiss.' It troubles thee to be remiss, does it not?"

"Of course, Your Grace. I have many tenets to follow in my calling, and I would wish to follow them all, and thus not be remiss. If I am remiss, then I have let down a member of my flock. And I have let down my Heavenly Father, as well."

"Thou dost state thy sin perfectly, Father. I could not have done better myself."

"Your Grace?"

"Thou hast been remiss, sir, and for quite a period. Ye have let down not just one, but two of thy flock, and it very probably makes the Heavenly Father decidedly put out with thee. I know full well that I am."

"Your Grace, please accept my apologies, but I cannot fathom what thy meaning is. I do not recall any time when I was remiss in tending to my flock. I take my positioon here very seriously, Your Grace."

"I know that to be true, Father. That is why I bring this to thy attention. Thou hast refused communion, confession, absolution and a host of other deeds that we in the Catholic Church practice. Thou hast barred from the Lady Alissa a seat in thy house. And the Lady Ariadne, as well. That is expressly why my maidens believe thou dost hate them."

"Your Grace, surely thou must know…"

"I have been reading a very interesting passage in this bible, Father. It seems that a shepherd was hurriedly attempting to get his flock of sheep into the barn before a terrible winter storm overtook them. He got all of the sheep he could possibly round up in the time he had available to him, and was indeed so long at the task that it became necessary to stay in the barn for his own shelter, as well. Having then just spent great pains in securing his flock, he took count of them, and discovered that he was short one lamb. Dost know this tale, Father?"

"Of course, Your Grace. Try as he might, he could not forget the one lamb he had missed, and finally braved the storm long enough to find the lamb, and return it to the flock. It is a parable, Your Grace; we who serve the Church are shepherds of our flock, and to forget one of the flock is tantamount to a criminal act. Dost thou feel that I have done this?"

"Yes, I do. And thou shouldst, also. In the short period of time I have been here, Father, I have taken note, both with mine own eyes, and from my maidens, that thou dost even refrain from speaking to them, let alone lead them to thy 'flock.' It is this paradox, in the face of thy way with Maritha, that did cause the Lady Alissa to weep."

"Your Grace, surely thou knowest that Maritha's sin was short-lived, and she confessed it and was heartily sorry for it. She met the standard for which the Church doth redeem her."

"I see. Then these absolutions are similar to financial transactions?"

"Of course not, but..."

"Then why hast thou left these ladies unattended? They are a part of thy flock, and quite frankly, I see thy treatment of them as being far more than remiss. I find it to be purposeful and injurious, and it doth anger me!"

"Now, see here, my good woman, what..."

Syrenya slammed her hand down on the table, making a crack that resounded in the tiny chamber. It brought Benedic up short, and he stood there, stupified. A tone that the father did not like crept into the queen's voice. She was furious, and she spoke in a very soft tone, which only lent weight to her words.

"I do thee the honor of addressing thee by thy title, *father*. I would appreciate it if ye would do me the same courtesy." Benedic's face reddened, as he realized what he had done.

"I am heartily sorry, Your Grace," he said contritely. "Please know that it will not happen again."

"I trust it will not. But ye still must justify to me why thou hast not seen to the souls of what those hereabouts have referred to as 'The Nudes.' I will have thine answer."

"Your Grace, neither the Lady Alissa nor the Lady Ariadne has confessed their sin to me, nor have they to any priest here at court; in fact, I do honestly believe that they do not even consider their practices a sin at all. In fact, I have noted upon their ring fingers recently matching wedding bands, as if they had somehow made a pact of marriage! I see thy hand in this, Your Grace, and it is my duty to tell thee that such a union is absolutely forbidden in the Church. If they maintain this sin, then they are lost forever. If they do not repent their sins, I cannot see to them. They are lost to me."

"What thou hast seen upon the fingers of my ladies are gifts from their queen, Father. They are identical diamond bands that mark their station; and in the event that I ever decide I need another lady, she shall receive the very same gift for her service. I fear, Father, that it is thine own bias that has brought thee to this unfounded conclusion. Art thou so quick to judge? And what sin is it that thou dost refer to, Father; are they proud? Slovenly? Full of avarice? Tell to me their sin."

"Their desire for each other is their sin, Your Grace, as I am sure ye art fully aware."

"I am of course aware of their desire for each other, Father. I cannot, however, agree that it is a sin."

"I know that thou hast taken these ladies to thy heart, Your Grace, but surely thou dost know that homsexuality is condemned by the Catholic Church!"

"I will ask of thee one question, Father, and I hope to receive an honest answer. Hast thou ever considered the possibility that those like my maidens are put here on on this earth, by God, for a reason? Hast thou even considered that?"

"I must say that I find it an affliction they are born with, and must work, within the Church, to overcome. Confession and absolution are given on the understanding that the confessor will work not to sin so again."

"So what we have here, two perfectly normal women, who are trusted, honest, and live in a harmonious and monogamous union, are nothing more than sinners, is that the Church's stance?"

"It is, Your Grace. Thou dost know it is."

"Then I throw the Church back in thy face, sir, for it doth offend me greatly!" spat the queen. She was obviously and thoroughly angry, though at whom or what, he was not sure. He held his ground but he also held his peace. In a moment, she had calmed somewhat, and asked of him another question.

"Hast ever entered the minds of those who work within the Church that God put such people on the earth to teach thee tolerance?" Benedic tensed, because he knew the only answer he could give was not what she wanted to hear.

"It is an affliction, Your Grace. Only if those so afflicted confess their sin, and take hold of God's mercy, can they ever be saved. That is how the Church sees them."

"Is the Church a human being, Father? Can it really see, at all? Can it see what ye see every day, that these children are good, kind, and loving individuals. Why dost their love offend thee? Should not we all be grateful for whatever love we find on this earth? Canst thou truly find fault with them? I firmly believe if it were possible, by some miracle, to change one of them to a man, then all of this discussion would be moot, would it not?"

"Well, yes, I suppose it would…"

"Then I have a charge for thee, sir. And I do not make it lightly. I charge thee, and yea, all of the priests here at court, to look on Ariadne as Animus. I do; and it doth not offend me. I ask that ye all try to do the same. By any account, I would have ye look on these two people as true, loving persons, who deserve far better at thy hands than thou hast giv'n. Look not that ye speak for the Church; I have no power over the Church. But like it or no, Father, I do have power over thee. And I would see thee give my maidens better than what ye have given them previously."

"Your Grace, what ye ask…"

"Oh, no, Father, mistake me not. I do not ask. I charge thee; I give thee a royal command. Father, hast thou wondered what has passed between the king and me in his chambers these past few nights?"

"I confess I have taken a moment to ponder it. But I would never take it upon myself to inquire. What goes on in the royal chambers is for nought but the royals to know."

"That is exactly the answer I wanted, Father, for it leads me to one more question. If it is nought of thy business what takes place behind the doors of those who rule this land, then why dost thou take it upon thyself to be concerned with what goes on behind any door in this castle—specifically Alissa and Aridane's?" Whether he was tired, or confused, or simply worn down by the argument, he could find no answer for his queen. He decided to try and do as she had charged him to do, and look on her maidens only while in sight, and not speculate on them when they were out of sight. But the decision caused a sigh to escape him.

"I will take it upon myself to attempt fulfilling thy charge, Your Grace. I will make every effort to do so."

"I am pleased that thou wilt. But surprisingly, that is not why I have asked for this meeting."

"It isn't!?" The Father's head was spinning now. Surely there could not be anything of more significance than the bending of the rules of the Holy Roman Catholic Church!

The queen was silent for a time, perhaps marshalling her thoughts. Whatever was going to be spoken of here, it was clear that, to the queen at least, it was a very grave matter, indeed. She let out a breath, and began.

"Father, art thou possessed of the powers of exorcism?"

"Wha-what?"

"Art thou possessed of the powers of exorcism? Canst thou perform one?"

"Your Grace, thy question stuns me. I have never been in need of the powers of exorcism. I would not know what to do with them if I were."

"I suspected as much. Then dost thou know of a priest who is, in Tabithia? Or even the surrounding countries?"

"Your Grace, I know not why thou shouldst ask such questions. The time when it was necessary to seek out the powers of exorcism are long since past. These are modern times. The minions of Hades found long ago that they were not the match for any exorcist, who may channel the wrath of God. And while I cannot speak with authority on this, it appears that Beelzebub does not concern himself with such matters. All of the creatures that have been driven out of possessed individuals have been documented as being demons. There hast never been seen a possession that was conducted by the Devil himself. Good gracious, dost thou not hear how uncommonly ridiculous this all sounds? The very idea of such a situation has long since been happily banished from thought. Dost thou actually have need of an exorcist?"

"No, Father, I do not. But the king does."

There was a long pause while Benedic recovered from the queen's flat statement.

"Canst thou tell me what has happened to make thee reach this conclusion, Your Grace?"

"Certainly. I have seen it, with mine own eyes."

"But where…"

"'The eyes are windows to the soul,' Father. When the king suffers his attacks, it is not because of something broken or awry with his body. These fevers are brought upon him when this demon doth possess the king's body. Ye must know that my very reason for being here is to relieve the king of these fits, or fevers, or desires, or whatever other incorrect name one may put upon it. I have seen this happen, Father. The very first night I spent with the king, his first words to me were 'if thou cannot relieve me of these demons, I fear I am damned.' That does not sound to me like a man suffering from fevers, Father. It sounds like a soul in torment. And when I worked to relieve him, it was not only the release a woman may give him I encountered. I felt something fighting to keep him from release. I could not identify it at the time, but now that the wedding night has passed, know thee that, last night, I looked into the eyes of my husband and saw the cold black eyes of a demon staring back at me."

"Didst thou tell the king of this?"

"Nay, Father, I did not. Demon or no, I am able, at least for the present, to stymie it. But the king burns when this demon is upon him, Father. When I lie with him under these conditions, his body is hot to the touch. Not just the added warmth of passion, Father. Hot. So hot that my normal body temperature cools him. It is this, as much or more than the release I can give him, that keeps this hellish imp at bay, for the nonce.

"And, Father, please know that ye may forgive the king for the horrrible ritual of First Night. Twas never he who planned it, nor he who set it in motion. The king that thou hast come to know since my arrival is the king ye wouldst have always had, were it not for this hellish creature."

"I shall hold a purification ritual for him tonight, Your Grace. He will be absolved."

"For reasons I cannot fathom, this demon only comes upon him fitfully, not entirely and permanently like those that would immediately demand the bringing of an exorcist. If thou dost know of any man, near or far, that hath practiced this skill, then I ask thee, Father, humbly, to contact him. Not as thy queen do I ask. I ask it for the king, my husband, whom ye serve. I understand, Father, from thy statements, that ye might not succeed; but the attempt must be made, and soon. My husband doth suffer greatly when this fiend is upon him, Father. Even more than thou and thy doctors are aware. It is as if he burned in hellfire. And if this devil should ever decide to again possess the king while he is at court or at business of the crown, then it may very well be that I would not be able to rout the monster. Please grant me two things, if thou wilt, Father. Try to find an exorcist with all thy power. And speak not a word of this to anyone, particularly the king."

"I shall do as ye ask, Your Grace, but, as ye say, we may very well fail. And I would never reveal what is given to me in confidence."

"Then I am glad that we are of one mind in this, Father. Search far and wide; within that time I will do what I can to contain the beast. May I request that ye begin immediately? For I have no other matters to put before thee."

"Your Grace, I will return to my rooms and begin tonight…"

"But?"

"Your Grace, in light of this information, now may be a bad time to discuss it, but…"

"Yes, Father. Go on."

"Your Grace, in thy role as Queen of Tabithia, thou art owner of a magnificent wardrobe. Wouldst thou not consider using it? Surely thou hast noticed that the ways of the people of Tabithia are different from those of thine own country." The queen, at this point, stood, and bent forward and touched the priest on his arm, and gave him a rueful smile.

"Poor Father. Thou must try, I suppose. But I am afraid I cannot do what ye ask, Father. And it is not only because I grew this way that I do eschew dress. The matters we have discussed here demand that I be immediately available to the king whenever this demon strikes, and I must say that the garb that is the standard in this country is mightily difficult to unravel. Nay, Father, it would never do. It is not for decorum, or the lack thereof, that I maintain my nudity. It is a matter of as swift and earnest a retaliation as I can mount against this foe. I hope that thou art satisfied with this answer, Father. I know it doth trouble thee, but it cannot be helped. Naked I am, and naked I must remain. At least until we can bring an exorcist to Tabithia."

"Then I will use every tool at my disposal, your Grace. And immediately."

"Father, one thing more. In the event it should happen, I would like to have a plan against this devil if he comes while we are at court. In the instant that it happens, I shall take the king by his head and kiss him long and deep. If I am successful, this can delay the attack momentarily. If ye should see me do so, as if for no reason, then I wish to have thee assist me. On that kiss as a signal, thou and two of thy priests must leave the hall on thy side of the king, immediately. I, with the king in tow, will be right behind thee. We must bring him here, to the antechamber, and then I will embrace my king. While I do, ye must stand close, and pray, aloud and long, all of thee. Invoke that wrath of God ye didst tell me of. Even if it is not entirely successful, thy added force will be a detriment to this monster's hold on Ballizar. May we lock this plan in place?"

"Certainly, Your Grace; thou art wise to have thought of it. But what will happen if we all leave the court so suddenly?"

"Alissa and Ariadne know what to do. They will straight to Lord Farraman, whom thou knowest is the king's most trusted advisor. Methinks he is versed enough of court that he may rule on the petitioners' requests. If what we spoke of here doth come to pass, I will of course explain these things to Lord Farraman. But unless it does, none at court may know of it. I think this is the best approach for all concerned."

"Your Grace, I feel the hand of God is with thee, for thy words art wise and kind."

"I thank thee, Father. For this service, I am truly in thy debt."

"Your Grace, thou art both protection and succor to thy husband. When thou dost take these duties so close to thy heart, and in peril, then I may do no less. There is no debt. We work toward the same goal. Let us be partners in this venture, for I do perceive that the greater task is thine. I will begin immediately, and I will pray for thee both, tonight and henceforth. I go now to begin. Goodnight, Your Grace. Go with God."

"Good night, Father. And my thanks goes with thee."

King Arthur realized he had been holding his bread between his plate and his open mouth, and he lowered it again.

"Darien, thy priest was, or is, if he still lives, a fool. Possession still takes place, even now, and it is not always a demon who doth practice it. Here in England, there are those who have been possessed by ancestors, vengeful spirits, malignant forces, and demons, of course, as well. So to dismiss it out of hand as he didst—Good God, man! He might have sealed the king's fate, then and there. Didst they ever locate an exorcist?"

"There was one man, Sire, who came to the castle years later, and told us he had been summoned by the priest because he was an exorcist. But even though we did implore him to stay some days at the castle so that he might witness the possesion, all was for nought. The entire time he was there, the king suffered no attacks, whatsoever. The man told us that the king was not, could not, be possessed, for it is the standard that those who are possessed remain so until the demon is driv'n out. He was fair put out for our bringing him so long a distance for nothing, and only gold would appease him. But after he went his way, not one hour after he was gone, the king was struck mightily, and the queen told me later that it was all she could do to keep the king with her, until his fire was put out. It made for a hellish tale, and I was fair horrified by it."

"So there was never an exorcism?"

"There was one finally, at the end, Sire; and if thou feels that Father Benedic was foolish, he did right by all of us at the end. But I have again raced to the end of my tale, leaving out the many things that the queen was able to do for the country and, specifically, for me and mine, while she did tend to our king.

"I myself was not told of the queen's battles until I was quite a bit older than I was when all this took place. It is not until the age of ten that I have a clear memory of her. At that time, she had been queen for five years. She, and her ladies, Ariadne and Alissa, did amongst the three of them look to my rearing, from that time. And it was a complete surprise to me when, one day, the queen brought me a sheet of parchment and, grinning a wide smile, had me read the document. I was completely shocked, for I had never expected such a thing. The document, all signed and official, stated that I was now the adopted son of Queen Syrenya of Tabithia, and as such, was the prince next in line for the throne. Sire, ye could have knocked me to the floor with a breath…"

CHAPTER 11

The Birds and the Bees

It was shortly after Darien's tenth birthday that he had his first direct contact with the Naked Queen. He had recalled staring at her, because of everyone present at court, she was the only one who was not wearing clothes. He wondered why that was. He also wondered at the strange internal feeling he had when he looked at the queen for very long. From his place at court with the other children, he watched her as court would proceed. It seemed to him that she was very intelligent, and very gentle. And it seemed to him, too, that the king and queen loved each other very much. He wondered if he would someday be as happy in a marriage as they were.

Once he reached the age of ten, his schoolmaster turned him over to the queen and her ladies. Their first meeting, they had all sat at a round table: him, the schoolmaster, the queen, and the Lady Alissa and the Lady Ariadne. Lady Alissa was almost directy across from him; she gave him a big smile and winked at him. This made him lose some of the anxiety that had built up inside him just prior to this meeting. He could not remember what was said, but it all seemed very cordial; and he did have the sense, when asked, to say yes, that he would very much like for the queen and her ladies to take over his schooling. This had not been a hard question to answer, because he liked Lady Alissa very much, and he did not like the schoolmaster very much at all.

It was about six months after that date, as Darien received many hours of daily tutoring by the queen and her ladies, that Syrenya had brought Darien that piece of parchment, which, due particularly to that schooling, he could read without difficulty. His eyes watered, and he held the queen with a look composed of part wonder, part warmth, and part elation. He dropped the document (which Ariadne deftly regained) and ran to the queen and hugged her, and she hugged him back. It was the first time in his life that anyone had said that he was wanted; for it to be the queen herself, he never would have dreamed.

Shortly after his formal adoption, he suddenly remembered that the document said that he was the adopted son of Queen Syrenya of Tabithia. It had said nothing at all about the king. He pondered this, and then he remembered to ask Alissa about it, one afternoon during his lessons. She told him that the king was ill, and that he might live a long time, or he might die soon. Since it was true and necessary that Darien be the ascendant even if only adopted by Syrenya, the king had thought that it was a better idea to leave himself out of the legal question. It was one of the very few times that he and the queen had argued in the entire lifetime they shared together. It was only when the king told his wife that, except for that one fact, he would be as much a father to the boy as she would be mother, that Syrenya accepted the compromise and moved forward with the adoption.

The day that the queen had chosen for Darien's birthday was February 14th. She told him that his own had been lost amid the terror and confusion of the cholera that swept through the castle, taking from him his father and mother in one stroke. Once the date had been settled, his birthday became an event as celebrated as the king's or the queen's, for he now was a part of the royal family, and all that entailed. He now was receiving advanced tutelage on the ways of an heir, his duties, his responsibilities, and all of the freedoms the royals enjoyed, as well.

His nurses became Alissa and Ariadne, and part of their charge was to tell him everything that had happened since the queen had come to Tabithia, and not simply once; many times o'er. The two charged him to remember it all, and at times had him repeat the tale back to them, so they could be satisfied that he knew it. The queen, his mother, often came and sat with him, and spoke of lore of foreign lands, of how the angels did surround the earth, and how each individual had a guardian angel, that watched over that person for all his life. These were fantastic flights of fantasy for him, for he had had, at the hands of the schoolmaster, only a rudimentary schooling, and as a result had not known the lore of Tabithia, nor that of any country. The queen and her ladies, therefore, looked to fill in the gaps that his earlier schooling had left, and he found that he was proficient with numbers. He did, on one occasion, give the schoolmaster quite a turn when he nearly beat the man at figuring out a particularly thorny mathematical theorem. Darien was taught the sports, the ettiquette, and the ways of the court necessary for one who would one day rule, and his days were full. At night, in his room, the queen would come and talk with him, and he was always left with some wonder to ponder, when at last she kissed him goodnight, and snuffed his candle.

Now Darien had just had his thirteenth birthday, and the queen marked it as a coming of age. His sense of male and female was now upon him, in his adolescence, and it was a time that was not lost on his mother and her ladies. Hugs there had always been, from Alissa, who was especially fond of him, and Ariadne, too. But while hugs had been plentiful from his mother, as well, at first, it was now becoming evident that her hugging a boy well on his way to manhood was becoming a touch uncomfortable for her son. He wondered why these strange feelings were overtaking him whenever his mother hugged him.

Alissa, who was especially fond of him, would give him his bath regularly; but now, when she soaped his chest, or washed his hair, or gave him a brisk drying with a big, fuzzy towel, he would react in a way that stupified him. His loins would grow hot, and his cock would grow hard and big and red; but Alissa, who was perfectly aware of the situation, told him that it was nothing he need worry about, because the queen would explain it all to him very soon.

He was also suddenly aware of how the girls at court would stare at him, and sometimes give him smiles that he knew must mean something, but what that something was, he could not fathom. And so it was that, one night, when the queen came to his room for their nightly chat, that the subject was something that his mother called sex. He was about to receive his lesson on the birds and the bees.

"Darien, sweet, thou art staring at my breasts. Dost thou like to do that?"

"Yes, Mother. I think that they are very pretty."

"I thank thee, my gallant one. But thou dost have something going on inside when ye do so, am I right?"

"Mother, I get all jumbled up inside. Like I do when Alissa gives me my bath. She told me ye would tell me what it was."

"Well, darling, it is a process that God gave us so that we may bring children into the world. He made men and women different, and he made each side very interested in the differences the other possessed. The reason that thou art experiencing these new feelings, is because thou art approaching manhood, and, I should say, faster than I thought ye would. Do ye like to look at Alissa?"

"Very much, Mother, and Ariadne, too. They are very pretty. I love them both."

"As ye should, Darien, for they are thine aunts, since thou hast no other aunts to coddle thee. The two of them will continue to spend a lot of time with thee, seeing to thy schooling. I expect that they will become even more dear to thee, once the process that is going on inside thee is completed. And, of course, we shall always have our chats in the evening. But after tonight, I will wear my scarlet cape when I come."

"Why, Mother?"

"Because the thoughts that thou shouldst begin to have shortly, while thou dost stare at my breasts, will be troubling to thee. Thou wilt begin to understand the relationship between the king and me, and also begin to understand why, when we have separate bedchambers, we do sleep together, in one bed or the other, but seldom one bed to each. Up until now thou hast slept in a bed by thyself, but soon ye will wish it were not so. Ye will find thyself wishing that there was some young lady who would lie with thee, as I do with the king."

"Mother, the girls at court are very strange with me. They want to smile at me and touch me, and I do confess that I like it, but I do not know why I like it."

"Thou art an astute pupil, dearest. Those looks and touches are the things that go on when a man and a woman are attracted to one another. Their real wish, beneath all the confusion, is to sleep together like the king and I do, and be able to touch one another when they wish to. There is a particular sharing that takes place between a man and a woman, when each decides it is the other they want to touch, and be with. Hast thou found a girl in court that thou dost feel that way about, Darien?"

'I think so, Mother; but in fact, I think I want them all to smile and touch me. It is a very pleasant feeling. But I feel like that is only a part of what I feel inside when they do touch me; like there is something I should know to do in return, but know not what it is."

"Yes, child, thou art correct. Hast ye watched the king and I, or Alissa and Ariadne, when we kiss?"

"Yes, Mother! It looks like something that is very enjoyable. But is pressing lips together that thing I don't know? Or is there something else?"

"Thou art too far in front of me, my precious. Yes, there is something else. It is that something else that makes me want to sleep with the king. It is called sex."

"Sex. What does that mean, Mother?"

"Darien, thou dost know the Lady Sarah at court, yes?"

"Yes. Mother. She grew very round for awhile, and then she was thin again. Is that what ye mean?"

"It is. Lady Sarah was pregnant, and she gave birth a little while ago to a new baby, remember? It was a very little person, and Sarah could carry him in her arms."

"Yes, Mother. And the baby seemed to make the Lady Sarah and Lord Farraman very happy. So it is babies that make married people happy?"

"Very special babies make married people happy. Lord and Lady Farraman are happy because the baby is theirs. It grew inside Lady Sarah until it was big enough to bring out. And when they brought the baby out, that's when Lady Sarah was thin again. Do ye remember the two things as happening at one time?"

"Yes, Mother."

"That is what we mean when we say that a child has been born. That it grew inside the mother until it was ready to be born. Follow?"

"Yes, Mother, but…"

"But what, Darien?"

"What makes her get big like that? Not all the ladies at court get big like that. Why do some get big, and others not?"

"We come now to the heart of the matter, my son. It is sex that makes the woman grow big. Sex is what nature uses to bring together two parts, one from the man and one from the woman, and combine them to make a baby. But the process is very odd, and it needs some explaining, dear. I will try to explain it to thee."

"Ye stare at my breasts, child, because they are a part of a woman's charms. These charms attract men to a woman. In order not to attract too many, both women and men wear clothes, like thine, so that, when a woman chooses to show her charms, they will be very strong medicine for the man she chooses to show them to. She does not show them to anyone until she finds a man she is sure will appreciate them.

"The man has charms that are attractive to a woman. His muscles, when he is big and strong, are very powerful charms. There is also a charm that is very important when a man and a woman make a baby. Thou hast one. It is between thy legs. Remember how it gets big and red when Alissa gives thee thy bath?"

At this point, a nod was all Darien could manage.

"It is big and red now, isn't it?" Another nod.

"And ye would like it to stop, am I right?" Still another.

"It is that way because ye can see my charms, dear. There is a particular young woman who is waiting for thee, so she can help it go away. And when she does, it feels very, very good. And when she helps you make it go away, the way it is done is the way babies are made.

"Listen carefully, my sweet, because this is both important, and difficulat to talk about, so I won't want to repeat myself. Ready?"

"Yes, Mother."

"Good. When thou dost find a young lady, and the two of thee decide that there is a bond formed between thee, then the desire to make babies becomes very strong. The way it is done sounds very strange, but it feels very good, so even though it might be strange, a man and a woman like to do it.

"I told thee that ye were uncomfortable because I am naked. And ye can see my charms. But the same reaction comes when Alissa gives thee thy bath. That is because thou art naked. The lack of clothing makes both men and women want to feel this good feeling. Ye said that it was nice when the girls touch thee, yes?" Another nod.

"And it is nice to touch girls back, is it not?"

"Yes, Mother, but only sometimes. Sometimes when I touch a girl, she gets very upset. If I try to touch Alissa while at my bath, she shushes me and makes me stop. Am I doing something wrong?"

"Nay, child, thou art doing nothing wrong when ye touch. But there are only certain girls who will like being touched. One of them who likes to touch thee likes it when ye touch her, am I right?" A nod.

"She wants to do this thing with ye that feels so good. When ye kiss this girl, do ye feel something happen inside? And does it seem like something happens inside her, too?"

"Yes, Mother, but there is only one girl at court who has tried to kiss me. When I want to kiss her, she wants me to. When I want to kiss other girls, they don't want me to. But if they do, then this one girl gets very upset. She hit me with her fan when she saw me do it with another girl."

"I see. Then thou hast already someone who is particularly attracted to thee?"

"Yes, ma'am. She is the Lady Stephanie; her parents are Lord and Lady Windover."

"Yes, I know who she is. She is very pretty, don't ye think?"

"Mother, Lady Stephanie is beautiful."

"Oh, she is, is she? Well then. I shall have to invite Lord and Lady Windover to join me at luncheon very soon. Answer me a question, love. Have the two of thee kissed often?"

"Only thrice. But I would like to kiss her much more."

"Hast held her hand?"

"Oh, yes, Mother, all the time. She likes it when I do that."

"My son, I think we have had this conversation just in the nick of time. Lady Stephanie wants ye to do with her that thing that feels so good, and that makes babies." Darien's eyes grew wide.

"Really? Ye know this?"

"Oh, yes. But there is one thing ye should know before we go further. Before ye and Lady Stephanie can do this thing, a proper setting must be arranged. Thy mother and Lord and Lady Windover must discuss this, and make sure that the proper setting is arranged for thee. Before ye do this lovely thing, thou must give Stephanie a ring. Knowest thou why?"

"When I give a girl a ring, I am asking her to get married. Am I going to marry Stephanie?" *Lady* Stephanie, thought the queen, though she did not feel it necessary to correct her son at this point.

"If that is what ye would like to do. Before ye can do this thing with Lady Stephanie, ye must decide to marry her. If ye should decide not, then thou wouldst have to find another lady at court to marry. Thou hast come of age, Son. And many girls at court would like to be thy princess. Is there any other girl at court that ye dost like as much as Lady Stephanie?"

"Nay, Mother. Lady Stephanie is very different than the other girls at court. She is very special. I didn't mind it very much when she hit me with her fan, because kissing that other girl didn't feel right. Kissing Stephanie feels right."

"Son, dost thou know that all the things thou art tellng me mean that thy wish is to wed Lady Stephanie?"

"Yes, I think I do, Mother. Does that mean we will have a sedding?"

"Yes, indeed, we will have a wedding. And it will be a very special occasion. But first there are still two things we need to talk about. First, after thou art wed to Stephanie, thou dost know that ye may do this good thing with her and her alone? No one else. Dost thou know this?"

"Yes, Mother. Alissa told me so."

"And what else did the Lady Alissa tell thee?"

"Nothing." He sounded disappointed. "When I asked, all she said was that I would have to ask thee. She said that thou wouldst tell me why I should not kiss Lady Melinda after I had kissed Lady Stephanie."

"Thou hast kissed Lady Melinda?" Mother sounded worried.

"Yes, Mother, once. That was when Stephanie hit me with her fan."

"Very well, then. Alissa is correct. Thou shouldst not attempt to kiss any of the other ladies at court after thou hast given a ring to thy Stephanie. It would upset her very much. And ye would get to feeling bad about it, and have to confess it to Father Benedic."

"Mother, dost that mean it is a sin?"

"Indeed I do, love. Father Benedic would be very cross with thee. So would Lady Stephanie, and so would I."

"This giving rings is a very serious business, isn't it, Mother?"

"Truly, my son. Ye will be telling Lady Stephanie that ye would like to do this special thing with her. It will perhaps make her cry, but they will be happy tears. But remember that when thou dost give Stephanie a ring, ye must ask if she will take it. She must say yes, she will take the ring; if she does not, then ye will need to find another lady at court to give the ring to, because Stephanie will be saying that she does not wish to do this special thing with thee. But I doubt, from what ye hast said, that she would do that. As I said before, I must have conference with Lord and Lady Windover.

"But now, this is the act that thou wilt be asking Stephanie to do with thee. It is difficult to do the first time, because ye have not yet felt the pleasure. But do not give up. Keep trying. Ye will manage it soon enough.

"First, ye must take her her ring. When she says yes, put it on her finger, this one, on the left hand. Understand?"

"Yes, Mother."

"Very good. Once that is done, the two of thee will be betrothed. That means that the two of thee intend to wed, and be husband and wife. This must be done with all seriousness, Darien. Ye and thy princess will afterwards live together, and ye will be her husband, and she will be thy wife. Dost thou understand these things?"

"Yes, Mother. I have thought about it, and I would be very unhappy if I could not wed Stephanie. I am certain that I love her."

"Ah, Darien, thou hast hit upon it squarely! And dost thou think that Stephanie loves thee?"

"Oh, yes, Mother, she has told me so. And I her."

"Splendid! Then all that is left is to give thee what takes place when ye and the Lady Stephanie do this very special thing that feels so good. Sometimes it is referred to as sex. Mostly it is referred to as making love. Hast heard the phrase?"

"Oh, yes, Mother! Lord Archie hast told me that he has been making love with Lady Agnes. He says it is a very, very good thing to do. He said he wants to do it again." The queen made a mental note. Twas clear she would have to take his parents aside, as well.

"All right, then. As I told thee before, when ye are naked, thou dost have that feeling, and that reaction. Dost thou have the same reaction when ye thinks on Lady Stephanie? Dost thou think of her as naked, as well?" This time, the nod was a little sheepish. The queen thought it was lovely.

"After we have a big wedding for thee and Stephanie, the two of ye will retire to a chamber that will have been prepared for thee. There will be many flowers, and sweetmeats to share; and it will be here that ye shall make love with Stephanie. And it should be absolutely wonderful for both of thee. But if it is not, be not discouraged; thy natural instinct will tell thee what to do.

"Something that Stephanie will like very much is for thee to undress her and make her naked. She will do the same thing for thee. By that time, ye will have had the reaction that I see thou art having now. Just talking about it makes it happen, does it not?"

"Yes, Mother. Just thinking about it makes it happen. The one thing I am very eager to do is to see Lady Stephanie when she is naked. She has such beautiful skin, and she is what Alissa calls shapely. It makes me want to touch her everywhere."

"Then that is exactly what ye should do, on thy wedding night. She will like it very much. And she may do things for ye that will make ye feel very good, and she should make thee very hard. Here is why. The two of thee may make each other feel as good as ye may like, for as long as ye like. But eventually the pair of thee will want to do this thing that feels so good. I am going to tell thee how it works, my son, and I will never show thee again. But thou must know these things, and why, if thou art to please thy bride on thy weddng night.

"All of the ladies, in fact all women everwhere, are different from all the men. Thou dost know this. Here is why they are different. The ladies have breasts like I do. Ye will want to touch them, and she will like it when ye do. But always touch them gently, for they are very sensitive. Ye will feel her nipple get hard, like mine is now. See?" And indeed the queen's nipple was hard. Darien marked it.

"It will make her feel even better if ye would kiss it, and stroke it with thy tongue. Dost thou know what I mean? Caress the nipple with thy lips and tongue. She will like it very much. Touch both her breasts that way, and use thy fingers to touch all the parts of her body, softly and gently, like this." She showed him how to do this by taking his hand and running it along her arm. "Dost thou see, my son? This will make her feel very good, and soon she will want to do this thing with thee very much.

"This will sound strange to thee at first, Darien. But as soon as thee dost do it, it will be very pleasurable. Thy wand is hard for a reason. Lady Stephanie, ye see, does not have one. She has a pocket between her legs, where ye has thy wand. At some point during thy lovemaking, she will want thee to put thy wand into that pocket. In order to do this, the two of thee must be in embrace; ye must be very close together. Once ye have done this, she will make thee feel very good. She will want to lie on her back on the bed, and ye should lie on top of her. Once thy wand is in her pocket, she will begin to move herself around, and it will make thy wand feel very good. What ye should do is move thy wand in and out, without coming out of the pocket. This will make Stephanie near mad with pleasure. If ye can do this slowly, it is better. But soon ye will want to do it very fast. Thy body knows what to do. Soon, two things will happen. Ye will feel something shoot from thy wand, and it will be an amazing feeling. Ye will want to make it happen very much, and very often. Stephanie will also have a special reaction; she might even moan or cry out, it will feel so good for her. Once this is done, once ye hast felt this feeling, it is possible that ye will feel tired, and want to rest. If ye do rest, stay atop her. Hold her in thine arms, and she will do the same to thee. Talk to her. Tell how good she made ye feel. Tell her that she must do it for thee often. She will tell thee about the same. If all goes well, then soon ye may be able to do the whole thing all over again. On the wedding night, it is possible for the bride and groom to spend all night in this fashion. It will make thee happy, and it will make thee feel more love for thy Stephanie. She will feel more love for thee. The more the two if thee practice this event, the happier will be thy marriage. Stephanie will bear thee children, and they will be princes and princesses.

"This is only a small part of thy duties as a husband, Darien, but it is so beautifully wonderful that ye will want to do it often, especially during the first months, hopefully years, of thy marriage. And the more that ye two can do this, the more comfortable ye will become with each other. But remember always to tell her how good she did make thee feel, and talk to her afterward, as thee lie there in thy bed. Talk about anything to do with the pair of thee; make plans for thy living together. Always talk; never be silent with thy wife. If thou art, she will think she has done something wrong. Always answer her questions, and always feel like your telling her these answers is a good and happy thing. Try never to do anything that ye would not want to talk to Stephanie about. She will become thy conscience, and thee hers. Do not allow her to remain silent, ever. Always ask her questions, and always answer hers. If ye can do these things, then thy marriage will be strong and happy, and those troubles that may happen to thy family will be easier to bear. She will make thee feel proud.

"This is a good marriage. But there are bad marriages, too. If ye do not follow these ways, thou might have a bad marriage. If thou dost think things are going that way, tell Stephanie first. Always tell Stephanie everything first; before thee can tell anyone else. If things still feel bad, then ye may talk to me, or Alissa or Ariadne, and we will try to put thee straight again. Ye may also tell Father Benedic, but I would leave him as a last resort. Go to Stephanie first with thy troubles; then me; then Ariadne or Alissa. We will all give thee the guidance of a loving family. Do these things, Darien, and thou wilt have a happy bride, and a happy home.

"Tomorrow, I will give thee a ring. Ye may wait until the proper time to give it to Stephanie, or ye might feel ye should give it to her right away. Either choice is a good one. But do not forget, ask her to accept the ring. If all that ye hath told me is true, then she will say yes, and she will be very happy, and the two of thee may do a lot of kissing. This is a good thing, too. But don't overdo it. There will be a long time for thee and thy bride and kisses.

"My son, from now until thou art wed, I will come to thee wearing my scarlet cloak. It is a present from my husband, the king. I do love to wear it, as thou hast seen at court. I will wear it when we talk, and hopefully thou wilt have this problem not again. But thou canst tell thy Stephanie that when ye think on her, it gives thee this problem. She may blush heavily, but she will like knowing it.

"Thou hast grown to be a man at court, my son. Soon thou shalt be a husband. Always remember, Stephanie is thy first and formost concern. She will become the most important person in thy life very soon. And once they come, thy children will be the next important thing. Only after thou hast seen to thy family, wilt thou be able to see to things at court. Court will begin to take up thy time, Darien, for thou art heir to the throne. Ballizar and I will have no children; his fevers have ruined him. So thee and thy lovely Stephanie will be our children, and thy babes will be our grandchildren. I know I will be proud of thee, my son. And be not concerned if I should cry at thy wedding; they will be happy, happy tears.

"I do love thee very much, my dear son Darien. Goodnight, and sleep well."

"I love thee, too, Mother. Art the king and thee as happy as thou hast described for me?"

"Very much, my son. I have grown to love thy king as I love nothing else. He is the most important thing in my life. Thou art my second. Good night, Darien."

"Good night, Mother."

"The next day the queen brought me an exquisite ring, a diamond of no small size within a cluster of rubies. As it turned out, I did not give it to Stephanie straightaway as I had thought I would; in the interim, my mother had spoken to Stephanie's parents. So when I presented it to her, unbenownst to us, our parents had already planned the occasion. Stephanie told me later that her mother was afraid she would refuse the ring; it was not every day that thine only daughter married a prince!

"Queen Syrenya arranged for a sofa to be brought into court and placed on the other side of the king, facing her ladies. It was my duty to be there, but Stephanie enjoyed the machinations of court, and often accompanied me. We had become quite the royal family. No one knew, at that point not even I, what hellish nights the king and queen struggled through. It was not until the fiend struck the king while I was there, in their chambers, that I learned the truth about the demon that haunted my family."

"The demon came upon the king only in chambers?" asked Arthur. "If that were so, it either had reasons of its own, or it was a very accomodating devil. We gather that the beast did not show itself during thy wedding, to be sure. But we cannot get over the idea that thee would be chosen for this role, knowing as we do that thou hast no clear memory of the queen before the age of ten. We keep coming back to that notion. There must have been a reason for't. Methinks that, with all the words these ladies poured into thy head, the reasons for such were not among them. And it may be something that ye did quite unconsciously, in thy youth.

"We must say, Darien, that thy court was a good deal more interesting than ours has been. All we do these days is settle disputes between neighbors, grant the marriages of the people, and hear their woes, ad infinitum. There have been times when we have wished of a livelier time of it. But to hear thy tale, methinks we will settle for dull and boring, rather than face the trials of thy family. Let no demons apply at this castle! My ministers are a bit more up-to-date in their practices, and more than one is versed in exorcism.

"So, thou wert married at age, what, 14? Tis a good age. We on the other hand, are not yet wed. As we understand it, in order to keep peace within the kingdom, we are betrothed to a young princess from one of our more volatile counties, whose name be Guineviere. We have yet to lay eyes upon her; would we had such a magnificent mother to guide us in our preparation. Our wedding draws closer by the day, and though we do see the purpose in't, we would fair be happier if we had been able, like thee, to choose our own bride. In that sense, we do envy thee, Darien. We trust that thy marriage was—is? Ah, good, is—as happy as thy mother did say it would be."

"Were it not for the king's affliction, Tabithia would have seen prosperous and carefree times, Sire. Apart from that, I am happy to say that my marriage has been a good one. My mother, as thou hast heard, did always give good counsel. But the black cloud that seemed to hang above the castle of Ballizar was not to be lifted for many a year, and at a terrible cost.

"The first sign of trouble came in the fifth year of my marriage, Sire. As my time at court grew, I noted that, more and more often, the king could not attend court. His fevers, as I had come to know them, would often strike him in the late morning, and in such a case, the king and queen would be absent from court that day. When that happened, Princess Stephanie and I would hold court, with an able assist from my aunts. It was so when the Intruder came, and this woman was the beginning of terrible times for all the royal family. My mother did dispatch her with alacrity, but what the bizarre woman was about, we would not learn until she was gone."

CHAPTER 12

The Intruder

With Darien's marriage to Stephanie, the amount of time he had to himself became almost nil. He did still receive his schooling from Alissa and Ariadne; in fact, after what the Lord and Lady Windover had seen of his schooling, they asked the two ladies if they might tutor Stephanie, as well. So it was that, between his schooling and his hours at court, and the long and educational evenings he spent with his new bride, his head sometimes felt as if it might explode from the addition of too much knowledge. Lady Alissa called such notions "nonsense." There was always more a person could learn.

However, he seemed to have learned his lessons from his mother quite well, for Stephanie took great pleasure in all the things that his mother had taught him; and she added a lesson or two of her own in the course of their first years together. Darien took extra care with his bride, for he took the queen's words to heart, and discovered that she was, indeed, correct. He did have a happy bride, and a happy marriage.

By the time that Darien had reached his ninetenth birthday, his dear wife had borne him two children, a son at first (which did fair please the king) and then a precious daughter. Darien took great care not to neglect any of his three family members, but he did dote upon his daughter, who, for reasons he could not explain, very much favored the Queen.

The Princess Stephanie was proving to be a marvel of her own, in fact. What Darien's aunts taught to him, and what they taught to her, were not at all the same thing. Part of Darien's schooling were lessons: history, geography, mathematics, and letters. But the princess was groomed to be the hostess of the family, and her lessons were those of etiquette, charm, and the art of commanding a man's attention just by listening to him. She did practice this art upon her husband during the evenings and nights they shared together, and Darien came to think of himself as one of the luckiest orphans alive.

The wedding had been in September, and their son came hard upon their first anniversary, in October. The child's mother chose his name, Randall, and he became the delight of the ladies at court, especially those the ages of his parents; there was already planning taking shape in many of the hearths in the castle, as to whom the young master might marry when his time came.

Randall was two when his sister arrived; his mother was fond of saying that this child was indeed a lady, for she gave her mother a far easier time at labor than did the young prince. Her father named her Lylanya; his bride took it to her heart as beautiful, as did the queen, for she realized the form was done in her honor. And if Darien doted upon his chldren, he was a distant third compared to their mother and grandmother. Darien came to spend more time with the king, something he was very eager to do; Alissa and Ariadne were able teachers, but there were things about being a king that only a king could know.

By the time Randall was four, he was already acquainted with court. As part of the royal family, he came not under the eye of the nursemaids; he was quite happy to spend time at court visiting with his grand-aunts, his mother and his grandmother. He was the most active of any child at court, and often spent some time upon his grandmother's knee, while she showed him the ways of court. The picture, however, caused Darien some confusion, for the sight was the very image of what he thought her afternoon with Darius must have been, and he stilll was unable to keep from trying to remember the incident as it would have appeared to him.

Lylanya, however, was quite content to remain in her bassinet beside the Princess, so long as there was no loud clamoring at court. The child, more often than not, slept though it all. Darien, in the meantime, was learning the ways of court faster than he would have liked; the king's illness often now kept him from court, and the queen insisted on staying by his side when it did. Thus the prince and princess—with Alissa behind the throne on Darien's left, while Ariadne stood to the right and back of the princess—held court in their parents' absence. Among the four of them, there was no case so difficult that they could not bring it to some proper conclusion; in the eyes of the court, this was impressive, indeed. And if such a quartet of decision-makers did upset the good Father, he was politic enough to remain silent about it. His attention was elsewhere, in any case.

But the prince and princess were quite unprepared for an event that took place right at the end of court one spring afternoon. Report was that the king was under the influence of his fevers, and so Darien and Stephanie had just managed to close out another day of court when something happened to make Alissa stiffen at Darien's side. Ariadne whispered something brief to the princess and fled the room; Stephanie reported to Darien that Ariadne had gone to fetch the queen. That was very good news to Darien, who was not quite prepared for the woman who entered the court near sundown, with wrath upon her lips and and nothing else upon her hide. Knowing the story, he realized that Alissa remembered the scene well, and it was one she did not like seeing from this vantage point. Nevertheless, the three upon the dais let the minister deal with the woman, while reinforcements were brought to bear.

To his surprise, and, if truth be told, relief, it was the king who strode into court from Darien's left, while Ariadne and the queen entered from Stephanie's right. The logistics of the change had been marked out long ago, and the changing of the guard was done quickly, and without a hitch. Thus it was the king who was addressed, when this woman turned with disdain from the minister and, striding several steps closer, hailed the throne. Darien, who had noticed the parting, was given a quick indication from the minister that the woman was quite the worse for drink, and he passed that sign to his mother, who nodded and bent to the king. Having been apprised of the situation, the king looked down sternly upon the woman and demanded to know what it was she thought she was doing.

"Woman, wouldst thou mock thy queen? Ye had best look to airing thy fogged brain, for if ye persist, ye will suffer for't." Then he lifted his head and shouted, "Dost know our mind on this?" And the woman, who had her back to the court, was near thrown to the floor with the wrath that came out in a mighty, "Aye, Sire!" Nevertheless, she held her ground and spoke to the king in a way that, normally, would have earned her a proper beating.

"My lord, what hath thou wrought? What hast thee to say to the women of this fair country? Wouldst thou take a foreigner to be thy bride, when so many of this land, thy loyal subjects, could serve as well as she? I was born in Tabithia, and I am thy loyal subject. I do charge thee, Sire, to forsake this woman of strange land who doth flaunt her beauty in the sin of nudity, and take me as thy bride. Am I not as fair as she? Am I not as bold? Cast her out, Sire, and take me to be thy legal queen!"

Had he been given to venting his own anger upon her, the king would have silenced that voice shortly after it began. But the queen, who had once more bent and whispered to him, indicated that it would be better to let her have her piece; twould bring the wrath of the court down upon her. And if she suffered that, as well, then the queen had something that might prove to this drunken female how different she and the queen actually were.

As it was, then, the king gave the woman a stony silence as she ranted, with each word stirring the ire of the court, who found this wench no more than some upstart crone. But the growing noise of the court seemed not to phase her at all, and as she reached the crescendo of her tirade, she was baffled into silence when it was the queen who spoke.

"My liege, look ye upon this lady with thy favor. She is fair, is she not, Sire? Indeed, quite a beauty. Wouldst thou enjoy her, Sire? For she has come to warm thy bed for thee; would she not be a proper sport? Look upon her, King Ballizar, and tell us what ye find in this woman." The king, following his wise queen's lead, gave the wench a once-over and considered that, aye, she was fair, though he had known fairer; and she was, to all effects, a game wench. But he would not touch the wretch until she had bathed. He told the queen, "prepare her, if thou wilt, and we may have her for sport, if nothing else."

This caused two things to happen simultaneously. The wench again began telling him how she would rid him of this foreigner and be his queen; and the court erupted, raining down epithets upon the wretch for her very presence. The queen managed to silence both the court and the usurper with a gesture, after which she spoke in an astonishingly friendly tone to her.

"I think the king doth look on thee with hungry eyes, Lady. If thou wouldst have a good scrubbing, methinks the king would deign have thee. Wilt thou come? For we may see to thy preparation." With these words, the queen took the woman by the arm, and they and the ladies left the courtroom. As soon as they had gone, the king put up his hands.

"Know ye, Lords and Ladies, that thy queen is wise. She may prepare her charge for sport in the royal bower, but ye should believe surely that it will never come to that. Methinks giving the queen about five minutes with the little snippet will bring this untidy little affair to a swift and effective end. Mark the time, milords, twill not take that long, if we know our queen. Be patient."

"Tell us thy name, Lady," said the queen in all innocence. "If ye would lay with the king, he must know thy name." The woman was beginning to sober; she had thought through what she would say to the king, but had not given much thought to what might happen after. Her mind was to discredit this Naked Queen by means of mockery; but it had turned out far different from what she had imagined. She was fair displeased with the turn of events; being behind the castle walls in the hands of three of the enemy was bringing her wits back amazingly fast.

"I do not believe thee, Foreigner. I know of what thee speaks. Ye would never let me lay with the king, not if thou couldst help it!"

"Dear Lady, the king is my king as much as thine; if he would have thee, there are none, including myself, who may say him nay. And he did say he found thee fair. But I do remember, as I am sure hast thou, that many women who would lay with the king when he was a bachelor suffer'd for't. Art thou prepared to do that?"

"I know what ye art about, Foreigner. I know of what ye speak. I am built for just such a man, for I have held men the size of which would bring thee down."

"Well, then, Ladies, it seems all is in order here. Let us prepare her for the king." Alissa and Ariadne, who had long since learned not to ask questions in the heat of the moment, followed the queen's lead, and headed for their quarters, as Syrenya had indicated.

"Ah! Hold, Ladies. I had fair forgotten; she must be measured to be certain." This was almost more than the ladies could take. They bowed themselves right out of the picture, and the queen took the wench to a small room just off the corridor.

"Thou wouldst do me mischief, eh, Foreigner? How wouldst thou 'measure' me?"

"Why, lass, I would measure thee in the same way as the king himself would."

"Ye cannot do this. How wouldst thou manage such a ridiculous charade?"

"As I said, lass, the same way as the king. Bear with me, and sit upon the table. That's good, yes. Now, just lie back. There, now. Thou must know what is in store for thee, must ye not?"

"I warn thee, touch me not. I have friends, Foreigner. Thou wouldst be wise to remember that. I have powerful friends."

"Oh, I do understand thee, lass. And I have no intention of touching thee further. I merely would like thee to know just what ye would be up against." At that instant, the wench felt the size of the king inside her, and she screamed. "He would wish to have thee like this, lass." And the pain doubled as she felt that monster jabbing in and out. Her screams echoed in the chamber. It was not possible for any man to be of that magnitude.

"This is treachery, Foreigner! Art thou a witch? How canst thou do this?!" She was in agony.

"I know not what ye mean, lass. I touched thee not. But if ye would lay with the king, then ye must be prepared for that ye will find. Thou canst imagine it, canst thou not?" An image of the king, and all he would bring with him, focused for one fleet second in her mind, and she screamed again, this time not in pain, but in terror.

"Nay! It cannot be! I would die; I cannot…I cannot endure… No. NO! No, no, no, no, no…" She pitched herself from the table, slammed through the door, and went at a dead run for the door to the court, not far away. She careened through it, and that was the last that the queen ever saw of her.

Syrenya summoned her ladies, and they returned to court together. They found that the king was in a merry mood.

"Methinks that we have racehorses that would be far outmatched by the speed of that wench!" cracked the king. He and the court had watched her as she streaked past them, clutching her breasts to herself with her arms and repeating over and over, "no, no, no…"

"My queen, we did allot thee five minutes," he told his wife. "Thou hast bested that time by nearly a full minute. We knew ye would be swift, but we knew not thy plan. Pray tell us, how didst thou convince the woman of her plight?"

"It was a very straightforward thing, my liege. I told her the truth." This, much as had the joke at the king's table so long ago, made little sense to the court, but the king bellowed his laughter, and the court joined in, mostly in relief at seeing this tawdry little spectacle dispensed with. But when the queen gracefully regained her throne, as Alissa and Ariadne took their seats, the queen leaned over and spoke briefly, with a deep concern in her voice.

"I fear that this is far from over, my liege." And until she could get her king alone, that was all she would say on the matter.

CHAPTER 13

Treason

The Prince and Princess nearly dined alone that evening, but Alissa and Ariadne joined them shortly after they began. The dining hall was full of noise; the court, having just witnessed the Intruder, was rife with speculation on why such an event would take place after the queen had already reigned for twelve years. Some held forth that she was a peasant woman, whom some fool bunch had besotted, and sent her on this errand as a sick joke. Others scoffed; no one in his right mind would do such a thing without careful planning. Their theory was that she was not of Tabithia, as she had claimed. Their conclusion was that one or more of the surrounding nations was trying to foment rebellion. Others still said nay to both; if there was trouble, it was from within Tabithia. No king or queen may reign all their years without making some enemies.

Darien, had he had his way, would have had both he and Stephanie with their parents, but the queen had insisted on complete privacy with her king. Benedic was sequestered with his priests; only heaven above knew what that was about. So Darien and Stephanie dined with Ariadne and Alissa, but it was a meal taken in near silence. None of the four knew anything else about the situation for certain, and all had the good sense to keep from useless speculation.

After dinner, Darien and the princess bade the ladies goodnight, to which Ariadne only replied, "Pray that it is, Darien. Pray very hard."

The children, at least, were sleeping; not so their parents. Darien was deeply worried; what had seemed only a morbid interlude had taken on a very frightening aspect. If the queen needed privacy with the king, it had to be that she felt this lunatic woman was only a precursor of things to come. And the priests never met in seclusion; his mother must have conferred with Benedic immediately after court, and stressed that he take this incident very seriously. But why, and what was it his parents were discussing, were lost to Darien, and his worry kept both him and his bride from sleep.

Father Benedic, too, went sleepless that night, but for different reasons. Immediately after court had concluded, the king had summoned him to the Royals' quarters, and what he had heard there was nearly impossible for him to believe. While the king stressed urgency, the queen charged him to meet with his priests, and see if any of them had heard anything about rebellion within the court. No event seemingly untoward was too insignificant; his was to assemble what facts he could, and see if any of them, unimportant in themselves, lent any truths when connected with other seemingly unimportant anomolies. He and his priests were up far longer than he at first believed was possible; what they had pieced together, in the light of the king's sense of emergemcy, was not a good picture at all.

Horses had gone missing from the stable, only to be found in their stalls again two days later. It had been noted by some that key personnel had been absent from court during that time. When Benedic's assembly connected names with deeds, their conclusion was unthinkable. Some who took confession on a regular basis from particular members of the court had not heard from them in weeks, despite gentle reminders. Others were quick to point out that they had felt vaguely uneasy of late, without knowing why. And John Paul, whom Father Benedic felt to be the epitome of calm, rational thought, flatly stated that he had heard comings and goings in the courtyard in the pre-dawn hours of some few mornings, it being his practice to rise quite early for his vespers. But only in the light of the suggestion that trouble was brewing, did any of the priests take particular notice of the irregularities they had witnessed. It was a very troubled Benedic who returned his findings to the king, shortly before sunrise the following morning.

During that time, the queen had marked several points that only she could have been aware of, since the intruder, as she was now known, had come into the castle and reached the very door to the court without anyone having noticed she had passed. Recalling the difficulty, and the stealth, necessary to complete such a deed, Syrenya deduced that either the woman had been within the castle, with knowledge of her route, before court had begun that day, or she had been led in by others who had that knowledge. Her conclusion was that it was the latter; she had to have been coached, and given her drink for courage; and whatever apparel she had worn prior to her entrance must be removed. Following that same line of reasoning, Syrenya concluded, once the woman's deed had been done, those who had used her for their purposes were apparently not worried about getting her out again. Syrenya had the troubling thought that, rather than send the wench on her way, she might actually have sent the poor woman to her doom. The queen could not now ignore the possibility that, had it not been for her own desire to put the fear of God into her, actually capturing and grilling the woman might have lent both vital information, and saved the woman's life, in the bargain. It was the first time the queen had acted rashly since her own arrival at the keep, and she now had to face the possibility that things were worse, rather than better, because of her own actions. Whoever had planned this lunacy believed that it would spur her to rash action, and they had been right. That someone could know her well enough to correctly predict her reaction troubled her far more than she let anyone realize. If those responsible were at court to see what she accomplished—and she was sure they were—then she was very vulnerable. It was a feeling that was brand new to her. She tried to console herself with the knowledge that she had discovered this insurrection specifically because of her reaction, but she could take only cold comfort from it.

The woman had referred to her as "foreigner." If that was what was stirring rebellion within Tabithia, it had certainly been a long time coming. To Syrenya, this gambit was a ruse, used to rally those with like thought from among the subjects of Tabithia. To those at the top of this insurrection, it seemed more to the mark that it was not just the queen who was threatened here; it was the entire royal family. That such a thing, an overthrow of the government, could be lurking in the shadows, was a possibility the queen had difficulty digesting. She and her king, therefore, waited, and hoped that the news brought by Father Benedic would prove them wrong.

Ariadne came to the door of the prince's chambers early that morning and told Darien that he and the princess were to meet their parents in the queen's chambers. Ariadne would stay with the children; Alissa was already with the queen, and Ariadne would hear the news of the meeting from her. It was not necessary for her to stress speed; the two left her standing in the doorway.

When they arrived, the pain on the queen's face confirmed their worst fears. There was trouble; and it would get worse before it got better. Darien felt woefully unprepared; his life at the castle had been blessed til now. To be plunged into turmoil at this point shattered what had been serenity for his family; to see his mother's grim countenance meant that serenity was suddenly far out of his reach.

Father Benedic had taken his conclusions directly to the king, and was still there when Alissa, Darien and Stephanie arrived. The queen summarized what little they knew, and the six of them attempted to draw up a plan of action. It was clear, from the priests' assembled information, that Lord Farraman was, for reasons of his own, bringing together an attempted coup on the royal family. His unaccounted absence from court, the selection of the stable's fastest horses, and a gradual change in his behavior since the birth of his son, now five years old, aimed the priests' conclusions directly at him. Syrenya realized that he had been at the forefront of the assembled court last night, quite a different position from his usual locale, a place near the far wall that gave him what he was wont to call "an overview of the room." This was confirmation enough for her. The king, who had trusted the man with secrets of the state, was livid, and his old temper was flaring. His first reaction was to lay hands on the man and try him for treason, but Darien suggested they instead try to smash the coup by following his movements. He suggested to the king the use of his knights; alerted to the situation, they could monitor the man's movements with little change in their routine, and therefore refrain from raising his suspicions. The queen, meanwhile, planned a visit to Lady Sarah, with the possible outcome of obtaining a motive for Farraman's actions, or at least discovering whether the man's wife even knew of his treason. The most troubling thing about this entire affair was that they could come to no conclusions at all on a motive for his crime. There was little more to do for the nonce; assuming their regular habits was the best action that Darien could suggest. While his mother thanked him for his cool reason, it seemed a woefully sad plan of attack to the prince. He was rising from his seat, his thoughts now turned to his children, when the king suddenly stumbled up, knocking over his chair and emitting a horrible cry. Darien froze; he suddenly felt completely out of touch with others in the room. He watched with horror as Father Benedic and his mother quickly stripped the robes from the king; the two then laid him out on the bed and the queen covered him with her body. Father Benedic then began a litany that Darien had never heard before. The queen wrapped her arms tightly around her husband and began pushing herself up and down on his body, all the while talking to him in language that Darien would never have dreamed she was capable of, urging the king to take her, stay with her, use her. Stephanie had cried out and turned away; Alissa was trying to comfort her. Then, having joined with the king, Syrenya began a terrifying litany of her own. As Father Benedic continued his prayer, Darien heard her words in a horrible descant.

"Release him, fiend. Begone! He is mine! Ye shall not have him! Ballizar, stay with me! Get out, monster! Get out! Get out! Get out!"

Frozen in a horrified limbo, Darien felt more helpless than he ever had in his life.

CHAPTER 14

Rebellion

Fully thirty minutes passed before both the queen and the priest stopped this unfathomable action. Darien, himself transfixed, heard and saw what was happening but felt helpless to do anything, even so much as joining his wife and Alissa. He realized that he was terrified; the queen's words had but one meaning. Someone, or some *thing*, had possessed the king, throwing him into one of his 'fits of fever,' as Darien had been taught to view them. His mother now lay with the king, who was holding her tightly; he seemed to be himself again. Benedic, whose own plan was to marshall the priests against the threat of a coup, now left to see to his task. Alissa, still with Stephanie, called to Darien, and he was able to turn and go to them in the corner. Stephanie was still weeping, and no wonder; Alissa whispered that she would go and wait for them with Ariadne; the two of them were now aware of the true cause of the king's 'fits,' and she felt it best if the family could talk alone together. Syrenya called to her son as Alissa left the chamber.

"Darien. Stephanie. Please come over here, if ye would. It is time ye understood what the king has been up against all these years, and even from the point of his first days of rule in Tabithia." The two went to the far side of the bed; his mother sat up and faced them, sitting on the side of the bed, her hand still outstretched behind her to Ballizar, who was now sleeping.

"I discovered this situation the third night I was with Ballizar, immediately after our wedding night. Shortly after that, I made Father Benedic aware of the situation, for I needed his help in finding an exorcist for the king. The facts defy all reason, so I can understand the looks upon thy faces. But there is no escaping the truth; thy father is attacked as ye have seen, by something we can only describe as a demon. We know not why or when an attack will come; Benedic and two of his most trusted priests have joined me in the fight against this beast.

"The first two nights I lay with the king, our lovemaking was as it should be between two lovers. I could cool the king and give him release from the fevers that sometimes possessed him. But on the third night, when his fevers came again, I sought out the king's eyes, for he suddenly seemed far from me. What I saw horrifed me. Locked inside the king's body was a devil; his cold and depthless eyes stared right back at me. I nearly screamed; I have never before experienced such things.

"It suddenly became clear why the king had concocted this First Night business; twas never him at all, but this horror who dreamt up such a lunacy. But even though I can, if I am swift enough, rid Ballizar of this monster, it has always returned; I cannot, even with the priests' help, banish this creature back to Hell, where it belongs. These possessions, for we can call them nought else, have plagued the king since his first days of rule. Ariadne and Alissa joined the court the second year of Ballizar's reign, and the king's 'desires' were already known to the court even then.

"This is why thy services at court have been so often requested. For hours after these attacks, the king is exhausted, and hot—'fevers' is certainly an apt, if erroneous, diagnosis for what the physicians saw. Ballizar burns while the beast is in him; it is a wonder to my mind that he has managed to survive for this long. Had I not come when I did, I suspect he would not have. And everything we know now would not have come to pass.

"I am sorry we have kept this from ye, my son, Stephanie; but there was no reason ye had to know, and I could see no good that would come of my revealing this horror to thee. As a result, ye have made a family of us. Both the king and I love thee very much. Now, when suddenly we realize a threat from within our own court, this evil only serves to exacerbate the trouble. I have found it increasingly difficult to be able to leave my king; his attacks seem to come more frequently now. So I fear I must depend upon thee, my son, to face this treason. Thy wise and cool thinking this morning gives me hope; ye did ascertain a plan quickly and succinctly. With both the knights and the priests as our eyes, I doubt that anyone will be able to surprise us with this insurrection.

"It is only immediately after Ballizar's attacks, when we have routed the fiend for a time and the king is sleeping, that I feel I can leave him. So if I am to see to Lady Sarah, I must do so now. Return to thy babes, my children; let us return to our regular habits, as thou hast suggested. Please tell thy aunts that I have gone to see Madame Farraman, and they may come to my chambers later this morning and find me. Heaven only knows they need a little time to themselves, as well.

"Thou must act as a king, Darien, and not as a prince, during this trouble. We have a strong number with us, and we know of the threat; that we are forewarned is half the battle. But this is going to be a very nasty business, and I fear blood will spill before it is all over.

"Go now. I am off to see what Lady Sarah can tell us—provided, of course, that she is not a part of this madness. I will come by and tell thee what I find. Be careful; and keep thy wits about thee. We will need every ounce of our energies and intelligence to bring us out safely on the other side of this. Kiss me, both; now, let us begin."

When Syrenya arrived at the Farramans' chambers, a servant answered the door. She immediately bowed the queen in, but looked up and down the corridor before she closed, and bolted, the door. She said nothing, but led the queen to the back, where her mistress was prostrate upon the bed. But for Sarah's sobs, the place was empty and silent; far more than it should be, in fact. Syrenya suddenly realized that the boy, Gerhard, was not here.

"Sarah," spoke the queen, urgently but quietly, "where is thy child?" Sarah suddenly twisted to face her visitor.

"Oh, my queen! He is gone! Edgar came into the nursery and tore him from my arms! He accused me of coddling the boy, and he said he was taking Gerhard with him. He's taken my baby away from me! Your Grace, I am near mad with grief! Edgar has changed since Gerard was born. Every day he has grown more fierce, more angry. And now he has gone, and taken Gerhard with him! Why? Why would he do such a thing? When they left, Gerhard was screaming! I tried to stop them, but Edgar turned on me, and I have ne'er seen the face he showed me. It fair paralyzed me. He has never done anything so evil!"

The queen had moved to the bed and was now rocking the distraught woman, to try and comfort her. She knew well enough how she would feel, if one of the family had taken one of the children and gone. Under the circumstances, she felt that Lady Sarah was weathering this storm better than was her right. But the theft of the child by his father was even more troubling than this insurrection already was. She calmed the boy's mother and tried to speak to her.

"Sarah, tell me truly. Hast thy husband stayed away from the castle overnight? And if so, where has he been going?"

"He has, Your Grace, and more and more often of late. And he tells me nothing! If ye knew the trials I have been through this past year..."

"Sarah, I believe that ye have not been included in thy husband's plans. We believe he is mounting a rebellion against the castle. We already have him under watch." Sarah stopped crying and looked at her queen with a look of misery that fair tore at Syrenya's heart.

"What? Tis true? I was afraid he was mixed up in something terrible! But this is beyond my worst fears! Why? He has shown signs of madness of late, but he would not speak of it. He very nearly stuck me when I pressed him upon it."

"We have not yet discovered his motives, but his actions are plain. He has already brought a blight upon the court. He has raised a distrust among the populace, and they have sent a most unusual envoy to enlighten us." The queen then described the Intruder incident, and managed to bring the point of it to Sarah without having to tell her too much of how the message had been uncovered. The poor woman went white when she heard of the naked impostor, and the taunt of 'foreigner' that she had hurled at the queen herself.

"Oh, my god. Your Grace, he has been speaking of 'that foreigner' for months, and getting himself more and more into a state o'er it. I would never have imagined he was referring to thee!"

"Sarah, I am afraid that merely confirms our conclusions on the matter. This wench was very clear with her words. 'Don't touch me, foreigner,' she said. 'I have friends; mark me, I have powerful friends.' I do not think she meant to reveal as much as she did, but by that time she was in a frightful position. If we at court had kept our wits about us, she would be here still. But thy husband saw her leave; if he is as clever as I suppose, then he is perhaps aware that we are onto him. We have already set our watchmen upon him, but if he is suspicious, he may himself become rash." She did not let Sarah know of her own rash actions. "But I doubt that Lord Edgar would harm thy child. If he felt it necessary to remove the boy from court, tis only to take him from harm's way, methinks. I believe we have done everything we can do to face this danger without tipping our hand; but we must bring our own weapons to bear, and soon. I have possibly made someone suspicious by coming here this morning."

"Your Grace, if what ye say is true, then my husband is...he is...a traitor, is he not?"

"Aye, Sarah; I am afraid he is." And she began to rock Sarah again, for the poor woman fell into another fit of weeping.

Even though Darien knew that the king had a militia at his disposal, he had never thought it would be necessary to use it against an inner enemy. Darien sent word to the captain of the company that he should arrange to meet with the prince, because Darien believed that the troops would be needed in the event of an attack. The message returned to Darien saying where and when the captain would meet him, but the prince later received another message from the soldier, reporting that, within the past two nights, a full third of the militia had deserted. Had Darien not contacted him first, he would have gone straight to the king, by nightfall.

The captain arranged to meet inside the castle walls, rather than in the field, where the militia was camped. Having made his way to the spot, only yards from the gate, Darien waited impatiently for Captain Tibbett to arrive. It was a quarter of an hour before the man made his appearance. But the news he brought was both an answer to their questions, and an immediate call to arms. The captain's conversation with a soldier returning to camp had made him late. It had also made him anxious to rally the troops.

Tibbett was a man bred in the military. He stood at attention even when relaxed; his back was ramrod straight, and he was quite comfortable in his uniform. He saluted the prince when he saw him; in less trying times, it would have amused Darien. "Beg pardon, your highness, but I am late only because I have important news, which I have only just received."

"Captain, I thank thee for the honor, but it is not necessary to refer to me as 'your highness.' I am still a good way from ascending the throne. Call me Darien, or, if it suits your military mind, 'sir' will do."

"Yes, sir. I thank thee, Sir. I was leaving camp to come here, when one of my soldiers, one of the ones who fled these past two nights, had just returned. He is a lieutenant, and until I found him gone I considered him a good man, and a good soldier. He did not disappoint. He undertook to go with the deserters to find out their destination, and their plans, if he could. He did well at both, and fears the men he was with are aware of his departure, and are coming here tonight to try and carry out their plans before we can organize against them. They could very well be on their way now.

"They were assembled at a small inn with a barn, just outside Barrowsmith, 20 miles northeast of here. Balmartin, my lieutenant, made the ride in just under three hours; his horse was very nearly worn out from under him. If they readied themselves and came immediately, they will not doubt be here this afternoon. We must organize and be ready for them when they arrive. If they have lost their advantage of surprise, then we are in a much more favorable position."

"Captain, let me discuss with you a plan that I have. I would like thee to divide thy men into two groups; can ye do that, and still give the impression that all of the soldiers are at the wall? I want to try and trap the brigands."

"What is thy plan, Sir?"

"Put half thy men on the balustrade immediately. Have them prepare for a long battle; plenty of arrrows and whatever crossbows and other weapons ye may have. Spears or anything. Then I want ye to bring the other half into the courtyard and surround the gate. While I would wish that your soldiers up top put an end to this attack, if they do not make short work of it, then I want to let the mob think that they can breach the castle and enter at the gate. With your troops on the ground, and the rest covering them from above, I think we could bring this horror to a swifter conclusion than we might have. Thy lieutenant deserves a promotion, Captain, and a rise in pay. If we have forced them to come immediately, then we have pushed their hand, and they will be more ill-prepared when they arrive. But we must make no mistake; this is rebellion, and must be treated as such. How feel thy soldiers about shooting at some of their mates?"

"A turncoat is a turncoat, Sir. We shall have no trouble at all."

"Excellent. Give this plan thy military knowledge and try to punch holes in it, if ye can. If we can seal up any openings then we might finish this by morning."

"Sir, I can find no flaw in thy plan at all. I assume ye will alert the rest of the castle. I will bring my men in immediately. At best speed, the attackers are still two hours hence. I expect about thirty-five deserters will be among them, but neither Balmartin nor I have any idea how much of a people's rebellion they have roused. We could be looking at well over a hundred men."

"Then let us prepare for them, Captain, with all speed."

"Aye, Sir!" The captain stepped back, gave a smart salute, and was gone. Darien returned to the castle and sought out the king.

"If what ye have devised against this rabble holds true, then perhaps God is smiling upon us, after all," said his mother. When Darien had arrived, he found that his aunts and the queen were all in the queen's chambers. Ballizar was sleeping in his room next door; the door to his room was open, and the queen sat so she could watch the king as he slept. Darien inquired after his wife first; Alissa said that she, and Lady Sarah, and the children, were all in Lady Sarah's quarters, with two of the king's knights. Even if the attack were to get into the castle proper, they would be safe. His mother looked on him with worry and not a little pride. He had taken his command now, and would see it through.

"My son, would I could let thee return to thy family at once. But I fear this is thy turning point, Darien. Thy valor has proved excellent thus far. We need thee with the militia, and in command. I agree with the captain; it is a noble plan. Pray that it works! Wilt thou take prisoners if they reach the courtyard?"

"Yes, Mother, as well as we can. But if a large number can get in, it will be hand to hand combat and no time for mercy. We will have to play it moment to moment. But if he is with them, Farraman will be spared. I want that man on trial with every fiber of my being."

"Thy thoughts reflect the king's. He has asked that ye do so. Very well, then. We give thee complete command of the castle, my son. Ye are in charge now; the king is too weak and I must stay with him. Our prayers are with thee."

"I will not fail thee, Mother." He leaned in to give her a kiss. "We are preparing already. The first shots will come from beyond the wall. That will be the signal that we are joined. In actuality we are preparing for what might only be an assumption; we have no real knowledge of the time they will arrive. But the captain is sure it will be before nightfall. I have put the knights and the priests to work; the knights have joined the militia on the wall, and the priests are preparing torches and ammunition. We are as prepared as we may be.

"I will stop in to see Stephanie and the children. If I do not return, know that I do love thee, Mother."

"I do know that, my son. And my love goes with thee. But I have good feelings about what ye have devised. It is sound and wise. Think not on thy grave as yet, my son. I know I will see thee anon. Now go, and speak to thy family. Return only when thou art done, and we have won our battle. I know it will be so."

"Thy words do sustain me, Mother. I will keep them in my head hence, and return as soon as I may. With this knowledge, there is no need to say goodbye. When I return!" And with that, Darien was off to see his family, and his mother was more afraid than ever she had been. To lose the king to a demon would be horror enough. To lose her son at so tender an age would be more heartache than she could imagine. She sent a prayer after him, and returned to Ballizar. She knew he would be chaffing at being out of the fray; twas not something he had ever had to prepare himself to face. The two of them would compose themselves, and wait.

Darien was upon the balustrade; the captain was in command below. There were four cannon mounted along the front wall. In all the years he had been alive, he could never remember them being fired. But the captain had judged them sound, and plenty of cannonballs and powder had been laid in. Without the element of surprise, it seemed to him this rebellion was doomed to failure; but Darien knew better than to be too sure of himself. It was only the forcing of their hand that was bringing them today; until now any actual movement had seemed weeks away. That may be the circumstance that spelled victory for himself and the captain.

They had been waiting four hours now; it was beginning to get dark when the watchman cried out. Darien could see the horses and the wagons, but he was unable to identify any of the men. It might even be possible that Farraman was not among them; if it had been him, and he had his son in his charge, Darien believed he might stay behind to fight another day. But he would know soon enough.

All the soldiers on the ballustrade were ready; and the knights manned the cannon. Bows, crossbows, and even spears were being used against this force; along with the cannon, that might be enough to reduce their ranks, and let them enter. But the wagons made Darien anxious; if somehow the rebels had gained firepower, then it would be a much more even match. He used the spyglass the captain had lent him. The wagons contained stone; all but one. That one carried a catapult. Darien felt his heart sink. If the cannon could not dispatch that thing, and quickly, the castle was at risk. But the wagons and their burdens certainly explained the mob's belated arrival. Darien called down below.

"Captain!"

"Sir!"

"They bring a catapult, and plenty to load it with. Any suggestions?"

"That is the focal point of the cannon, then, Sir; their job is to eliminate that threat. One solid hit will do the work, but a few near-hits will do just as well."

"Thank thee, Captain. When it looks like we can allow them to storm, I will come down and give the order. And captain?"

"Aye Sir?"

"I know that thou wouldst rather be fighting than waiting. But I need thy experience on the ground. Those who wait in battle, do battle nonetheless."

"Aye, Sir. Thank thee, Sir."

It was clear that Farraman was as aware of the cannon as was Darien; the approaching throng stopped well out of range. The positive thing about that was, if they were out of range of the cannon, then the castle was out of range of the catapult. It was a waiting game now; they might try a nighttime attack, or wait until morning. The sun had already set; there was a blood-red sunset along the horizon. Darien tried not to think of it as an omen.

Torches were being lit along the hillside; twould be a night raid, then. Darien's heart was in his throat; he simply wished to get on with it. Then he could stop all this thinking and get down to some honest doing. The noise outside was picking up; the brigands were advancing.

"Steady, gentleman. Let them begin; we have the better barrier. Let them get as close as they will, and pick thy marks. Make every shot count. If we can reduce them to less than thirty, I will let them in. Crandall!"

"Aye!"

"Hast seen the catapult?"

"Aye, sir. We have it located."

"That's thy target, then. Without the catapult, their wagons are worthlesss to them, and they will advance on foot. How many dost thou make out on horseback?"

"Scarce ten, Sir, unless they have more at the rear."

"Gentlemen, the horses go down first. Stand ready."

All the men along the rail watched as a small bundle of torches advanced on the castle. The torches broke into individual lights as they advanced, and there were at least fifty of them. Darien watched as they approached, watching for that first sign of attack.

"Crandall."

"Aye."

"We will hear that catapult before we see anything fly. Canst aim those cannon by sound?"

"Indeed we can, Sir. 'Pon the first shot, we have three cannon ready for response."

"I leave the cannon to thy good judgement, then. The sooner, the better."

"Aye!"

Darien had wondered how he would be able to fight an onslaught by night; he discovered he would not need to. With blazing torches both inside and outside the castle, the red glow made the darkness light. He had no trouble seeing the approaching throng; and he was certain they had no trouble seeing the castle or the men along the ballustrade. All that he could hope for was that the darkness would confuse the issue enough so that no one outside would know how few men he actually had along the wall.

The first attack on the castle was indeed from the catapult. There was a snap, wood banging against wood, and then the sound of wind. The shot was actually short, the result of his foe's own caution. But the firing of the catapult loosed the tide of men, and the battle was joined. Volleys of arrows arched across the wall or struck the stones just below. A cannon shot, and another just behind it, rocked the castle; he was prepared for neither the noise, nor the repercussion; he nearly lost his footing. There was an explosion, and Darien could see that one shot had struck directly in front of the catapult, taking out many of the men who were advancing its wagon. The other landed to the left, with the same result. But the catapult itself remained intact.

From the moment he had heard the first snap of the catapult, everything seemed to slow down for Darien. Arrows floated over the wall;

the catapult's wagon was now trying to negotiate the blasted turf made by the cannonballs, inching forward almost painfully slowly. He could see several men on horseback within the opposing forces, but if Farraman was among them, Darien had yet to pick him out. He was ready to give Crandall the order to fire again when a double blast again rocked the castle. His men had done well with their recalibrations; this time, one ball struck the front of the catapult, immobilizing it. The other landed so close to the right side of the wagon that many men were brought down. Now, with the catapult still, the real fray would begin.

"Crandall!"

"Aye!"

"Keep one cannon firing on that thing; I want it out before they can fire it again. But put the others to use against the throng; the more we can eliminate, the better things will go at the end."

"Aye!"

Another clatter of wood against wood, a sound of rushing wind, and suddenly, with a barrage in the ears, the castle itself seemed to stagger. They were using smaller ammunition now; the catapult was suddenly showing its muscle. Another like that one at the forward wall, and they would be in serious trouble.

His men were well-trained and disciplined. Runners kept supplying arrows and bolts, powder for the cannon, and laying more spears along the wall. They would only be needed directy before the gate "came down." He could see men falling outside, and tried to count the remaining number. He could also hear a cry very near his ear, when one of his men was struck. The image nearly made him ill. He forced it down again, picked up his spyglass, and swept the field. There were still far too many; Farraman must have garnered at least 150 men. The cannons spoke again, and a cheer from the wall went up as the catapult was smashed; bless the knights and those long-unused cannon, thought Darien. The core of this rabble's strike was eliminated before it could fire its fatal shot. Two more cannonballs flew, and fell among the bowmen. Darien saw two horses go down.

The throng was pressing forward, spurred on by the horsemen. Volleys of arrows continued over the wall, and Darien felt every arrow that struck a man. Stacks of his own arrows disappeared quickly, it was all the runners could do to keep the men supplied. Darien found that his best part was to keep the ground in view; he would have to count men and horses before he could loose his trap. Too many, and the trap would be his own. In the next minute, three more horses went down. Fallen torches were scorching the field and gave the enemy an eerie backglow; it reminded Darien of demons. He made a conscious effort, and pushed that image down deep.

It seemed as though it had gone on like this for hours; Darien was sure dawn would appear at any moment. He continued counting horses; there were still five running. They were leading a charge on the castle, and as he swept his glass across them, Farraman's savage face crossed the lens. Two more horses and another dozen men were blasted by cannonfire. That left three horsemen and roughly two-score men. He needed one more horse and another ten men; but he still hoped that Farraman made it inside. He would have that man's neck in a noose, not yeilded up in battle, a hero's death. No martyrs would rally another such attack; none of the men outside the wall would return home this night. Darien swore it. He counted again. A score and eight men and two horses. Twas enough. He clambered down the wooden ladder and found the captain, who, Darien was pleased to see, had had bowmen at the slits. He reached the captain and told him it was time to spring the trap.

The knights had very carefully planned just how this ruse would work. They had rigged the heavy gateway so that it would slam down from the top upon any strenuous effort. The resulting momentum would power the men inside before they could realize it had been far too easy. Except for five bowmen along the top of the wall, all of Darien's men now stood, weapons at the ready, along the walls and in the shadows. There had been one rush against the door; upon the second, the gate would fall. It would be hand-to-hand for those who remained standing. His mother's words came back to him; indeed there was blood to be spilled, and unless this ruse worked, it could very well be his own.

The second wave struck the gate, and down it came, with a thunderous crash. Men came rushing in; the first dozen went down from arrows fired too near to miss. Bows were dropped and knives and swords appeared. The soldiers directly beside the gate dispatched the second horseman as he entered. Now it was Farraman only, and he was wreaking havoc, sweeping the courtyard visciously with a mace. Darien lost all his reason at that point, and began fighting his way toward the thundering horse. He went through two men, then a third. "I'm killing mine own people!" he thought. But he would reach Farraman if he had to go through twenty men. Then, as Darien saw an arrow hit Farraman's shoulder, he also felt the pain of a bolt in his right thigh. As he went down, he saw two of the knights pull Farraman from his horse. From that point, he was lost in the dust and tangle of men.

Darien, now down and bleeding, began to drag himself to the shadows, when a thought struck him. Go to the servants' entrance; it was a sentence in his head. The entry in question was scarce a dozen yards away and in shadow; in the clamoring he would go unnoticed. Though it took him an interminable time, he managed to reach the door, and rested his back against it.

"Thou hast done well, my son. The enemy is dispatched. Lie still; help is coming." Darien shook his head. He would have sworn he'd heard his mother's voice. Another moment, and the door swung inward. Lying on his back now, he could make out the face of Lord Windover, his father-in-law, who was leaning over him.

"Well, my young soldier, thou hast received a hero's memento of this fracas, I see." He bent down to help the prince stand, but Darien would not budge from the spot.

"I have to know if we got Farraman." He told Windover.

"Fear not. Two of the knights hustled him through a passageway only moments ago. I am sure that thy captain knows how to handle the rest. Thy job is over. All ye need do now is heed the physician." Leaning on his father-in-law, Darien limped his way into the castle. By the time Windover had gotten him to the dispensary, he had passed out from the effort.

When he again opened his eyes, Darien was in a room full of people. The first face he recognized was that of the doctor.

"Well, gentlemen, ladies, our fair prince is back among the living, I see. How dost thou feel, Darien?"

"Drugged, actually." His voice felt suspended, and slurry.

"Ye passed out on the table, which was just as well. I did not want thee awake when I removed that shaft. What ye feel is a sedative I gave thee for rest. It is wearing off now; soon it will pass. But there are people here to see thee, Prince of Tabithia. Let me see if I can get this pillow under thee…ah! There. There is a young lady here who is very eager to see thee."

The doctor was actually brushed aside as Stephanie rushed into her husband's arms. Tears and kisses flew, and for a few moments that was his world. Next came the queen; the king; the captain; and several members of the higher court, as well. In good order, the captain spoke first.

"We have six prisoners and a mighty pile of bodies, Sir. But we lost only eight of our own men, and Farraman is under guard. Congratulations,

Sir; thy plan was excellently drawn, and went, if one could call it that, smoothly."

Applause filled his ears; it took him a moment to realize that these people were clapping for him.

"Prepare a heroes' burial for thy men, Captain. They will be honored by this court. I am humbled by their bravery, sir. They have given their lives so that we may be standing here. They will not be forgotten." The captian smiled a sad smile and moved away. The king came next.

"Well, my son. Thou art a wonder, m'lad. Just don't be bringing any more sticks into the castle, hmm?" He was holding the shaft that had just recently attached itself to Darien's leg. It made the prince laugh; it was a sudden bark of laughter, and it surprised him as much as anyone. "We will see thee decorated anon, my honorable son. The Prince of Tabithia has won the day. We are mightily proud, Darien, mightily proud. But for the nonce, I am taking this horde and departing. Methinks there are two royals here who would like a few moments alone with thee." He moved quickly away, gathering up people as he went. A cursory check, and the physician departed, as well. Darien was alone with his wife and his mother. He had not had time to think about when it was over; he believed that this was the best he could hope for, and then some.

Stephanie, who had the advantage of getting to her husband first, now sat near the head of his bed, her hand tightly gripping her husband's. The queen took up her place upon the opposite side of the bed. She leaned over and gave her son a kiss, then took up his left hand much the way Stephanie had his right.

"My dear son," spoke the queen, "what a marvel thou art. There has not been an attack on this castle in over a century. And ye dispatched it by midnight. Thy warrior's skills are very acute, my son. Where they come from, I can only wonder!

"But we two are very happy to see thee here, and safe. When I heard ye had been shot…" She stopped, her eyes filling with tears. "I am a foolish old woman, to wet thee such, my son. But I am so terribly happy to see thee!"

"Mother, I have a question. When I was shot, I heard a sentence in my head. 'Go to the servants' door,' it said. Just like that. A complete sentence."

"Twas thy own innate cunning, my s…"

"And then, just after I reached the door, I can swear I heard thy voice. Ye told me that help was coming, and to stay where I was."

"Methinks ye were hearing part of my prayers, Darien. I was praying mightily hard!"

"We all were," joined Stephanie.

"How are the children, Love?"

"They are completely oblivious to all this, my love. They have been happily playing in their hostess's kitchen, with their aunts to keep them company. By now Alissa and Ariadne have carried them home. But twas all I could do to send them there. They had a child each and were headed for thy side. My promise that I would bring thee back with me was the only thing that stayed them."

"I need to see my babes sorely, Ladies. How wilt thou transport me?" Darien's doctor entered at just that point. He was pushing a chair that had wooden wheels attached to its legs.

"Here is thy chariot, milord. Mayhap these fine ladies will be thy horses, and bear thee home." Syrenya and Stephanie took up their places, and with the physician's help, Darien hobbled into the chair. The trip to his quarters was swift; it seemed to Darien that this must be what it is like to fly.

"By Jove!" swore King Arthur. "My friend, that is a stirring tale, a stirring tale, indeed! How didst thou work out such a plan, Darien?"

"Sire, I know not. It must have been the urgency of the moment, Sire, for, one minute I had no plan, and the next, there it was, and all laid out to the last detail. Truthfully, Sire, I would swear it was divine providence, for I had very little tutelage in battle strategy. It could just as easily have gone the other way; I must put most of it down to the valor of the men who fought alongside me. The lives of eight militiamen stung me hard, Sire. But the captain said that such losses were a fact of battle, and that each man was prepared for it. It was little consolation, but I did see their memories honored; their battle medals still hang in a casement at court. Tis little enough for a shrine..."

"For a Royal to smart so much for the loss of men at war is a rarity, Darien, and we do think well of thee for't. We also think thou art a bit too modest. Indeed, sir, twas a mighty plan! We would have been proud of it, ourselves!"

"Sire, I thank thee. Tis praise from a very high source."

"Tut, my lad. It is deserving. And ye did bring this Farraman back to stand trial, eh?"

"Indeed we did, Sire. But we could never have imagined what his motives were..."

CHAPTER 15

Courtmartial

It was quite a period of time before the court was able to return to normal; indeed, there were those who felt the court would never again be as it had been. It was sobering, after so long a period of unbroken peace, to suddenly find oneself attacked, and by thine own people.

The soldiers took up the task of clearing the battlefield. They were able to identify most, but not all, of their former compatriots. This troubled Darien, but not so the captain. There had been several bodies mangled by cannonfire; those missing were probably among them. In the days to come, Darien and his family would preside over the soldiers' awards for valor, a commendation for their captain, and an honoring of their dead. But the king had a surprise in store for his son. Immediately after the decoration of the captain, the king called for Darien, Prince of the Ream, and awarded him a Medal of Honor for his service in battle, and a Purple Heart for his injury. There were cheers all around, from the soldiers as well as the court. It was a time to rejoice, and thank God for their good fortune, and for the restoration of peace. But it would be many a fortnight before Darien himself could rest easy.

It was not only his leg that bothered him. He had been able to identify several of the bodies as men from the court. It did not surprise him, for these had been the closest friends of Farraman, and a clique within the court. But their families had suffered, not only the loss of husband or father, but also the shame of treason. Darien would make sure that these families were provided for, and Father Benedic held prayer meetings with them. Darien promised each of them that no stain would be upon them, as long as he was at court. He felt it was the least he could do.

But finally, after more than a fortnight of gruesome clean-up, the court finally returned to a semblance of order. And so it was that upon the third week, Ballizar and Syrenya presided over the choosing of a jury, for Farraman was still fuming in gaol, and Daren was determined to get to the bottom of this man's lunatic actions.

The queen had granted Lady Sarah a visit with her husband, for it was uppermost in Sarah's mind that her son be returned to the castle immediately. But Farraman refused to tell her anything about the whereabouts of their son; he instead hurled epithets at her, calling her foolish, and soft, and a stain upon the name of Farraman, until he drove her, weeping, from his cell. He would smart for it before it was over, Syrenya promised her. But Sarah begged the queen for mercy; the inconsolable woman was still, even after all this, in love with her lord. The queen relented, and promised instead to have the entire kingdom searched, if necessary, to find and return Gerhard to her. This was far happier news for Sarah, who chafed visibly at the separation from her child.

She would be asked to tell the court all she had told the queen about her husband, but beyond that, she was excused from the proceedings. The prisoner would earn himself a slap across the face for continuing to abuse his wife during the testimony.

Lady Sarah told the princess that it would be blessing to sit with the children, if Stephanie wished to join the other Royals at the courtmartial. So it was that the Prince and Princess, the King, his Queen, and her ladies all sat at their places while the prosecutor—Father Benedic's good John Paul, who was versed in such proceedings—laid out the case against Lord Edgar Farraman, charged as traitor to the realm and this court.

Darien would not have traded places with anyone on that jury. To hear this testimony—some for the very first time—was visibly a shock to many of them. And they, too, had friends among those who had followed

Farraman to their doom. There was not a man among them who believed in the man's innocence; what these proceedings were about was discovery. Before they were done, they would know the reasons for what they all considered a maniacal undertaking.

It took the better part of the first day to recreate for the jury what had put the priests on the scent of Lord Farraman. And, even though most knew the story already, the record showed the visitation of the Intruder, and how it was deduced by her presence that a plot was brewing.

By the time it was told of Farraman departing with his son, the prisoner was becoming agitated. He was hurling epithets at his prosecutor and the witnesses, and he again lit into his wife, earning him another slap with a gauntlet. It became necessary to post a guard by the prisoner, who was himself bound, hands behind his back, or he would have hurled himself bodily at the priest several times during his prosecution.

The basis having been well established, the prisoner was then set in the dock, and forced to answer the priest's questions. They were short and to the point; Farraman's replies, however, were anything but.

"Edgar Farraman," asked the priest, and it was not lost on those listening that the man had already lost his title. "How dost thou plead to these charges against thee? Dost thou admit to these treasons?"

"I admit the actions, yes. But I am guiltless of treason. I am the only one left in this court who is *not* guilty of treason. All of thee are traitors to Tabithia, and her pure heritage!" Divine retribution would not have shocked the court as much as this statement. The priest pressed on.

"Give thy reasons for such a statement."

"Then listen well, ye milksops, and know thy sin. How canst thou be ignorant of the base and wicked persons ye do call the Royal Family? Thy king is mad, and his family are bastards, all!" This earned him another backhand. He would earn many more before he was done.

"I held my piece when first the wicked sorceress, Syrenya, did cast her spell upon this court, for I believed then that she was benevolent, and she did rid this place of the lunatic First Night, deamt up by this madman! But she was clever, indeed, ye lords and ladies, and did pull the wool over thine eyes, all! She dost still sit there, upon a Tabithian throne, and insult the eyes of this court with her sin of nudity!" He was again punished by the glove, and debased by the court with taunts and threats. But the queen motioned for silence. She would hear this madman out, and see where his ravings were taking them. But she did have to hold hard to the arm of her king, or he would have gone for the prisoner himself, so insane were the man's lunatic ravings.

"And that is the least of her guilt, for she has altered the good and proper ascendency of the Throne of Tabithia with her brazen ploys of adopting an orphan child, and lavishing upon him the pleasures of royalty, and setting him up as the ascendant to Tabithia's crown!

"Twas necessary that she move quickly, for the rightful heir to the throne was already born when she began her plottings. Had it not been for her wicked deeds, then this lunatic king would have died of his fevers, and the next in line would have ascended, in true and proper fashion!"

"Thou shalt name this 'next in line,' sirrah!" The derogatory fair turned Farraman around, and he again glared at the prosector.

"Canst thou not guess? Art ye all blind? This court is accursed, and spellbound! She is the one! She is the Foreigner! Only she! Are not we all Tabithians born? How canst thou allow this upstart to bedevil thee? It is she who smacks of treason, ye fools! She who wrested this court from its proper heir by treachery; and holds it in her grip even now! Dost thou still not see?

"Oh, yes, she was quick; not a full moon had passed before she was working her wily ways. Canst thou all miss the very timing of her sin? Did she not go adopting an orphan child, barely more than a snot-nosed boy, and not a month within the birthing of my son?!

"Were it not for her, we would not now have the evil King Ballizar, and the women on whom he placed his blight; nor would we have this witch in our midst, nor her bastard son in line for our precious Tabithian throne!" By this time in his rantings, Farraman had wrestled himself to his feet, and stood screaming at the jury box.

"Can ye still not see? She did rob Tabithia of the true Tabithian ascendant! She did snatch from our very fingers the right of ascendancy to the only son of the king's most trusted advisor. She did steal away the crown from *my son!!*" A stunned silence followed, as Farrraman stood, shaking in his rage, spittle pouring from his mouth.

Only after several seconds did the prosecutor remember his role, and level his accusation.

"Then thou hast done all of this, in order to see thy son set upon the throne of Tabithia?"

"Yes! Of course! There is no other reason! *My son* should be the rightful king of Tabithia!" The prosecutor motioned to the prisoner's guard, and the man was forced to return to a sitting position. He continued to mumble to himself, with interjections of "fools!" and "devilry!" King Ballizar rose resolutely from his throne, and this time the queen did not stop him. He stepped down the dais, and stode with purpose toward the dock. The priest tried to talk the king out of it, but he was brushed aside. By the time the king came to a stop, he was only a foot from the prisoner. Farraman was still bound to his chair; otherwise the man would have gone for the king's throat, for his madness had now caught up with him, and he was tense and tightly wound, like a leopard ready to spring. But the king startled the entire court by calling to him in the familiar.

"Eddy! Damn it, Eddy, art thou there?"

"Aye, Sire, I am here," replied the prisoner, in a voice barely above a whisper.

"Eddy, where are ye? Where is thy bride? Where thy son, Eddy?"

"Sire, I am here," he said again. After a beat he continued. "But here is not with thee, Sire. I know not this place. And Lady Sarah, the queen mother, she has fled from me. But my son is safe, Sire, ye may rest assured. He will not be taken by the wickednes of thy helpless court. He is alive and safe, and when thou art in thy grave, he will rule thy lands as ye would have him do. For he is thy rightful heir, Sire. There simply is no toher. Thou dost have no children, no heir. I did provide thee with one, though, Sire. And he is safe, and well. And when the time comes, he will come forth, and claim his rightful crown."

"Eddy, how came ye to this thinking? Art no blood relation to us. By what right do ye claim the throne for thy son? We will know this, Eddy. Ye will not keep this from us."

"Nay, Sire, of course not. But there truly is no other way. Thy line will die with thee, for thou art childless. Thou hast no queen, no babes, no heir. And I could provide for thee what thou hadst not. I could give thee an heir, and I did so, did I not, milord? Is he not a fair and true Tabithian born?"

"Eddy, where are thy senses? Ye are wrong, Eddy, totally wrong. For we would not die without providing for the state. We have done so, Eddy. Thou knowest we have. The Prince of Tabithia has been here nigh upon a score of years, Eddy. Nay, old foolish friend. Even if our Syrenya had not come, we would have never left Tabithia without a rightful ascendant. But, Eddy, thy child would never become the King of Tabithia. Hear us, Eddy! Never thy son!"

The prisoner's head had sunk upon his breast, but with this from the king he did raise his head up, and from deep within there began a low moan, and it did grow until it was a scream, and did blight the ears of the court for an awful time. Finally spent, Farraman collapsed again, and his head returned to his breast, and he was still.

The king was himself still for a time, and not a breath was heard. Then he drew himself up, and turned to the priest, John Paul.

"Father, thou has served thy duties as prosecutor, and done them well. Thy duty is at an end. I thank thee for thy help." The priest took the king's proffered hand, and silently resumed his seat. The king then turned to the jury box, and he spoke thus:

"Gentlemen of this jury, we thank thee for thy service. We do now relieve thee of thy charge. This man, for all his sin, cannot be judged by his peers, for he has passed beyond us. Only God Almighty may judge him now. For that which ye see here now is a madman, and not Farraman at all. Lord Edgar Farraman has departed, and left this shell of a man in his place.

"We must pity Lord Edgar, for he was in his time a true and proper advisor, and a close friend. Though the result of his madness has brought terrible loss to the kingdom, we must pity him. He shall be removed to the asylum at Shepherd's Crossing, and shall live out his life as a ward of the state. Scribe, make of this a royal decree. This shall be done. And his wife and his son shall also be provided for. And now, friends, let us end this madness. Let us return to our hearths, and praise God for our good fortune, that we have not set our own foot upon the twisted road of madness. Friends, go to. This court is ended." The king's head fell, upon this decree, and he waved his family to join him, and together they all slowly departed the courtroom.

CHAPTER 16

Sarah's Child

Immediately they left the throne room, Syrenya again looked to her son.

"Darien, ye must ready the knights for a singular mission. Ye must know that Gerhard is still with those of the same mind as Edgar. He must be found, and returned to his mother, before he is spirited out of the country, or is killed to cover the tracks of his captors.

"My son, thou hast done this country service enough in these past weeks, but thy charge is not over. We must find Gerhard, for Lady Sarah's sake if for no other. Wilt thou take this task upon thee? Wilt thou go?"

"Of course I will, Mother. We will leave after nightfall. I think I may have a good starting point. But if he has been moved, we will be gone for a long—perhaps a very long—time. I will put Crandall in charge of preparations. I shall be with Stephanie and thy grandchildren until the hour. We will commence after sunset; the fewer who see such a party leave the castle, the better. It may be that, even now, the castle is watched. We are still not sure how many people didst join with Farraman in his attempt. We will have to work with stealth, but I think I have a ruse that will work, once the child is found.

"Father, Sire, how didst thou know what ye would find in that poor man's head? I have never seen anything like thy rational, indeed, inspired, course of action. We might never have brought all this to light, if thou hadst not acted. Or he might have done thee harm, bound though he was. Yet thy words went right to the source. I stand amazed!"

"It may surprise ye to know, my son, that when we left the dais we had no more idea what we would do than thee. Thy mother had us quite by the arm until that time, and a good thing, too. We would have done the man mischief, so towering was our rage. But when Edgar seemed to collapse, we felt thy mother's grip loosen, and before we knew it we were face to face with the man.

"But we did know, as surely as we see thee now, that somewhere in that shattered form, the spirit of the true Farraman, our friend and advisor, still remained. When we called him by a name that dates between us and him back to our youth, we did find him. But twas all for nought; he had already moved too far beyond us to retrieve. Tis just as well, however; had we been able to return him to sanity, there would still be the question of treason. Twould be of no good use to restore him, only to see him hanged." Ballizar's voice was low—so low, it seemed, that now the trial was over, Darien could feel his father's grief at the loss of a friend who had been for so long a trusted confidant.

"But thou wert so strong, my liege, that I was mightily proud. Ye did show thy court today that thou art still the rightful King of Tabithia." The queen's voice was warm and loving, she too, aware of the king's loss.

"Indeed?" said the king in mock astonishment. "And was there any doubt?"

"Only in the mind of a madman, my leige, and never else."

"The king and queen will dine in her chambers shortly, my son," continued Ballizar. "Bring our Stephanie and we will dine together."

"That would please us both, would it not, my love?"

"Truly, Sire; we thank thee."

"Tut. Can not a king dine with his family when he likes?" And he herded his family down the corridor. For the nonce, the evil madness of Edgar Farraman was forgotten.

Darien spent the rest of his afternoon in his chambers, but twas not only to be with his family. When the prince and princess returned to their rooms, Lady Sarah was happily rocking Lylanya, while Ariadne and

Alissa, who came to these chambers immedately after the trial, were in the kitchen, where a happy young boy was sampling their handiwork.

"Young man," asked Darien. "Dost thou bedevil thy aunts?"

"Yes, Father!" exclaimed the lad, laughing, to which Ariadne added, "Nay, Darien, not a whit! He hath taken on the role of taster for their luncheon. Twould never do to have them turn up their noses at all our hard work!" This sent the boy into more laughter, and it continued as Stephanie scooped up her son, and carried him out to Lady Sarah.

"Thou art most kind, Sarah, to stay with the children. How are ye holding up, Dear?"

"Nay, Princess, twas a blessing. Thy children are passing sweet, and never so spoiled as I fear my Gerhard is..."

Before Sarah had a chance to react to her own statement, Darin cut in.

"Sarah, the knights and I leave tonight, to find thy son. I promise thee we shall not return until we know his whereabouts. Upon that time, one of the knights will come and tell thee where we are, and thou must bring thyself to us, straightaway, in thy royal robes and with as much noise as possible, so that all of the people shall know it is thee who leaves the castle. Thy messenger will stay behind, and follow later upon a circuitous route. He will catch up to thee out of sight of the castle and lead thee to us. Canst thou do this?"

"Of course I can, Darien. I await the moment."

"Good; so do I. I will have further instructions for thee when we meet at that time. Be strong, Sarah; we shall find thy son. Should it take a year, we shall find him."

There was a party of ten on horseback who left the castle under cover of darkness. With them came a covered wagon, with two more knights upon the driver's seat; the twelfth knight watched their back from inside the cover of the wagon. They had dressed themselves as nomads, groups of which were known to pass through Tabithia from time to time. By daybreak they would be well on their way, and no one watching the castle would be the wiser.

Leaving the keep, the troupe began on a southerly route; if they could rumble through Crossroads and Shepherdswick without stirring the populace, they could continue north, on a direct path toward Barrowsmith, the last known place the rebels had met before the attack on the castle.

Barrowsmith was the largest of the three towns in the North, which was made up of the River Quadrant to the west, and the Mountain Quadrant to the east. The only other location having more than 150 inhabitants was Crevice, and it was located high on the side of the tallest mountain in Tabithia, Sorrow's Peak. The mountain had been named by the people of Crevice, in honor of the ill-fated explorers who were Crevice's founding fathers. Leaving the camp of about twenty, the four men leading the expedition had attempted to reach the mountain's summit. They never returned, and their bodies were never found. What began as an attempt to find them turned into an overwhelming desire to remain at camp, rather than returning to the lowlands without their leaders.

Over the years, Crevice drew many who wished to leave their old lives behind and join this now-self-sufficient town. With the foods they could not grow themselves brought up from Pine, at the base of the mountains and located in the River Quadrant, Crevice was slowly able to shut itself off from the rest of Tabithia. While it was still accessible by means of a major road coming from Barrowsmith, Crevice took less and less part in the country as a whole, feeling itself a city/state whose home was the mountain, not Tabithia. In time, the populace was able to cut a mountain road west, leaving the bounds of Tabithia in twenty-three miles, and exiting into Tabithia's neighbor to the north, Norway. Their reason for this was their own. Except for the residents of Pine—who were now as dependent on Crevice as Crevice was on them—rarely now did another soul in Tabithia cross paths with the mountain men. So the disguises that Darien and the knights wore added to their credibility. If they had to travel to Crevice during their search, nomads they must be. Were these travelers not vagabonds, their presence in Crevice would have been suspect, indeed.

The troupe traveled northward without incident, doing their best to play their roles by attempting to trade with farmers they met upon the road, or leer at the women who may have been traveling with their husbands or fathers. Thus they rolled into Barrowsmith, without any ado, to find that somehow their imminent arrival had preceded them, and that many of the shops on the main street had been closed and shuttered, despite the fact that it was not yet closing time. The one place that Darien counted on remaining open was the tavern, for it was there that the Captain's man had met with the other rebels. It was also known that those nomads who possessed the money to do so could drink a man's saloon dry, and the barkeep who closed his doors to them would probably get his door battered down, in the bargain.

Darien himself, who was a good bit younger, and still a great deal less hairy, than his mates, was left "to guard the wagon," while the knights went inside to play their roles. From the sound of the din they were making, they did a fairly good job of it. One of the knights, Brontaine, brought Darien a pint, but only to report that, from all they could ascertain, all aspects of the rebellion had either left, or gone completely underground. There was not even a word of it, though broad hints had been dropped. Crandall had spun a yarn that "they had overheard in Tabit's Mill" that a few weeks before, a gang of cutthroats had attacked the castle. All it got him were blank stares.

"It doesn't matter," Darien heard himself saying, "Gerhard is not here."

"Sire?"

"Take some time to wrap up, and let's leave without arousing any suspicion; what we seek is not here."

"Aye, Sire. I'll tell Crandall." The look on Brontaine's face clearly revealed his confusion.

The wonderment in Brontaine's voice was only a little less than that which now weighed in Darien's own head. The words had left his lips before he himself had known what they would be; it was hard to tell, from Darien's view, which of the two of them seemed the more surprised. It was a good bet that Crandall was going to be more than a little curious.

It took about half an hour to wrap up the effort, and then the knights returned to their horses. Darien nodded to Crandall, and the two of them took the reins of the wagon.

"Sire, I must confess I am right well perplexed at what ye told Brontaine. Art thou sure that the boy be not here?"

"Crandall, I am not sure how I know it, but I am as sure Gerhard is not here as I am sure thy beard is red."

"Thou dost know not the reason?'" It was clear that Crandall was doing his best to be polite to his prince, but this was beyond the pale, and it showed in the man's voice.

"I will tell thee something, Crandall, and I will also tell thee that I know not how these things happen. On the morning we learned of the rebellion, the king was for laying hands on Farraman and trying him. But I came forth with another plan, which proved to be the right one; to follow him and his minions and find out his intent. I have no idea where that plan came from. During the campaign, when it came to me to rig the castle gates, I know not from whence it came. It appeared in my mind, as complete as when we executed it. And during the attack on the castle, when I took the bolt, I heard a sentence in my head: 'go to the servants' entrance.'

I didn't figure it out. I was told. It may have been my mind that told me so, but I was told. I have no experience in battle, nor in campaigning; where could such ideas come from? I tell thee, Crandall, I cannot explain these things to thee; I cannot even explain them to myself. But I know that Gerhard is not here. That is the long and short of it."

Crandall, silently, took up the reins and moved the wagon into the column behind the horses. He remained silent for a long time. When he spoke, it was in a hushed and almost reverent tone. "Sire," he said, "I am heartily glad that thou art on our side."

It had been decided that Clover would be their next stop. The small farming community was the last gathering of populace before the road led out of Tabithia into Sweden. While they all were aware that the boy could well have been spirited out of the country, any intent of such might have been ascertained by the honest folk of Clover, and information might be forthcoming there. Thus the column headed northeast, and after camping just five miles beyond Barrowsmith, the knights remained where they were while Crandall and Darien took the wagon into Clover the next morning. The two had agreed to play father and son, and stock up on supplies at the feed store.

During the purchase, Crandall, who Darien had begun to realize had a slick tongue indeed, began to engage the shopkeeper in conversation. It was the first time Darien had heard the man speak Swedish; somehow, it did not surprise him.

"Do you speak Swedish, man?" asked the knight.

"Indeed I do, sir. Do I have your order correctly?"

"Yes, most certainly, and I thank you. But I thought since you are a resident here in Clover that you might know something of a tale I heard on the way into Tabithia. There was a band of vagabonds headed into Sweden, and they told my boy and me that, not a month ago, there had been an attack on the king's castle here. Do you know if that story has any truth in it?"

"Indeed I do, Sir. There was a most fearsome battle, from what I heard, and the king's soldiers wiped out the brigands, to a man, sir. They captured their leader and hanged him, sir. That they did. Some of the folks I know from Barrowsmith brought me the news, sir, and they're as honest a family as you will ever meet. They told me those who planned the insurrection were right there in Barrowmith, and that they fled when they heard, right up the mountain into Crevice—or beyond. It wouldn't have surprised me, sir, to hear that they were well out of Tabithia by now. Well out, Sir."

"Seems a long way around just to slip out of the country," countered Crandall. "If it were me, I'd have come through here, and on into Sweden. Twould have been a far sight faster."

"Oh, yes, sir, I agree, and I can see how you, being from Sweden and all, might think such a thing. But let me tell you, Sir, if that bunch had attempted to come through Clover, well, by the time they were done, the whole town would have known. And we learned of the insurrection not a week later, Sir. Had we seen anything, well, the king would have heard from us, and you can count on that, Sir."

Their business quickly concluded, Crandall and Darien turned the wagon around and started back to camp, heading west. Darien agreed with Crandall. The shopkeeper appeared an honest man, and both took him at his word. Therefore, if those who held the boy had fled Tabithia, they did so by another route. So it was back into Tabithia that the "nomads" would travel. Darien, knowing it to be the second most direct route out of the country, suggested Crevice as their next stop.

"It would be a spectacle, indeed, if such a band were to pass through Crevice," said Crandall. "Methinks that it might not even be a safe passage. It would be more to the liking of the residents if those who arrived in Crevice did so to join them, rather than pass beyond them."

"Should we try another direction, then?"

"Nay, seems wise to me," answered the knight. "Heaven only knows how such a bunch would stick out, if indeed they have gone that way. And having come to join those who are so apart from the rest of the country, they might well believe that no one would think to look for them there. Nay, I say let's do it. We can pass around Barrowsmith by the northwest, and pick up the main road before we begin the ascent. Anyone who sees us will simply put us down as daft nomads. Tis the way of the locals hereabouts, anyway."

"Crandall, there is always the possibility that this group merely went east from Barrowmith and right into Sweden. Once there, I fear Gerhard would be lost to us."

"Aye. The thought had occurred to me, as well. But I think we must stick to Tabithia, and pray they have kept him close. Sweden is a big country; I don't like the thought of them having spirited him out..."

"I like Norway no better, Crandall. And if they passed beyond Crevice, whether the townspeople did them mischief or not, then we have the very same situation."

"Well, then, Sire, I think we had best do as ye say, and try to stick to Tabithia. If he is outside of the borders, he may be lost to us already."

"Crandall, I would be grateful if ye would address me as Darien. I still think of 'Sire' as my father. This royalty ceremony, while dressed in such attire as this, seems a bit unnecessary."

"Well, then, Darien it shall be. And wouldst thou have all the knights address ye so?"

"I would indeed, Crandall, I would indeed. Thou art knights; thy commander is the king. There is no need to stand on ceremony where I am concerned."

"I'll say it again, Darien," spoke Crandall, only this time with a broad grin. "I am heartily glad thou art on our side."

Even though the road to Crevice was only 38 miles long, it was up, and it was in no way straight. The journey into town took three full days, and as it turned out, those provisions picked up in Clover would be far more necessary than the ruse they were meant to be. By the time the search party arrived, they were worn and ragged, and even Darien had no trouble passing for the gypsy he professed to be.

The horses and wagon moved slowly down the main throughfare of the town. Darien, now on horseback near the front of the column, kept looking about him as if hoping to see Gerhard. Crandall wondered if he was looking around for him mentally, as well.

They stopped at the livery, but got the barn door slammed in their faces. The same thing happened when they tried the General Store. So it was to the tavern that the band headed, despite the rude and angry stares that met them from all the townfolk; the publican might still be willing to serve up some ale.

To Darien's relief, the man was more than happy to see them. The tavern in Crevice did not get a great deal of patronage from overnight guests, to be sure. Strangers in town were a treat for this fellow. So there was always the possibility...

The men's coin was readily accepted, and drinks were passed around. After some more of their ruse was played out, Crandall used the same tale he used in Barrowsmith to try and draw the barkeep out. He seemed more than happy to oblige. Unfortunately, he was completely unaware that any such event as an attack on the castle had ever taken place. So Crandall altered his story just a bit, and suggested that, since the rebels had come from Barrowsmith, it might be that they had come through Crevice to escape into Norway.

"Only if they were completely daft, man. Thy band being traveling fellows and all, I can see how ye wouldn't know a bit of this, but nobody uses that road unless the Council of Crevice gives them express permission, and I can tell you, that has never happened, to my knowledge."

Crandall appeared shocked.

"Art thou telling me, man, that we cannot take that road and travel into Norway? For that is exactly what we had planned to do."

"I'm not telling thee anything, Sir," said the barman quickly. "But if that is thine intention, then it's going to take a bit of work to get the permission ye'll need to do so. That road is for emergencies only, Sir. Crevice sits in the middle of an avalanche area. If it becomes necessary for the townsfolk to pick up and flee, then that's the route we'll take. That's why it's there, and that's when it'll be used."

"And just how do we go about getting permission, as ye like to call it?" asked Crandall, with a rumbling growl in his voice. The look on the barman's face made it seem he was rightfully glad that the bar was between him and this large and angry man.

"It would be at the courthouse, Sir. Ye'll have to confer with one of the Aldermen. But—I'm sorry to have to say it, Sir—I don't hold out much hope for thy chances."

"Yer telling me that no one has been granted access to that road for… how long?"

"The road was built about eighteen years ago, Sir. And it was a hard row to hoe, let me tell you. All mountains and all forested. To my knowledge, except for maintenance, no one—especially anyone who is not a resident of Crevice—has ever been allowed to use it since that time."

"And if one of those Norwegians who be on the other side of that river should decide he'd like to use it, what then?"

"He'd have a pretty tough time of it, too, Sir. We maintain a gate at the river."

Crandall shook his head as if in disbelief.

"Ye know that every citizen of Tabithia thinks ye people are all daft, do ye know that?"

The bartender drew himself up to his tallest height and dared gaze directly at Crandall.

"Frankly, Sir, we *do not care* what the citizens of Tabithia think." And that was the last that the man would say on the subject. So the men headed back to their horses, and Crandall and Darien conferred for a moment.

"We'll have to at least try to get permission," said Crandall, "else our entire purpose here comes under suspicion."

"I agree entirely, Crandall. But if nothing else, we have learned two things: first, why it is that Crevice built that road in the first place, and second, that those who have Gerhard did not come this way."

"Ah, any...thoughts...on whether Gerhard is about the place?"

"Nary a one, which only means that the question did not arise, I suppose."

"Well then, the only route left open to us is the road down into Pine. If the elders here are as adamant about their road as our host suggests, then that's the way we go."

When getting the answer they all knew they would from the elder at the courthouse, the knights put up a pretty fair ruckus. You would have thought that Norway was their destination all along. Darien believed that the men were beginning to enjoy taking on their roles. But after some bit of din, the men stomped out, mounted up, and headed down the mountain to Pine, leaving those who witnessed the event to shake their heads in continuous wonder at the lunacy of all those who lived "downhill."

Pine was the only town in the northwest, or River Quadrant; except for the lower mountain range that led the men down from Crevice, the entirety of the quadrant was forestland. The chief business in Pine was pine—pine lumber, to be exact. The only other place of activity was Pine Mill, fifteen miles west of Pine and located on the Shallow River. Pine Mill it was indeed; it was here that the wood that had been cut and hauled was sawn, loaded for export, or floated downriver to the port of Sedwick, where it was sold through Sedwick offices to the surrounding countryside, or loaded onto ships for delivery outside Tabithia. Pine was one of the chief exports of Tabithia—that, and some exceptionally fine wool sheared from Tabithia-born sheep. Except for the logging industry, and the constant resupplying of Crevice with its out-of-town needs, there was no other business in Pine. Except, of course, a tavern. In a town like Pine, lack of a tavern would mean lack of loggers, and that would never do.

The usual plan was to go to the tavern and play their roles, expecting to get some sort of reaction, but the column and wagon rolled through Pine and never even stopped. Darien had again perceived that Gerhard was not here. The group continiued on to Pine Mill, which caused a bit of anxiety on the part of Crandall; how were these nomads, having once reached Pine Mill, going to explain their turning around and returning to Pine—and beyond? Darien believed he had a plan, and told it to Crandall; what he got in response was a roar of laughter.

The plan ran something like this. Having reached Pine Mill, and probably realizing that the boy was not there, either, the column would begin to continue their trip westward into Norway. But Darien told Crandall that one of the men—who could be the knight's choice—ought to ask if the bridge over Shallow River had been blessed. Once the question had been asked, it would become essential that the entire column know if the bridge had been blessed by the Goddess; in other words, was it safe to cross? Knowing the answer they would get--that no such of a thing had ever been done and would likely never be done--the entire group would have to shy from crossing the bridge and grumble badly that they would have to travel south through Sedwick. Crandall called the knights around the wagon and explained the ruse, and there were chuckles and slaps of comraderie all around. Crandall turned his head and gave Darien a wink. The plan would work fine, and could be continued, if need be, in Pine itself.

But that's not how it happened.

Pine Mill had a total of four buildings facing a central logging-yard: the mill itself, a large barn-like structure in which lumber was cured, the— quite ample—home of the miller, and a small store. This latter served as a trading post and bar for those coming to the mill for service. The road passed through the logging-yard on the diagonal, with the store, and then the home of the miller, on the right side, and the mill and the wood-barn on the left. It then very quickly reached the bridge in question. As the column pulled into the yard, passing the store and heading for the mill, Darien grabbed Crandall's arm.

"He's here," whispered the prince. "He's here, Crandall. I'm not sure where, just yet, but I know he's here. My guess is the house or the store."

"Well, checking the store is no problem. We'll do our usual. After that…"

"Crandall, listen. Let's not change our plans all that much. Let's go ahead and see if the bridge is blessed, but when it isn't, insist we have to stay here until one of us can go get someone who can bless the bridge. That way we can stay here and surreptitiously explore the area while we wait for our emissary—and the Lady Sarah—to arrive."

"Excellent, Darien. We'll make a campaigner of thee yet. Anyone in particular you want to ride off for our 'blesser?'"

"Whoever can get back to Tabit's Keep the fastest and return with a royal coach without associating himself with it."

"There's going to be trouble getting a royal coach through Pine."

"They'll have to circumvent Pine. Tell your man to have Lady Sarah bring two guards with her; she may need them to keep her going. If— *blast*—who do you plan to send, Crandall?"

"I'll make it Gravaine. He's our best horseman."

"All right. Have Gravaine circumvent Pine to the south along the logging roads. His success will aid Lady Sarah in getting back to us without arousing suspicion in town. Have him direct her through Marketsborough. That will keep her out of Barrowsmith altogether. You have *no idea* how glad I am that we did not stop in Pine. It would have been into Norway and gone for Gerhard if we had. Or worse."

"Who do ye suppose is keeping him here?"

"We don't know. It could be the citizens of Pine themselves; we have no way of knowing who decided it was time to revolt when Farraman brought his plans to Barrowsmith. The presence of anyone here who looks out of place—barring ourselves, of course—should be an indication. But I don't want them; let them off scot-free for all I care, as long as we get Gerhard back safely."

"That's surely the most expeditious plan we have, although I doubt anyone here would have it so. Let's get ourselves inside the store and see what we're up against. We'll keep someone 'guarding the wagon,' so if anyone makes a move outside the store he can let us know."

"Good. Let's go."

A dozen men descended on the store, ready to bedevil the inhabitants with their nomadic ways, only to find that there was but one man inside— the storekeeper himself. And he wasn't at all happy to see them.

"And just what is it I might do for ye, ah, gentleman?" he asked gruffly.

"Ale, man, ale! I'm as dry as a desert, and could drink a well. Unless," Crandall said, just as gruffly, "yer not particularly fond of this here coin." Since the nomads' money was indeed Tabithian, the storekeeper made the best of the situaton, and put up drinks all around. The knights made their usual ruckus, but not a word was said of the boy or the battle at the castle. Darien himself took a pint out to the wagon, and their guard reported that all was still in the yard, and had been since they had gone inside.

After they had drunk their fill, their host hinted rather broadly that perhaps they ought to be gettng on their way. Crandall let it make his suspicious.

"Thou art in a particular big hurry to get us out the door, mister. Is our money not good enough for ye?"

"Now, Sir, it isn't that at all. But as thou canst see, there is not a wagon or a dray in the yard. The mill is shut down, the barn is closed, and I was just about to shut down here myself. There's no lodging here, and I could plainly see that ye came from Pine. So I thought ye would want to get on into Norway to find thyselves a place for the night."

"Well, sir, now that ye mention it, it does seem that night is approaching. Alright, men, let's get it done, then. And we can leave this tiny little kingdom to its inhabitants."

The sigh of relief that the storekeeper released was cut short, however, when one of the men spoke up with their expected question.

"Thou wouldst know, would thee not, Host, if thy bridge is blessed or not?" The question drew a complete blank on the part of the storekeeper.

"If the bridge has been—what?!"

"Blessed, man, blessed. Hast thy bridge been blessed? For I'll tell thee truly, Sir, I'm not crossing that Styxian river if it not be!" General agreement came from all around.

"What kind of an insane question is that? There is no need to bless bridges! If we blessed every bridge that we built, the priests would have no time for preaching!"

"Not by a priest, man, by a Priestess; by a daughter of the Goddess. Art thou completely ignorant of Pagan ritual, Sir?"

"By a—a *what*?!" The storekeeper could not contain himself; he burst out laughing. "Thou dost think that Tabithia—fully a stout and loyal supporter of the Holy Roman Catholic Churh—doth waste its time on Pagan *ritual*? Ye be a case for Shepherd's Crossing, that's what ye be, man. HA! A Priestess! What next?"

This caused a general hubbub among the nomads, and the storekeeper suddenly wished he had kept his wits about him, said simply, "of course," and gotten this band of roughnecks out of Pine Mill. What was to happen now? Could he get them to backtrack though Pine? Or at least far enough back to get them out of Pine Mill—the miller would have his skin if he caused a band of nomads to camp on the mill's doorstep. By all the Saints in Heaven! He would have to talk quickly, and try and convince them of sense.

"There are but ten horses and one wagon in thy band, gentlemen. I have myself seen drays loaded down with lumber that would dwarf thy weights travel across that bridge regularly without a single incident. That bridge is as sound as modern science can make it."

"Which is nary sound enough, my good fellow," replied Crandall. "Unless that bridge be blessed, we'll have to stay here—at least long enough for one of us to go and bring a priestess so she can bless that bridge."

"But, Sir, as I have told thee, there is no place for thee here! This is a business establishment! Do ye wish to have our regular loggers turned away because they cannot get their lumber into the millyard? Nosir, ye will have to go back to Pine…"

"Not as long as I'm leadin' this band, my friend. Nomads do not travel backwards."

"Can ye not at least take thyselves back a mile or so in that direction? We need to have this road open for lumber! Ye can't be residing in Pine Mill!"

"We have no intention of 'residing' anywhere, man. We're just going to camp out back for a coupla days, until one of my men can get back here with a priestess. Fer Chrissake, man, there's a priestess in Marketsborough! It won't take our man two days—provided, of course, that she's available. But the blessing of a bridge is no small matter, man. She'll come. And we shall stay here until she does." Crandall let it be known by the tone in his voice that argument might prove painful.

"Then can I ask ye to please go down to the river behind the store? Ye'll be comfortable down there, and cause no consternation to our regular customers. Can I ask ye to do that? For if ye don't, then it will be all my position is worth here at the mill. The miller is going to have my skin for thy presence, as it is. Can ye not at least do this for me?"

"Why, of course we can, man. Ye needn't worry one bit. We'll be as quiet as church mice, now, won't we, fellows?" His question was met with guffaws by the men, and the storekeeper now found himself in the very uncomfortable position of having to go to the miller's house and explain why this band of gypsies was about. Far better that he go over there with the news, than make the miller come to him.

Crandall, meanwhile, sent Gravaine on his way, and the rest of the band took themselves and their horses and wagon down to the river, to wait. Once night was upon them, Darien planned to take a walk. If Gerhard were here, as he firmly believed, and he was not in the store, he had to be with the miller. Perhaps a surreptitious stroll back up the hill would prove the question, one way or the other. Darien certainly hoped it was the house. In the home of a miller, at least, a boy would never be suspect and would receive, hopefully, a semblance of proper food and shelter. If they had the boy in the barn or the mill, then he was a prisoner, indeed, and his life was in danger. But even if he were not, what his captors were doing about explaining to the boy the extended lack of either of his parents was a question Darien could not answer. The prince found himsef wishing to meet this miller, to take the measure of the man. Who he was might lead Darien to learn how well he was tending the boy. It would also tell him whether his original plan would work, or if the knights would have to take the boy by force, and restore the rage that had caused this northern district to revolt, in the first place.

The men had their camp well under way, fires lit and food prepared, before Darien began his ascent to the miller's house. There had been no further contact from the mill since the band had come down to the river, and Darien suspected that it was the presence of the boy that kept the man the barkeep seemed so much to fear at arm's length. If Darien was to see anything at all, it was up to him to advance on the house, and try to ascertain what he could.

The house was in view and the lights shone brightly from within when Darien realized he had been quite correct, and Gerhard was inside. He again wondered with a part of his mind how he might know this, but he was sure of it nonetheless. He stood still in the darkness, when something suddenly clicked, and he heard himself utter one word in his head.

Mother! Abrupt silence, as if he had suddenly interrupted something— or, in this case, someone.

Yes, my son?

Art thou a sorceress? What are ye doing in my mind?!

A sorceress? Nay, my son. I have what thou may call a curse; others, a gift. It depends on how one wishes to use it. Thou dost have it to a degree, else ye would not have been able to detect my presence. I cannot explain it all to thee at the nonce, but suffice it to say that I can travel with thee, through thy mind, and use thee as mine eyes and ears.

Then it is thee who hast been able to say whether Gerhard is within our purview?

Yes, my son, thou art correct. Darien found himself growing angry.

And art thou also the one who hast spoken in my head ere now, planned out these ruses, and led me to the servants' entrance during the fray?

I can see why thou wouldst be angry, if ye did believe it so. But nay, my son. Thou dost do both of us a disservice if ye believe such. I am here solely to aid in finding

Gerhard, and am heartily glad we have done so. I have guided thee not at all; I am only able to sense his presence. All else—ALL else—is of thine own devising. Thou art a warrior born, my son. I cannot use thine intelligence or thine instinctive grasp of a situation; that is thine alone. But, if it doth help thee, I will tell thee that what ye possess of this gift is perhaps a part of what gives thee these talents.

What is this gift, Mother?

Those who have it, those who can make use of it, refer to it as a "sixth sense," another means of sensing the world around them. If ye can learn to use it, and not think it a curse, it will aid thee well, for it doth give thee an advantage over any foe, and an additional aid in helping a friend. As thou art doing now for Lady Sarah. But we cannot seek a physical reason or logic behind it, my son. Those who have it, deal with it. But no physician can answer what it is, who it might effect, or how. It is rarely spoken of, even by those who use it well. As thou didst so adroitly state, it is indistinguishable from magic to most folk.

This is not happening, thought Darien. I am suffering from delirium.

Nay, not so, my son. Thou art quite sane. But ye art still exploring thine own boundaries as a man. Do not rule out thine own innate advantages over thy fellows, Darien. Thou art in line for a crown. There be reasons for it, even if we know not what they are, or why. Thou knowest that God works in mysterious ways.

For a time, Darien was silent. So, too, was his mother's voice. After he had given himself several moments to calm himself, he spoke again within his own mind.

So what happens now?

Methinks thou dost know already. Thou hast sent for Lady Sarah, and ye have a plan for when she arrives. Meet with her as ye have devised, and give her thy counsel. I am anxious to see what thou wilt do; I am also most anxious to reunite mother and child. I have fulfilled my purpose, Darien. Gerhard is found. I hope that thou canst forgive me this subterfuge; but it was not worth trying to explain. Discovery of me is a discovery of something thou dost carry within thine own self. Think on't. I wish thee success. Trust thyself, Darien; I will see thee upon thy return, which I hope will be soon now. Thou art but two days' ride from the castle. I will see thee anon. Farewell!

Mother?

Yes, my son?

Nothing. I will see thee soon. Darien actually *felt* his mother smile.

I love thee, too, my son. Anon.

On the morning of the third day at Pine Mill, Gravaine returned to camp, and informed Darien that Lady Sarah and he had indeed returned through Marketsborough, and that she awaited him in her carriage, just out of sight of the millyard. Darien walked out to meet her, and swung himself up into the carriage beside her. Her sudden start reminded him of his appearance, and he spoke quickly to reassure her.

"Lady Sarah, tis I, Darien."

"Darien! Ye do look a fright! What hast come over thee?"

"We are playing at being nomads, the knights and I, Sarah. It is the ruse we have devised to let us travel freely about the kingdom. And it has worked; I tell thee thy son is within yon house. Ye are about to go and claim him."

"I?" Lady Sarah seemed a bit taken aback at the thought.

"It is a move designed to demoralize them, Lady Sarah. If thou canst march into the house in all thy regal stature and demand the return of thy son, with every confidence he is there, it should take them so by surprise that they will have no defense. Demand it; thy station in Tabithia says thou must be obeyed."

"And if these be rebels truly, and they will not comply? What then?"

"These people have no idea we are aware of the boy's whereabouts. It is my belief that the miller, who holds thy son within, will either immediately comply, or else try to stall thee whilst others try to spirit the boy out the back. If the latter, they will be met by Crandall and the knights, and brought immediately back in again. One way or another, thy son and thee will be reunited."

"Then I am ready. Wilt thou ride with me?"

"Nay, I will walk back and observe. With speed and determination, Sarah. Give them no quarter. Thou may be sure he is within. I tell thee straight."

"Then what are we sitting here for, Darien? Out, I say; I am gone!"

Darien had time to see the carriage pull smartly up to the walk of the miller's house, saw Lady Sarah step from within and walk determinedly up to the door. By the time she was let in, he had reached a place nearby and could hear her within. She confronted the miller himself.

"May I help thee, Madame?"

"My name is Lady Sarah Farraman, wife of Lord Edgar. Thou hast my son. Ye will give him up to me straight."

"Nay, Madame, truly!"

"Nay, what, rascal? That thou hast my son, or that ye will not give him up? If the one, thou liest; if the other, I shall have thy scalp."

"Now, see here, Madame..."

"What, Lout, wouldst thou quibble? I shall beat thee with my horsewhip, sirrah, if thou wilt not obey me!"

Darien, who could stand it no longer, moved to see inside the house. At that moment, a youthful voice cried out in glee, "Crandall!" And a mighty scuffling was heard in the room beyond, before the man himself appeared, with a youth by the scruff of the neck in one hand, and the boy in question by the other. Behind him came the other knights, spilling in from the rear entrance of the house. The miller himself, who still cowered from Lady Sarah, tried without success to be angered with the trespass.

"Gerhard!"

"Mummy!" The child shot across the floor and into his mother's waiting embrace. Once united, the two were quickly gone, without another word. Crandall, meanwhile, advanced on the man who now seemed more confused than nought else.

"Thou hast earned thyself a sound thrashing, mister, separating a woman and her child as thou hast. Given half the chance, I would do it myself. But twould serve no purpose, other than to make me extremely happy. Thou art a lucky man, sirrah, for thou hast escaped unscathed. Keep thy peace about what has transpired here, for if ye cross the crown again, it will go doubly bad for thee. Rue the day ye find me on thy doorstep again. Do ye understand me, man?"

By this time, the miller could only nod dumbly. Crandall snorted, and led the way out of the house. As if by command, the band of men retrieved their horses, drew up the wagon, brought themselves to in front of the waiting carriage, and began the odd-looking procession that would carry them all home again. What might have taken weeks, or months, had taken the knights a mere twelve days; and before a fortnight had passed, they would all be home in their beds again. But not before fate had dealt them one more peril. They would still have to deal with the rebels of Pine.

"Hold hard, there, Darien," spoke King Arthur. "Ye mentioned this once before and we let it go, but now we must say something. Twice now thy mother has told thee thou art ascendant to the throne. And thou hast said both are now dead. Why art thou not on the throne of Tabithia as we speak?"

"I cannot undertake the role of king until I know what I do not know, Sire. I am on this quest for the very reason that I must take on that yoke, and soon; but until I know the answers to how these events have unfolded, I am unable to do so."

"But who is in control of thy country while thou art about learning these secrets?"

"Prince Randall currently wears the crown, Sire, as would be expected; he is next in line. But the queen mother is still very much in evidence, and she can rule as well as I. And she can have no better advisors than the two who were ladies-in-waiting to Queen Syrenya."

"Then thou hast not abdicated?"

"Nay, Sire; at least, not as yet. My wife and I argued long about it; but she could not dissuade me. Randall agreed to take the throne temporarily, and the Royal Family remains intact. I have given myself a year; and having traveled in many a country since that time, my year is nearly done. I have but a month before I must make up my mind."

"Well, we are pleased to hear that, at least. But thou hast misrepresented thyself, Prince Darien. Had ye not come cloaked, as it were, ye would have received a more royal welcome. It is not often we can meet those who rule as we do, in countries abroad. Unless it is upon the battlefield. We are well pleased to have thee here, but we would have made thee far more comfortable, had we known that we entertained an equal. Good God, man; ye brought not even a horse upon which to ride!"

"Many thanks to thee, Sire; I am touched by thy hospitality. But I am not yet a king, and may never be. And I choose to travel light; weighty baggage tends to catch the eye of thieves. And I would no more wish to die unenlightened than I would to rule."

"Then have on, Sir, and we will do what we can to aid thee!"

CHAPTER 17

On The Way Home

The procession rolled along sedately through the pine forest, as the sun crested and began its descent. But before the group could reach the point where Gravaine would take them off toward Marketsborough, they were blocked by a band of about fifty citizens who armed themselves with a variety of farm implements, and they would not let the group pass. Cradall was leading the men, and stopped the line with a shout and a raised hand. The column came up short. Darien, who was riding in the back alongside Sarah's carriage, moved slowly up the line until he could hear what was going on.

"And what, may I ask, is this all about?" asked Crandall roughly, to no one in particular. He was answered by a young man who stood roughly in the center of the road, and carried a bow. He was the only one who did so, but it was loaded and ready.

"We are the citizens of Pine. Thou hast robbed Tabithia of its heir, Pagan. We are here to get him back. Ye shall not pass until we do."

"Seems to me that thou art the ones who did the stealing, Youngster. That boy has been reunited with his mother. Thou canst have no objection to that, surely."

"We have a mightily large objection. Gerhard will rule Tabithia when the Foreigner is o'erthrown. His mother is a part of that faction that keeps her on the throne."

"*That faction*, as ye like to put it, sirrah, is the Royal Family and all those good citizens of Tabithia, save for that small band ye seem to have gathered here."

"Mock me not, Pagan. Thou hast no business in this. What is thy reason for putting thy nose in the business of this country?"

"We put our nose in, sirrah, because we were *asked* to, that's why. Now suppose ye get that rag-tag band of would-be soldiers out of the way and let us pass. For I'll tell ye straight, armed as ye may be, ye are no match for a pillar of Nomads. And we will give up neither mother nor child. So I suggest you lot get out of our way."

"Wouldst thou do battle, Pagan?" By this time, Darien had had enough. He goaded his horse and rode smartly up alongside Crandall.

"My name is..." But before he could utter his name, Crandall had lifted up his right leg, and smacked Darien smartly on the hip with the heel of his boot. Darien was thrown from his horse and landed with a resounding *thud*. Before he could regain his stance, Crandall spoke gruffly.

"No one is interested in thy name, whelp. Cooler minds than thine will handle this. Now get back in line!" Darien, who was taken by surprise more than anything else, held his bruised ego in check. It took him a moment, but he realized that Crandall was in charge here, and that the Nomad game was what he planned to keep in place. So he sullenly remounted and returned to a few paces behind the third knight in line. Here, he could keep an ear on what was going on. He prayed that Crandall could keep the situation in hand, and that they would need not take up swords against the citizens of his own country, again.

"Thou wilt give up Gerhard now, Pagan. We outnumber thee five to one, and we shall not let thee pass this point until we have our king back again."

"Thy king, Zander?" rang a voice from behind Darien. "Methinks thou wouldst not refer to him as such, wert thou not in so public a gathering." Having gained a horse from one of the knights, Lady Sarah rode up alongside Crandall. Having seen her do so, the other knights, still on horseback, filled in behind her and blocked the road, themselves. The two guards and a pair of knights remained behind the horses, with the carriage, protecting the boy. Seemingly oblivious to these mechanations,

Lady Sarah continued her address to the youth who stood, shocked, at the head of the gang of Pine.

"Why not refer to him as your brother, Zander. For that, of course, is who he is."

"Silence, woman!" bellowed Zander, a touch louder than perhaps he intended. Lady Sarah paid him no heed.

"Thou wouldst like to silence me, perhaps, would thou not, Zander. Heaven knows I have felt thy resentment, despite the fact that, since thy mother's death, I am the only mother thou hast had these seven years."

"Thou art my father's Royal Wife, and nought more, woman. Thou hast given Lord Farraman the means to rid us of the Mad King, and his witch of a wife, and for that we thank thee. But thy task is done. Meddle not in the rightful ascent of a Tabithian to the throne. Gerhard is Royal Blood, and a Tabithian born. And beyond the king himself, his is the closest there is to an ascendant line. No adopted son of a Foreigner will change that."

"Thou knowest the name of the prince, Zander, as well as I know thine. His name is Darien, and he is a prince born, and of Royal Blood, as well. If thou hast listened at all to what thy father told thee, ye would admit that."

"I admit nothing, woman. My father tried to tell the king he had delivered him an heir, and he was rebuked. The king is entranced by the spells of that witch, Syrenya. And when Lord Farraman tried to return the court to its rightful status, the Mad King took my father, his most trusted advisor, and had him killed!" The rebels growled their agreement, menacing. Lady Sarah took no notice.

"Your father did nothing of the sort, young man. And I trow that thou dost know it, though most of thy mates do not. What did Lord Farraman promise thee, Zander, that thou didst swallow thy pride and become a champion of the Royal brother ye hate? Did he promise thee a place at court, if thou didst assist him? A position of authority, perhaps? Even my husband knew of thy resentment, Zander. He knows, as well as I do, that thou dost resent that he lived at court, and thou, because of thy mother's lineage, do not."

"I said silence, wench!" shouted the youth, his face contorted and red with anger. "My father came to us and told us of developments at court, and we agreed to aid him in restoring order. Canst thou not admit that the king, with all his 'First Night' horrors, is mad?" Lady Sarah dismounted, and took three bold steps toward the screamer.

"Thou hast the wrong man, Zander. The king is quite sane. It is thy father that is mad."

"Thou liest! My father is a martyr, who fought to restore Tabithia to its former glory. He died in combat at the Battle of Tabit's Keep!" More assent from the mob, who waved their implements above their heads. Only a motion from Crandall kept the knights from drawing their swords. For his own part, Crandall kept his eyes glued upon Lady Sarah. She now held control, and if she could dissuade this youth who appeared to be her husband's son, then maybe all would be well. If she could not, she would be the first to fall in the battle that ensued.

""So thou speakest the language of a warrior, eh, my son? And thou hast christened the battle that thy father's madness brought on? What better way to keep the lie alive, and keep the rebels thou hast duped at a blood lust? Do they not know that thy father lives, and solely at the discretion of a king who is greatly saddened that he lost his best friend and advisor?" The crowd continued its noise, but there was a question now, as if this was new information to them.

"SHUT UP!" Zander was thoroughly agitated now, and his body trembled. "Call me not thy son! Ye are not my mother! Father promised me that all of thy kind would fall under the truth of our cause!" He took up his bow in his right hand, and pulled back the arrow slung there. "If thou wouldst not die in the road like a dog, release Gerhard to us! Else I will kill thee myself!"

"What thy father promised thee, Zander," said Sarah quietly, "was simply a poor plot in his own mind. Thy father is mad, Zander. I know it, and so dost thee. He sits at Shepherd's Crossing, ye know full well, a ward of the state, and he is very well looked after."

"NO! Thou liest! He died in battle! He is a hero." The crowd behind Zander was now growing restless. A few voices came forward and challenged Zander's words.

""What about this, Zander. Is thy father alive?"

"What did he promise thee, Zander?"

"What say ye of this, Zander? This is not what thou hast told us."

"Listen not to this woman!" Zander was on the verge of tears. His control was nearly gone. "She stands with rogues and pagans, and tells thee lies! Believe her not!"

"Good citizens of Tabithia, heed him," responded Sarah. "Listen not to me. Go thyselves to Shepherd's Crossing, to the asylum, and see Lord Farraman thyselves. Gentlemen, thou art the victims of a madman, just as thy fellows were. The only evil to Tabithia is in the mind of my husband. Go to him, and he will tell thee so. He hast told me often enough." Despite the fact that Zander now held her in his sights, Sarah seemed unconcerneed. The crown continued to grumble.

""You, Pagan!" shouted a large, bearded man from Pine, addressing himself to Crandall. "Know ye of any of this?"

"I know that a madman stole this woman's child, and that we were asked by the King of Tabithia to restore him to her. And I know that the man they call Lord Farraman was that man."

"Zander!" spoke the beard. "What have ye to say to this? Hast thou lied to us?"

"No," whispered Zander. "My father is dead. He died so our cause may live."

"Not so, Zander. Thy father, ill though he is, is alive. And I know that ye know this, for all relatives of my husband were contacted, and advised of his fate. It is the law. Thou knowest it is." And with this quiet chiding, she advanced on Zander and pushed his hands aside. He released his arrow, and it buried itself in the ground.

"But he promised me..." whined the youth, crying openly now. "He promised I would live at court..."

"Fool," muttered the beard. The crowd grew in its own mutterings, and as they saw him do, they began to turn and head back in the direction of Pine. What had begun as a mob now disbanded, and slowly drifted away from the knights, Sarah, and Zander.

"NO!" screamed Zander, "No! I forbid it! Stand for Tabithia! Do not let her win! Do not let her take the Crown Prince of Tabithia!"

"Go home, Zander!" someone shouted. But no one stopped. Zander turned with fury in his eyes and flung himself at Sarah.

"What hast thou done?!" His forward motion drove both of them to the ground, and Crandall and another knight quickly dismounted and pulled Zander from the Lady Sarah. Strung between the pair, he continued his screaming at his stepmother.

"What have ye done? Wilt thou continue to keep me from my rightful legacy? Lord Farraman is MY FATHER! I BELONG at court!"

"I'm sorry, Zander," whispered Lady Sarah. "I truly am. But we have had this conversation before. I could no more bring thee to court than thy father could. It is time ye accepted that." She placed her hand alongside Zander's face, but rather than accept the gesture, he attempted to bite her hand. She withdrew it, slowly, and with a look of sorrow upon her countenance, she turned and walked back to her carriage. Zander, spent, merely glared at her retreating figure.

"Alright, Youngster," said Crandall, shaking the youth, "wilt thou behave?"

"Burn in Hell," spoke the youth.

"No doubt," retorted the knight. "But not today. And just to be sure, I'm going to borrow this." He picked up Zander's bow and slung it over his shoulder. "I'll not have any stray arrows come flying in our direction, when we leave ye here."

"NO!" Zander screamed. "Ye can't leave me here! Arrest me! Take me back to court to stand trial! I'll tell the entire court of how they have been duped by this Mad King and his witchy wife! I'll tell them all!"

"I'm just a Nomad, boy. I have no power to arrest ye, and no mind to do so, either. Ye be a fool, boy; keep going the way ye be headed, and ye'll be as mad as thy father one day."

"No! Please, leave me not here! I cannot return to Pine! Please…" The pillar of Nomads again took up their interrupted way, and left this troubled lad, now alone by the roadside, in their wake. It would be another two days before all of them would find their weary bones back at Tabit's Keep, and be able to sleep at peace in their own beds. Gerhard had been returned to Lady Sarah, and now, finally, Darien would be able to rest, and put this whole sordid ordeal behind him. It had been a very long time since he had been able to look forward to a peaceful night's sleep, without the whole troubling adventure hanging over him. They had finished this final leg of the journey in only a fortnight, and managed to do so, Saints be praised, without any loss of life. Darien looked forward to home, and family, and a fire in the hearth. They all had earned it.

King Arthur sat silently for a moment, scowling down at his hands in his lap. When he raised his eyes to Darien, he had something of a glint in his eye.

"Well, Darien, ye told us ye had an amazing tale to tell, and we must say there has been quite a lot to digest, what with demons, and nudes, and 'sixth senses' and the like. But this last tale ye have told us is the strangest of all. Art thou telling us that one small woman held an entire mob at bay while a whole line of knights stood by and watched?"

"Sire, it is indeed quite a bit to swallow. All I can tell ye is that, as I promised thee, I speak the truth, and even more so in that this is truth I witnessed first-hand. I would never have believed, knowing the woman as I did, that the Lady Sarah would have been capable of such bravery. I wonder, truly, if I would have been. All I can tell thee is that, in everything I have learned in this lifetime, one of the surest is, there is no one more stalwart than a mother in defense of her child."

"Too true, Darien, too true. But thou knowest that Crandall saved thy life, do ye not?"

"Aye, Sire, well do I know it. Had I announced my presence, I am convinced that arrow would have been for me, and no time at all to contemplate it. Had I had my senses about me, I would have held my peace. Methinks I still have a bruise where Crandall's boot struck me, but I wear it as a badge of luck, and with thanks."

"As well thou should. So, this concludes the Adventure of the Mad Advisor. Whence goes thy tale from here?"

"It is already in the prime of the afternoon, Sire. While I could regale thee with many a tale more, I think it is time we moved to the saving of the king. It is a tale that is remarkable and frightening in its own right..."

PART IV

The Freeing of the King,
and The Quest of Darien

CHAPTER 18

The Danger to the King

In the years that followed the insurgence of the Renegades of Pine, life at Tabit's Keep would have appeared, at least to the untrained eye, to be as carefree as a ruling family's castle could be. It had been a total of seven years since the king's chief advisor had retired to Shepherd's Crossing; Darien and his family had all seemed to take the years in stride. His children had grown; Randall was now eleven and about to embark on the sometimes treacherous road into puberty. Lylanya was a darling child of nine, the apple of her father's doting eye, with light hair that matched her father's, rather than the darker strands of long hair worn by her mother. And Princess Stephanie had blossomed, to Darien's everlasting wonder, from a lovely young girl into a beautiful woman, whose grace and poise were unrivaled by any at court, save Queen Syrenya herself. King Ballizar was prone to wondering, at those times when he and Darien found themselves alone, who the luckier man was, between the two of them.

While the king had aged perhaps more than he should have in those eleven years, he was still firm of step and mind, handing down his even more tempered wisdom from the throne that still sat to the left of his raven-haired Queen. And Syrenya herself, who had become known far and wide as the land's fairest lady, seemed not to have aged a day. Indeed, the only sign that over two decades had passed since her arrival was a thin graceful lock of white that began at her forehead and swept back through her otherwise still-dark hair. In Darien's eyes, and indeed most everyone else's, that one simple punctuation seemed, if anything, to make the queen even more stunningly beautiful than before.

But signs of aging within the court there were indeed, and one need not look far to find them. Father Benedic, who had looked quite the chubby friar in the days before Darien's nineteenth birthday, had grown not only thin, but gray as well, and those within the priesthood at the castle feared for his health. While he seemed as energetic as ever, he did not eat as well as he had once done, and he was often softly chided by his brethren for working late into the night, and missing what they felt was much-needed rest. But Father Benedic had a charge that only a few at court knew, and it seemed that that one item was, almost literally, draining him of his strength. Those within the royal family knew all too well, and it was a secret they kept as closely as did the Father himself.

While Darien well knew the toll that this secret had on the Father, what cut him more was the fact that this secret also preyed on the minds of his dear aunts, as well. During the years since Syrenya's arrival, Alissa and Ariadne had passed from their mid-twenties to their mid-forties, and while their youth may have fallen behind them, they were nevertheless still sharp of mind and wit, and Darien still depended on them for loving advice and counsel. It touched and saddened him that their youthful beauty was waning; but this was a thought he kept well to himself. Darien had learned long ago that to commiserate with a woman over her aging was not a safe thing to do, especially within arm's reach. But of all the royal family—and indeed Darien could not think of them as anything else—it seemed that the king's condition weighed most heavily upon these two. The pinched look in their faces, as well as the often sad and worried looks behind their usually-twinkling eyes, belied the jovial personas they attempted to show the world outside their own room—and most of the rest of the family. Though they were now completely accepted, at least within the keep's walls, as members of both the court and the royal family, the joy they once held between them had waned. Darien, who had tried several times to draw one or the other out concerning the situation, succeeded usually with drawing only sighs from his dear aunts. And their discussions, when alone within the family, dwelt almost exclusively with the toll that the king's "affliction" was taking. To Darien, and to Syrenya as well, it seemed that both Ariadne and Alissa were taking this terrible problem all too much to heart. It was the one thing Darien wished he could do something about; he was cut to the quick by the downtrodden looks of his troubled advisors.

According to the priests, the year was 1141 A.D. Darien marked this year as the beginning of the end, because it was in the autumn of that year that a most unexpected visitor—to Darien, at least—appeared at the keep, a man so unforeseen that even Syrenya was surprised, and delighted. Once she realized that the man was the answer to her prayers, she wasted no time in seeing that he was apprised of the situation regarding King Ballizar and his terrible secret.

But for now the spring of 1141 still lay upon the land, and outside the keep the rigors of spring planting and the joys of the season were at large. Darien took it upon himself to let his mother know just how upsetting to him was the weight that sagged the shoulders of his aunts. He found that, on this subject, his mother was of the same mind as he.

"I am unable to understand why they dwell so upon it, Mother. I know that both they and the Father are intent upon releasing Father from this devil, but there is little that Alissa and Ariadne can do to help him, save pray, and they seem unable to do even that. Just this week, when another of my questions drew only sighs, I asked Ariadne to kneel and pray for the king's salvation with me. She burst into tears, and fled the room. I cannot fathom it!" Were the entire situation not so grave, Darien would have put this down to yet another aspect of the female psyche he would never understand. But there was too much at stake here to believe that this was merely a whim on the parts of his suffering aunts.

"Darien, sweet, I have tried myself to draw them out, both singly and together," replied the queen. "But though they will come to my arms and weep most bitterly, they will speak not a word of it. Whatever secret they carry, they are unwilling to part with it. It preys upon my mind, almost as much as does the king. And, for that matter, Father Benedic. Thou hast seen the shadow he has become of the man he once was. It is as though this plight were burning him up from the inside. He wasteth away."

"I have seen it, Mother. But though the Father causes me concern, I have spoken with him; he is alert, and intent, and inquisitive, and bent upon his task. If he is causing himself physical harm, it is in a good cause, and he tells me his loss of weight is a boon to him. He says he never felt so light. But Alissa and Ariadne are miserable, Mother. I wish it to be not so." His mother had been sitting with Darien in her rooms, at the table where often the family dined. He, however, could not sit. He paced, and while it seemed to affect his mother, he could not stop himself. For her part, Syrenya sat and stared into the fire, a study on her face of he knew not what. Suddenly she shook herself, bringing herself back from someplace far away, and looked up at him suddenly.

"What was that ye said?"

"I said they are miserable. What are we to do about it?"

"Nay, my son, earlier. Ye spoke of thy conversation with Ariadne. What did ye say?"

"I asked her to pray for the king with me, and she not only refused, she fled the room."

"That's what I thought ye said. Come, my young prince; we are about to beard the lionesses in their den." With that, Syrenya rose and started down the corridor, covering in no time the distance that separated her quarters from those of her one-time lovers. Darien, taken aback by the sudden change in his mother's demeanor, was hard-pressed to keep up. Syrenya rapped twice, sharply, and entered the room immediately, for the second time giving Darien a start. Never before had the queen entered the women's room without first being bade to do so. Once inside, however, it was Syrenya's turn to be brought up short. What confronted her was the visage of Ariadne and Alissa packing their belongings, in preparation, obviously, for departure from the keep.

"Children, what in Heaven's name has gotten into thee?" was all that she could manage. It elicited a wan smile from Ariadne, who rejoindered as best she could.

"Syrenya, thou hast not called us children since the day ye arrived here." But she said no more; she merely returned to her packing. Syrenya, however, reacted with alacrity.

"Stop this, both of thee!" she barked, and reached out and took a bagful of clothes from Alissa. Alissa simply complied, and turned a calm but desolate eye on her queen.

"Both of thee have been silent far too long," continued Darien's mother, taking Alissa by her shoulders and sitting her firmly on the bed. Ariadne sat in a chair and looked at her mate, then turned just as unhappy a face to the woman who, years ago, had made the two one. Syrenya did not let the looks stop her; she sped forward.

"What, exactly, is it that the two of ye plan to do?"

"We are leaving the keep, Syrenya. We do not belong here."

"Posh and nonsense!" cried the queen. "Ye belong nowhere else but here."

"There is no other way, Syrenya. We love each other. We aways have. Ye above anyone should know that it is true. We tried to talk it through, to see if by chance we could live here together without intimacy. But we cannot." Alissa's statement was causing her yet more tears. With her final word, they broke forth. "So we have to leave!" This flat statement brought her to her feet, as if she were intent upon completing her task. Syrenya was incensed.

"I have had just about enough of the pair of thee! Now sit down here, Alissa, and tell us both why ye have the insane notion that ye must leave thy home! Nay, Alissa, I have been more than patient. In the twenty years that I have been at this place, the two of thee have not even ventured beyond the gates. And now ye think it is 'necessary' to leave here entirely? Nay. Nay, I tell thee. Now; I am thy Queen. I command thee both, to tell me the truth. What secret hast thou been keeping that has caused thee so much pain and grief?"

"We cannot part, Syrenya! Dost thou not see?" Ariadne's face contorted in anger. "I will not leave Alissa, even if I burn in Hell! But we can leave this keep, this land, and let the king live in peace!"

Darien was shocked, but Syrenya was stunned into silence. She stared at Ariadne open-mouthed, before regaining her composure enough to stutter out a response.

"Thou--. Art thou of the belief that *ye two* are the cause of the king's attacks?!"

"What other reason can there be, Syrenya? It has gone on far too long, and it has made not a whit of difference what ye, or the priests, or anybody or anything else that hast been done for him. As long as we live under his roof, as long as we are outcasts from his faith—then he lies in a devil's grasp, and even thou canst not help him!" Alissa was adamant, standing and addressing her queen with strength, but tears poured down her face. Syrenya could not believe her ears, and did not know whether to weep in relief, or knock the heads of these two together in her exasperation. She did neither; she merely sat on the bed across from Ariadne and reached for Alissa's hand.

"Oh, my sweets, has this been the load that thou hast carried within thee for so long? It has been twenty-two *years* since I came to this place, and then as now, there has not been another pair of people in all of Tabithia as pure of heart, as innocent of guilt, as the pair of thee! Have nearly a quarter century of my words to thee meant nought? Whatever the reason for the king's possession, that devil and Hell alone know it. Why on earth wouldst thou take on such a burden? With the exception of the family that has supported King Ballizar, thou are the most stalwart and devoted members of his court!"

"And that is exactly why this possession has gone on for as long as it has, dearest Syrenya. For thou hast been able to fight this demon. But we are the reason he is here! What other reason can there be? We are sinners in the sight of God, for all thy preaching; thou dost know, even after thy conference with Father Benedic, that none of the priests, and particularly not the father, hast ever approached us for inclusion in their blessed 'flock.' Despite our honor at court, we are still outcasts in our own home."

"This is not something we have just hit upon, Syrenya," added Ariadne. "The signs of the decline of the king have grown stronger every year. He hath aged beyond his years; more and more, dear Darien here hath found it necessary to mount the throne in place of his father. And it hath long been our belief that our very presence upon the dais, while he and Stephanie sort out the petitions of the subjects, heightens the weight upon the king's shoulders. There is a batallion of priests in this place. With thy holy help— and I can think of nought else to describe it—they should have been able to rout this monster long ago. But he is *still here*, and the only thing that has remained the same throughout his hold on the king has been our witness of the event. I have come to believe—I am sure—that if Alissa and I leave this place, then the recovery of the king is, if not assured, then at least given a far better chance than if we stay."

"My darling Ariadne, methinks the darkness behind the eyes of thy dear mate hast invaded thee, as well. Nay, Alissa, speak not; I have known of it from the beginning. It is a dark spot behind thine eyes, and it has been there from the first day I saw thee. I had suspected then, and I know now, that—despite everything I know and that has been proven since I arrived—thou art afraid that the priests may be right, and that thou art nought but sinners. It hath colored every single thing thou hast done all thy lonely life, and now I fear that a piece of it hath embedded itself in the mind of thy love, as well.

"My darlings, listen to me. Remember ye not the conversation we had the very first night I came here? Twas thee, Alissa, that admitted to me in front of Ariadne that thou didst believe that the king did love thee. Well, I can tell thee truly that he doth. And he is not alone. I, too, and Darien and Stephanie, and thy niece and nephew love thee dearly! And while I cannot point to any one item to support it, I would wager that the twelve, even though more aged now as they are, love thee as well. Hast ever seen any one of them take on the colors of another lady? I have not. Never once to this day. And I suspect that they would have taken on *thine*, were they not afraid of offending thee. Thou art beloved, my sweets, truly!! I cannot accept, and will not allow, that thou wouldst leave the comfort of the only home thou hast ever known!" The ladies stood together now, listening; but their heads were bent, their eyes downcast, and Syrenya could feel the wall that was now between her and them—something she had never before felt, and it was palpable now.

"All that thou hast said is true, Syrenya," whispered Alissa. "But it changes not the circumstance. Love him as we do, we can do nought else. It is a pain that is deep within me; and Ariadne, too. But if the king is to be free, we must go from this place."

"Darien, for the love of God, say something to thy aunts! They obviously are not going to listen to me!" Darien felt anger from the queen, but he knew it was at the pain felt by his dear old friends, and not at him. A thought suddenly struck him, and he moved up and forward as he caught the eyes of his beloved advisors. It was an idea that had never fully formed in his head before now, but now that it was there, he knew that he had known its veracity, all along. He reached for the right hand of Alissa, and Ariadne's left, and he put the one physically into the other. Then he reached for their other hands, and held the two in a triad. Looking deeply into their eyes for a moment, he held his peace until he was sure they were listenng to him. Then he spoke in a very soft, loving tone that Syrenya had never heard from him before. No one had, save his beloved Stephanie, for it was a tone he had reserved for her alone until now.

"My two darling aunts—my beloved sisters—what is it that hast brought thee to this crossroads? Never in all the time that I have known thee hath there ever been a harsh word from thy lips for anyone; even those foolish people who have fought against thee have come to see the error of their ways. Thou art not the burden of thy king. Thou art his joy, and always have been. Imagine the thoughts he must have had when, knowing the ever-slimming possibility of ever having daughters of his own, he was met with the two of thee staring back at him like babes from a cradle. Can there be any other reason why he would clasp thee to his own fortune with such alacrity? And thou dost know, if ye stop and think, and mark the time, that the first of the king's attacks preceded thy arrival by fully a year. To my mind, if there can be any reason at all why any devil must possess a man, it must be, here, that Ballizar was taken because he *was* king, and for no other reason. And the fact that he remains the king, despite all, is not only because of his devoted wife; it also is because of thee. Thou dost sustain him, loves; to leave him now would cause him more harm than good.

"As to thy so-called sin, I can repeat my mother's words: posh and nonsense. I am a *man*, and I cannot see it. Thou dost live for each other, wholly and faithfully; that is a command that doth come directly from the wedding vows. Never hath thou strayed from each other; thy love is as strong today as it ever was, if not greater. Knowest thou why the marriage between Stephanie and me is as strong as it is? Canst thou guess? It is because I vowed long ago, when I took Stephanie's hand, that if I could keep our love as strong as thine, then nothing would come between us. And all the while I was learning to love her, I had thy guidance. Not just in thy teaching, for which I am blessed, but also in thine example. Thou art holy, my sisters, dost thou hear me say it? Speak not of priests, or churches, or God or devils. God knows. He knows as well as I do that thou art as blessed a couple as any in Tabithia.

"And as to God, what of that? Hast ever thou heard that God doth turn to the Devil to do His dirty work? God is working on the king's problem, rest assured. But thou hast no part in why or how the king doth suffer, I tell thee truly." Now Darien let some warmth and humor seep into his voice. "And to find thee both of a mind that thou dost, makes me worry for thy sanity! Why, how couldst thou take thy belongings and leave Tabit's Keep? It cannot be, and for one simple reason. I would have to go with thee, and that would never do!"

Both of the women were staring at him with longing; it was obvious to Syrenya that these were, indeed, the words they needed to hear—but to have them come from her would have proved less than effective. To have it come from Darien—their charge, their "nephew," and, aye, their brother—was the very aspect of this speech that would drive it home to them. But in the second that it took for Syrenya to think this simple thought, Ariadne broke the sudden silence with a bark of laughter, and threw her arms around Darien's neck.

'O, thou reckless Prince, who taught thee to have such a silver tongue? And why did we not think to confide in thee from the start? Oh, I never thought I could say this, but thou art a blessed, blessed man!" Alissa, for her part, said nothing, but was very eager to share in the embrace started by her love. Neither was she sure whether to laugh or cry, so she did both. Syrenya let them remain for a moment; then she cleared her throat and spoke with some royal authority.

"Ariadne, Alissa. Come here at once. I must hold conference with my Ladies-in-Waiting." Darien made to leave the room, but was caught by his mother's words. "Nay, Darien, stay. I will need thee as witness. I am about to give these two a royal command, and it will be one they will not wish to obey. But if thou art witness to it, there can be no shilly-shallying. So please remain where thou art. My thanks." The women now stood in front of the Queen, who still sat upon the bed. They were of a confused state, having never heard such words from their queen before; never had it been that they would not do what Syrenya asked. And the words that she gave them threw all three, Darien included, into turmoil. Having just now stopped the two from leaving the castle, it seemed that she now wished them to depart!

"I have been thinking of thee two for some time now, wondering what it was that kept thee so downtrodden. I am both relieved and perturbed that it was so small a thing. But, to believe that thou canst be the cause of someone else's possession is a sign that both of thee still feel that thou art outcasts from this world. I wish to prove to thee that is not so. Thus, here is the command I wish thee to take up. Upon the provision that thou *shalt return*, I am ordering the pair of thee to go. Thou shalt have a carriage, an escort—take four of the knights; I daresay they will clamor for the right— and ye shall be gone wherever thou shalt wish to go for as long as thou wilt. Be it a fortnight, a month, a year; it is of thine own choosing. Thou hast remained inside the walls of this castle for a full quarter century. It is time that ye felt the sun upon thy faces, wind in thy hair, and the freedom to go about as thou wouldst wish. Ye are royals; there will be absolutely no stopping thee from whatever it is thou shouldst wish to do. And there is absolutely no reason why anyone, who does not already, should know of thine intimate relationship. Two royal ladies abroad in the land will raise no eyebrows; it happens almost daily. Thou hast a large purse—I shall see to it—and a long vacation ahead of thee. That is what I command of thee. Thou art already packed; wouldst thou shy from thy journey, now?"

"Syrenya, we were going to protect the king. Having been within the walls of this keep, we have felt safe, at least from those people from whom we were taken in the first place. We believed it necessary, but it scared us, nonetheless. To go for what is really no reason at all, is all the more terrifying. We have been like canaries in a cage, well cared for. The wide world frightens us both."

"What was thy plan, Ariadne, as to what thee would do when ye left? Surely ye would have taken horses, a carriage, some conveyance. And where wouldst thou have gone?"

"We were going to take a pair of horses and the dray wagon that Arturion uses to haul hay. He is a dear man, and he promised us that it would easily get us from here into Sweden, and beyond. We were going to blend into the scenery, disappear. Beyond that, we had not really thought."

"It surprises me not," snorted Syrenya. "Having never traveled before, thou knewest nothing of the necessities of moving about the countryside. First, thou must have ready cash. How didst thou plan for that?"

"Uh, actually, we hadn't…"

"Exactly. And what of safety? Any two ladies traveling might just as easily meet rogues as well as gentlemen. What of that?"

"We are both equipped with daggers, Syrenya." This was calmly stated by Alissa.

"Eh? Are ye, now? And knowest thou how to use them?"

"Aye, my queen. We were taught well by Branton of the knights. Crandall suggested that he teach us, after we told him that, being ladies in waiting to the Queen of Tabithia, we felt ill-prepared to defend her should the need arise. Branton pronounced us model pupils."

"And this was…?"

"Quite a few years ago, Syrenya. We were earnest in our concern, at the time. It simply serves us now that we are so taught. It made our decision easier."

"I can see the two of thee now, knives between thy teeth, becoming highway robbers to gain thy support. I should have had to send the knights after thee in any case, what? Now answer me. Wilt thou go? I believe it will do the pair of thee a world of good."

"Darien? What thinkest thou?"

"Alissa, far be it from me to insinuate myself between anyone and a royal command. But for what it is worth, I must agree with Mother. I think it would do thee both good to see what is beyond the walls of this keep. If thou canst remember, Tabithia is beautiful in May. And I might suggest that a trip into the mountains, and a visit to Crevice, might do thee a tonic. The people there are most self-sufficient, and a room in the mountains is a lovely retreat. Ye might ask the four who accompany thee about it. They will tell thee amusing stories."

"It is settled, then," spoke Syrenya authoratatively. "We shall speak with Arturion, get thy dray changed into a carriage, and ye shall pick the four who will escort thee. I want thee both at dinner tonight; I shall have thee a proper goodbye before thy travels. And ye are free to begin thy vacation at whatever time tomorrow thou shalt choose." Syrenya smiled for the first time since she entered the room. "My sweets, know thou art so dear to me! I could not bear it if thee were gone from this place. I shall count the days until thy return. But ye must stay at thy liesure, for as long as thy wishes and thy purses allow. Then thou shalt be welcomed home with open arms, and we shall have no more talk of thee causing any danger to the king. Knowest my mind on this?"

"Aye, Your Grace!" chorused the two, and all four of them made merry over the joke.

CHAPTER 19

The Arrival of The Spectator

At dinner that evening the banquet hall was full to bursting with well-wishers for the queen's Ladies in Waiting. All the royal family—save the children, whose bedtimes made their appearance problematic—appeared on the hearth to join Alissa and Ariadne, toast their upcoming 'vacation,' and join in the celebration that ensued. If there was still any doubt as to the affections of this court for the two, this gathering of nearly all the lords and ladies banished those doubts from Alissa and Ariadne. The smiles that were firmly painted on both the ladies' faces were smiles Darien believed were a long time coming, and thoroughly well-deserved. The king himself raised a glass in salute, and his toast was rousingly supported by these revelers. Alissa was at one point so overcome that tears ran down her cheeks, though her smile never dimmed. Only Ariadne and Darien noticed; Ariadne took her mate's hand under the table, and after a moment the tears had ebbed. Dinner had long since been cleared away, but the kitchen was kept busy by the banquet, that would stretch long into the early morning hours. If the two had made plans for an early getaway, the hour they retired was so close to the sunrise that the actual departure did not take place until mid-afternoon.

Both the queen's ladies were struck dumb when they entered the courtyard. While they had taken Syrenya at her word when she told them a carriage would replace their dray, they were still unprepared for the Royal Coach to stand before them, laden with their luggage and sporting the usual two footmen that always accompanied it. Their queen had once again succeeded in rendering them speechless; they boggled at the queen, who shrugged, said she would not be needing it anytime soon, and reminded them that there was no time limit on their meanderings. They would know when it was time to come home, she told them, and she would impatiently wait until she received word of their return before making any further plans on their behalf. Darien and the king each took their leave; the king took extra care to let them know how much they would be missed in the interim. As Crandall and three of his fellow knights mounted up and formed a column ahead of those two snow-white steeds, the gatekeepers opened the high wooden doors and the procession began its stately departure. Heeding Darien's suggestion, the two had made plans to wend their way toward Crevice; the higher elevation would be a welcome respite from the coming summer heat. Stephanie had brought the children out with her, and they chased after the coach, waving and shouting happily, until the coach cleared the castle walls. All told, the ladies and their knights would be gone only four months; but, unbeknownst to anyone at the time, those would be a very trying sixteen weeks, indeed. During that seemingly brief period of time, the king would be struck down a total of 18 times.

In conference with Father Benedic, the queen could see that she needed not press him on his continuing search for an exorcist. Using a spiral pattern and a large contingent of messengers, Benedic had made good his promise of looking under every stone for one. Sadly, however, it seemed that the Father had been right during that first late-night conference with the queen so long ago; finding a church-sanctioned, honest-to-God exorcist was proving futile, indeed. But the Father had still not given up; he reported to the queen that he still had one more avenue open to him, and that he had already sent an urgent letter to the Pope by messenger. While the Father could not say what exactly would be the Pope's response, he did state that his entreaties had been adamant, detailing their search and stressing that the king was in peril if something was not done. He hoped with all his heart that it would be enough for the Pope to send him the man they sought. The messenger was slated to reach the Vatican in three weeks; the return, through some very diligent forethought by the Father, would be much faster. The emissary carried with him a homing pigeon, and word of the Pope's decision would be on the wing as soon as a scribe could put pen to parchment.

Syrenya and her priests—at one point she smiled to herself that she now referred to them as *her* priests—had their hands full during the weeks that her ladies were away. Syrenya was heartily glad that their mistaken assumptions regarding the king had been dispelled, and they themselves had been removed from the vicinity, during that time. If their unshattered fears had kept them here, these long and tortured weeks would have quite possibly done them in. As it was, it was all the priests and the family could do to keep their unsuspecting court in the dark; the physicians, priests, and the queen herself seemed quite unable to leave the king's bedside. Lady Sarah kept the children with her, where they played innocently with Gerhard, during the time that Darien and Stephanie held court. During those hours, Darien sorely missed his two stalwart counselors, and prayed that the prospect of their being gone as long as a year was mistaken.

Despite the Father's careful planning, it was beyond six weeks before he was notified that his winged messenger had actually arrived. The note, necessarily brief, stated only that the priest's emissary had been successful, and that a detailed account was to follow. But the international mails in the year 1141 were utterly unreliable, and the missive his emissary promised could be several more weeks, nay months, in coming. Both the Father and his queen hoped against hope that the emissary, himself, could be back by that time.

All told, their messenger did not return to the keep for a wrenching nine weeks. Though the long and detailed missive he sent ahead of him did arrive before he did, it was not by much. He had had to wait for an audience with the Pope's Cardinal despite the urgency of the Father's written plea, and it was deemed necessary that the Pope confer with his advisers before a decision on how to proceed could be reached. Once the messenger had received the Pope's decision, he did two things in rapid succession: first, he completed and sent the missive that would barely precede him, and second, he made haste to get himself back on the road to Tabithia. He assured the Father that he had not spared the horses; it had been necessary, in fact, to replace one of them in order to bring him home as quickly as possible.

The messenger was prepared to dump everything in the Father's lap as soon as he arrived; but the priest held him off, if only long enough to send for Syrenya and have her attend their conference. According to the emissary, the Pope received him personally, but only after conferring with his counselors. The decision the Pope had reached was not done in haste; in fact, it would take some time for the Pope to send a gift he had for the King and Queen by a special messenger. The reason for the delay was two-fold, both because it would take time to prepare this gift, as well as some time for this particular messenger to be found, apprised, and sent on his way. When pressed, the emissary could only tell his Queen that the Pope felt strongly that this gift would be exactly what she, and her king, required. But as to what, exactly, that gift was to be, the Pope remained mum. The queen had no time to chafe over the matter, however, because both she and the Father were again summoned to the king's chambers, and they left the poor messenger where he sat.

It was already September, and the leaves had begun to turn, when a weary but happy procession pulled through the gates to bring Alissa and Ariadne home. But it was immediately clear to them both that all was not well at the keep, and they quickly reported to Syrenya in her chambers. The eighteenth attack had occurred only the night before, and both the queen and her king were spent. Syrenya apologized for what was less than a happy homecoming, but the two would hear none of it and begged to hear of the trials during their absence. They immediately wondered if the news had reached the court, and Syrenya was able to reassure them that Darien and Stephanie had proved immeasurably fine at their task of holding the court at bay. Despite a harrowing and bone-wearying time of it, everyone who had to know had been sworn to secrecy, and the court at large still was not aware of the actual 'malady' the king suffered. Ariadne used a phrase Alissa had not heard her use before: "Thank God for small favors." Ariadne told her she had been told it by the Host at their stay in Crevice; Syrenya labeled it 'extremely apt.'

The Ladies' reunion with the prince and princess was happier, though muted, nonetheless. They both regaled Darien and Stephanie with the wonders they had discovered during their time away; Darien was quick to reply that, though he firmly believed they needed and deserved their time 'abroad,' he was heartily glad that they were back. The ladies stayed long into the evening, as they had missed Randall and Lylanya sorely.

Nonetheless, neither child would allow them to leave until they had promised that, yes, they were indeed returned, and would see them on the morrow.

By the time court was convened the next day, Syrenya had been able to fill both her ladies in on the Father's news. Happily, the king was somewhat rejuvenated, though Ariadne and Alissa mourned over how the past four months had aged him. He and Syrenya again sat on their thrones before the court, and once again the Prince and Princess, and now the queen's ladies, held their respective couches. For all the court could tell, all was right with the world. It would be another three weeks before news of the pending arrival of the Pope's special emissary, and his long-awaited gift, reached the keep.

Twas a brisk autumn day in only the month of October, but in the Scandinavian north, winter's winds already braced the trees. Today was a day that Darien would mark in his own history as a turning point. Early in the morning, news reached the keep that a special emissary from the Vatican was on the road to Tabit's Keep. The long-awaited arrival of the Pope's gift was at hand, and the family and the priests, all of whom now knew of the Father's correspondence and its deeper meaning, eagerly made ready to welcome their guest. Queen Syrenya, especially, was eager to meet with the soon-arriving agent, for in the news arriving that morning the identity of the man was revealed. It had taken many a day for the Pope to reach him, but now, twas The Spectator who bore his gift to Tabithia. This pending arrival had all the court agog, for tales of the Spectator and his many exploits had reached their ears long ago. This was a day to celebrate, for such luminaries seldom graced the court of such out of the way places as Tabithia.

Syrenya, however, had a particular reason for having a conference with their notorious guest: it was imperative that she inform him of the circumstances requiring his arrival, for if he was not the man they sought, precious time may have been wasted. She cloaked herself and went to meet her illustrious new arrival; private conversation was imperative before he was presented at court that afternoon.

The man known as the Spectator was as much eager to meet his hostess as she was to meet him; tales ranged far and wide, in every corner of Europe, about the infamous Naked Queen. Not only was her beauty sung and touted; her poise, grace, and intelligence also was legend. When she met him at his coach, he felt a rush of conflicting emotions. The cloak caused a stab of disappointment; it was not every day that a man was going to be able to behold, in all her glory, the most celebrated beauty in the land. But the fact that she, and she alone, was on hand to welcome him was an honor he could scarce ignore. So the smile he wore as he stepped down was genuine.

"Your Grace, Queen Syrenya of Tabithia, I come at the behest of His Holiness the Pope; it does me no small honor to be met by such a beauteous and regal lady."

"Sir, ye do me honor with thy presence. But it is essential, before we present thee to an eager and anticipating court this afternoon, that ye be apprised of the true reason we have asked the Pope for this audience. We are much in need of thy services, if ye be the man we seek. Pray join the king and me for some light refreshment; after our conference, we shall let ye rest after thy long trip."

"Thou art most kind." The Spectator's Norwegian, a form of which was the spoken tongue in Tabithia, was nearly flawless. Leaving his coach and baggage to the servants, he offered the Queen his arm, and they made their way to the King's Chambers. The king was already prepared with a tray; Father Benedic was also in attendance. Introductions were brief; the queen was anxious to get to the point.

"What is thy given name, Sir?"

"Michael, Your Grace."

"Michael, my name is Syrenya. We must know immediately. Art thou versed in the art of exorcism?"

"Nay, milady, but let me put thy fears to rest. The Pope has already briefed me on the condition of King Ballizar; and the gift that the Pope has given me for thee is, I believe, what ye seek. I have it here..." He reached into the satchel slung over his shoulder and withdrew a large and ornate tome. "This is the Holy Communion that is the means of routing evil such as thou art experiencing. It is the specific incantation of Exorcism. The volume is in Latin; I trust the good Father is versed..."

"Indeed, sir," interjected the cleric.

"There was no one at the Vatican who could conduct an Exorcism; sadly, the one priest who was in residence as an exorcist lay on his own sickbed upon the arrival of thy messenger. It is said he is himself not long for this world. I spent a lengthy interval with the Pope himself over this volume. It contains all the relevant scriptures, all the chants, and all the processes necessary to mount the attack on thy foe. I am told that the Father himself should lead the ritual; I am to observe, and take back to the Vatican the results of the rite. I have in my luggage three vials of Holy Water that is to be used in the rite; all the priests must take part if this monster is to be vanquished. The Pope wished me to assure ye all that a week's special study is all that is required. Father, I wish to lend my own support to thy cause. Take up this volume, and meet with thy fellow clergy; time, I need not tell thee, is of the essence." The priest took up the volume with a reverence; he silently bowed his way out, and was gone.

"Sire, let me say ye look astonishingly fit. I pray that thy strength is sound, for twill take every ounce of thy stamina to survive such an ordeal."

"Our strength sits at thy elbow, Michael. It is she, and she alone, who is the reason I am still alive; were it not for her, there would be no reason for thy trip."

"I am hoping that the beast bides his time, Sire. For if he strikes before the priests are ready to confront him, I fear the worst."

"Michael, I believe that the Pope held back nothing in preparing thee for thy charge. It sounds as if ye are familiar with our—distinctly singular—circumstances."

"I am, indeed, Your Grace. The Pope had me read thy Father's document before we began. It left no chance for misinterpretation."

"That is the Father's careful way. Well, Michael; I am sure that thy rooms are ready for thee. If it is thy charge to witness the event, then thy stay might well be a long one. Pray make thyself at home here. Thy presence is most welcome. Oh, and Michael; if I may ask, wilt thou bring thy hammer when we introduce thee at court this afternoon?"

"I will indeed, Your Grace. Will I see either of thee before that time?"

"I think not, Michael; but I want my son and a few chosen others to meet with thee; I will have him meet with thee in thy room at say, noontime?" Syrenya rang a small bell upon the tray, and a servant appeared almost instantly.

"I look forward to it, Your Grace. Sire." He rose, bowed, and allowed this servant to lead him away.

"My Queen, thou art unhappy." It was a statement, not a question.

"Not unhappy, my liege, merely worried. I would have felt quite a bit better had the Spectator been an exorcist himself; I can only pray, now, that Michael is correct; that, and that Father Benedic is up to this monumental task." The queen then turned the topic to more pleasant matters; she regaled her king with several choice deeds she knew to be among the Spectator's exploits before his arrival at the keep.

The chapel bell had not finished its tolling of the noon hour when a tapping alerted The Spectator to the prince's arrival. In the interim, Syrenya had sent Michael a note, informing him of the prince's desire that Michael call him by his given name, rather than stand on ceremony. Thus Michael greeted Darien as requested, and a firm handshake cemented the introductions.

"I wished to speak with thee about court this afternoon, Michael," Darien intimated, adding, "and the queen wished me also to explain their absence between now and the three o'clock hour. As well ye know, it is she and she alone who can stay this fiend if he strikes, and she has been almost inseparable from the king for many months now. Beginning this summer and for eight weeks after, the king was struck down a total of eighteen times, and the queen fears another attack, which as ye know may come at any time."

"Darien, relay my thanks to the queen, and inform her that I will expect to see her at court this afternoon, as she told me when we met. But I understand that this will be true only if there is no attack in the meantime."

"If there is, only the Princess Stephanie and I will be at court; both Ballizar and my mother will stay out of sight until the king has recovered. *If* he recovers."

"I pray that the demon will not strike until thy Father Benedic is abreast of the very salient volume I have been sent here to deliver. If thy priests are up to the task, we may, with God's grace, rout the beast permanently. It is the hope of the Pontiff himself that it shall be so."

"It is the hope of us all, Michael, and very fervently, too. But let us speak of this afternoon's festivities. If all goes well…" The Spectator and Darien were in close conversation for another half an hour before another tapping alerted them to another visitor.

"Ah, Michael, I wish to present thee to the Princess Stephanie, my wife. She has been most anxious to make thy acquaintance…" It was hard upon the two o'clock hour before the prince and princess left Michael's room; the time between their departure and court, Michael knew, would be one of intense preparation. His presentation this afternoon would rock the entire court to its very foundation.

When the hour struck three that afternoon, there was not a seat to be had in the Royal Hall. King Ballizar and Queen Syrenya entered to a chamber that fair rang with enthusiastic talk of the Spectator and his gift, direct from the Vatican itself. Prince Darien and Princess Stephanie were in their seats, and even young Prince Randall and Princess Lylanya were on hand, each bubbling with the excitement that was surrounding them. As the king and queen took their seats upon the dais, King Ballizar addressed his minister.

"We understand, Sebastian, thou hast a most august personage to present to this court. Pray do so now."

"Emissary from His Holiness, the Pope, direct from the Vatican in Rome, Your Highness. Sire, Your Grace, and members of this Royal Court: we present a most honored and long-awaited guest; we give thee The Spectator." Michael entered exactly on cue, wearing the robes that marked his station as the Pope's envoy, and carrying with him a most impressive-looking implement. Worn slung over his right shoulder was his messenger's satchel, but in his right hand, as he had promised the queen, The Spectator carried his renowned hammer—a weapon that looked far heavier and more unwieldy than this man's handling of it made it seem. Upon his entry, the queen rose, and addressed him.

"Good Sir, thy arrival has been a Godsend to the people of this court. Thine exploits precede thee; it is not only for thy charge from Rome that we welcome thee. Thy deeds are legend, as is the hammer that attends thee. Many a tale has reached our ears of the magick that it is said to hold. May I inquire as to how ye came by it?"

"Your Grace, it is a tale that in itself is a topic of much speculation. But if I may, I will present it to thee; it is not overlong, and one, I am told, that will enthrall thy descendants for quite some time hence."

"We are all agog with anticipation, good Sir. Pray proceed." The Spectator doffed his cap, stepped a few paces closer to the throne, and began to sing in a clear, vibrant baritone.

> Night fell around me and I fell forward in time
> Twisting in search of something to hold until
> I felt myself traveling as if with wings
> Over countryside until, looming before me
> There stood a mansion of stone in grounds
> Immense and full of life.

I sensed more than saw the multitude of
Varied creatures who shared their lives
Within this garden, and I knew
There was accord here.

I entered the palace ghostlike and stood on
The landing of a great staircase; and I looked below
Into a parlor, rich with beauty and containing
But one frail figure.
Her aged hand moved slowly to light each candle,
Holding the taper loosely in her crooked hand,
Her other holding tight to the top of her cloak,
Until the evening ritual was complete, and the room
Was warm and glowing.
She looked at her reflection in the mantle mirror, and
I saw the lines of time, trial, and age that filled her face.
Yet she smiled, and smoothed her hand over the tired flesh,
And there was a glow in the tiny eyes that was not age.
She moved to the sitting bed and sat as if waiting;
And as I sensed another present in the great chamber,
I turned and saw above me on the stairs
A man of Youth and Power.
Yet he saw me not, but smiled down into the parlor
A smile of warmth and love.
She sensed more than saw him, and she turned her
Eyes to meet his, the same loving smile tracing her lips.
He moved slowly, and I descended with him the stairs
That separated them. I stopped so as to view them,
For there was more in these eyes than a mother
For her child, or a son for his bearer.
And as I watched he approached her,
And she released her grasp on the single garment,
Allowing it to fall loosely to the floor about her ankles.
And her form was youthful, no longer held by the lines
That held her face, a face full of tenderness for her lover.
His smile never left his face as he approached her,
And as they embraced, the lines that held her face
Released their grip, retreating back into the years

That were now removed, and as they kissed
Her face, too, became young and beautiful,
His body flowing into hers the youthful vitality
That the years had deprived her, until she stood before us,
The dazzling woman of her youth.
And I realized that I was again The Spectator.

Yet I moved not to depart, for I knew that there was
A reason for my presence, which I knew not.
Their arms entwined and they moved to the bed-chamber.
I followed behind them, slowly, silently, aware that my
Presence to them was not known, when
From the shadows there stepped the figure of jealousy,
Who wielded before them the Hammer of Hatred,
Threatening the man.
The woman again began to age, quickly, rapidly,
Unable to hold what had been hers for so short a time.
The man released her and cowered in fear; and then
I knew the reason for my presence.

I moved between the two men and my presence
Became known to them. A shadow fell across
The face of the attacker, but seeing my form,
He began to laugh, dropping the hammer and
Holding before him his hands.
On each knuckle were bound three tiny metal bands,
And the hands themselves were mammoth, able
By strength to snap me in two, so large were they.
I did not yield.

He moved toward me and I flung myself at him,
Feeling his hands crush me about the waist, yet
I could feel no pain.
Only strength, flowing into me like youth did
Flow into the woman, and I fought with savageness
Unequaled by any man, fought until the man's body
Lay crushed below the open balcony.

> I turned and re-entered the room, finding the hammer
> And flinging it to my shoulder.
> The two were again embracing, and again
> The transformation was complete.
> And again my presence was unknown to them.
> And I knew my task was done, and left them.

For a brief moment, there was an appreciative silence; the Spectator took that moment to bow deeply to the dais, acknowledging the boon granted him in allowing him to tell this, albeit true, self-aggrandizing tale. Before the King could acknowledge this courtesy, the court erupted in ear-splitting applause; the tales that preceded the Spectator to this place were not nearly as impressive as this one brief encounter. It was many a long moment before the din abated enough for the king to be heard.

"Knight of the Vatican, ye bring a stirring and nearly miraculous tale to these old ears. It is, indeed, one we might tell our grandchildren. I trust that the purpose of that hammer is now one unlike it was when ye first laid eyes on it."

"It has taken on a new purpose, Sire; as my hand is guided by the One on high, so too is the power of this mighty weapon. It is now a powerful tool for all that is good and just; I pray often that it will remain so, long after my time upon this earth is done."

"It is a grand and noteworthy tale ye have brought us, Sir," added the queen. "It makes me wonder what news of the couple thou didst defend; hath there been any further news from that source?"

"I fear not, Your Grace. It is a land that I have not revisited; my duties have taken me far and wide, across Europe and beyond, but this land and its inhabitants I have not come across again."

"I am struck by thy description of flight, Sir; is this a sensation thou hast had often?"

"No more than the one time, Your Grace. When it is clear that time is of the essence, which is not often the case, the means by which Our Lord transports me is far quicker than even the means of flight might serve. I can only liken it to a boy playing with his toy soldiers. When it is necessary for me to be transported away, it is somewhat akin to that boy picking up one of his toy soldiers, and putting it down again in a place that, to the soldier itself, is far, far away."

"Hast happened often, that ye must be thus borne away?"

"Nay, Your Grace. Those times when it has proven necessary are few; I can count them on the fingers of this hand. More often that not, my task is one that proves to be of a much longer duration; whenever this is so, speed is not the most important factor to be considered. It is rather that I must glean the problem at hand, and find that course of action which will bring about the best outcome."

"Then by all means, let us return to the charge that brings thee from Rome. We know that Father Benedic sought the Pope's advice on how best to approach the fevers which have, for many a long year now, beset the king. We have been informed that the Pope would not respond to us at all until he had enlisted thy services. For thy help in this grave matter, we are all in thy debt. Pray, tell us; we are all waiting to hear of the news that brings thee to Tabithia."

"Your Grace, thy welcome humbles me. Indeed, I bring tidings from Rome; I come to answer that which has reached the Pope and his counsel, of the many years that King Ballizar has suffered, under a malady that neither thy priests nor thy physicians can name. We have been told of the effects of this malady by medical reports included with the weighty missive sent by thy good Father Benedic. The medical findings of the king's symptoms, and the Father's own detailed descriptions of the suffering of thy king, sent the counsel into the most serious of deliberations. I fear that the word handed down of their findings on thy case is grave, indeed. I cannot find any way to soften the blow, O King: it is the opinion of the counsel that, when Ballizar suffers from these 'attacks,' as Benedic described them, that he is possessed of a demon from Hades."

The reaction from the court was not anything like the reaction Queen Syrenya had expected at this proclamation; for many a moment, there was not a word spoken. To a man, the court was thunderstruck. The queen took it upon herself to snap the people out of their musing.

"Envoy, this is the most grave news ye could bring us. Father Benedic feared that it might be so, but there were so many other possibilities that it seemed far-fetched, indeed. Can there be no mistake in the findings of the counsel?"

"None whatsoever, Your Grace. It was many a long hour necessary to reach this conclusion; but there can be no other. Thy reign, O King, is beset. A demon is the cause."

By this time the court had indeed been snapped out of its stunned silence. Further, upon hearing this news, Father Benedic and his priests had fallen to their knees in fervent prayer. Many a citizen of the court did the same; those who did not, crossed themselves in the hope that this proclamation might be stemmed by one of the Spectator's marvelous remedies. But the hubbub that ensued was one that would not subside; it was necessary for the king himself to bring the court to order.

"Lords and Ladies of this Court, hear the words of thy king. Long has it been that the fears of the Father and his priests were known to us; it was a chance that was always one that must be considered, notwithstanding the unlikely possibility of it actually being so. In the cold light of reason, we must accept these findings as true. It is, as the Pope's counsel has found, the only conclusion that covers all the facts. These fevers, as ye all know, have long baffled the physicians, and the best medical minds of this modern time have been unable to find any cure, indeed any remedy at all, that would stem or even reduce our suffering. We have heard the findings of the counsel, as brought to our ears by this most honored guest, at the behest of the Pontiff himself. Sir," asked the king, again addressing himself to Michael, "we must ask of thee: is there any remedy that the Pope can give for this—we shudder at the word—possession? Pray give us all thy news."

"Sire, I have here a gift that has been given me by the hand of the Pope himself. It is a holy relic, one that has been a part of the history of the Vatican. It is a Shepherd's Cross, one that has been carved from stone. It hangs upon a chain of the purest gold, so that it may hang from thy royal neck to protect thee from this minion of Hades. I offer it to thee now, with the Pope's own blessings; it hath been thrice blessed with the anointing of Holy Water. There can be no stronger talisman than this gift from God, which is offered to thee with the Blessing of the Lord, and the fervent prayers of the Pope and all his Ministers." The Spectator had taken the cross from his shoulder bag as he spoke; he now covered the distance between himself and the dais and, bending to one knee, he offered up this Holiest of gifts. Having bade the king remain where he was, the queen rose and came down to accept it from Michael. She lifted it up high, so that all the room might behold it. It was heavier than it looked, and seemed to shine of the purest white. The cross stood taller than a hand, and was nearly as long from side to side. In the center, spanning the arms in four equal arcs, was a halo, and the cross itself was inscribed with runes that even the queen herself could not interpret. She remounted the dais, stood behind her king, and reverently lowered it over his head, so it now rested against his chest. Father Benedic had long ago prepared a blessing for just such an occasion; once it had been intoned, both the Father and his fellows began a long chant in Latin. Though few could understand it, all stood in reverent silence until it had done. In all the time he had spent at court, Darien could not recall a more somber, nor a more crucial, event as ever taking place. This court was now finally aware: there was indeed evil in their midst.

As Darien had predicted, all thought of any hearing of the people's petitions was banished. Without even being told, with only a beckoning from the priests, the court slowly, almost reverently, filed out of the hall. Having cleared the room, the priests followed suit. In no time, the royal family was alone with the Spectator.

"They did not even consider that this talisman would not be the cure they seek." The queen, who knew better, now began to examine how best to inform the court, once it became obvious, of the necessity of exorcism. She prayed aloud that Father Benedic be allowed his full course of study. If the monster struck before all was properly prepared, she did not want to think what the final result would be.

Despite their knowing, from the very beginning, that the king was indeed possessed, having it all out in the open now was a sobering, indeed terrifying, realization for all the royal family. Alissa could not hold back her tears; indeed, for once, Ariadne joined her. Syrenya, too, was struck by the realization that tears wound their way down her cheeks, as well. She took the arm of her king and the two led the way out of the chamber. Stephanie had long ago left with the children; Darien took each of his aunts by the arm and escorted them, gently, from the hall. None of the family wanted to part after this harrowing afternoon; carefully planned though it had been, it was now an open declaration. It had taken a full quarter-century to reach this point. Now, the final battle between the forces of Good and Evil in Tabithia was at hand.

News of the king's dire situation had cast a pall upon Tabit's Keep. While life did go on, it did so with a sadness, and a dread; while the court did fervently hope that the king's talisman would protect him from further attacks, few had the faith to believe it to be completely true. This was, of course, the understanding of all the family; even before Father Benedic and his clergy were sufficiently versed in the teachings of the volume from

Rome, plans had been made to try to stay any further attacks until the priests declared themselves ready for the beast's appearance. Holy water there had been at the keep even before the Spectator arrived with his own; vials of it were on hand in the king's chamber, and preparations that had been detailed in Father Benedic's text were implemented. The holy water brought from Italy was to be reserved for the exorcism itself, but massive amounts of the purified liquid were prepared by the clergy. Holy water was one of the staples of this rite; it would be a strong impetus to make the demon release its grip on the king. Without revealing their preparations to the court, the clergy set about preparing the king's bedchamber for the coming battle. Candles, crucifixes, and holy images of Christ and the Mother Mary covered every surface. The formidable drapes that covered the king's favorite part of this room, a wide and high latticed window that tapered to a point almost five meters above the floor, were drawn back so that the windows could be opened during the rite. The frigid air of Tabithia's winter would aid in cooling the king. As was instructed by the text, loops of rope were fastened to the king's four bedposts. It would be necessary to immobilize the king once he had been taken. Syrenya and Ballizar spent the days after the Spectator's arrival in her rooms, and it was often that Michael himself joined them there. Not only was he there in his official capacity; both king and queen welcomed him as a distraction. His witty repartee and intriguing tales of adventure were a tonic for them both, and Michael was happy to oblige. Though the king fully understood the necessity of remaining close to his chambers, he chafed at what was almost unbearable waiting. The beast was in no hurry, now that his adversaries were assembled; Syrenya recalled the time that another man had appeared at the keep, one who claimed to be an exorcist. The beast had not appeared at all during the man's stay; only after his departure from the keep and, indeed, from Tabithia itself, did the monster attack again. Syrenya told this to Michael, who commiserated with her and Ballizar in her rooms.

"The beast knows of the preparations we have made to greet his next arrival," explained Michael. "It is another tactic he uses to keep us off-balance. But Father Benedic keeps a sentry here in the hall, and the priests will converge on thy rooms immediately, Sire. Everything that can be done is being done; I am ever hopeful that all our planning will prove triumphant."

"I see that ye keep thy cudgel with thee at all times, Michael. I am grateful that ye both are with us in this—AH! I know not what to call it!" Frustration emphasized Syrenya's words.

"I know what to call it!" quipped the king. "I call it a damned nuisance, that's what I call it. And I can think of a few more choice descriptions, as well."

"'Damned nuisance' is a rather bland description, Sire. I have heard a whole host of other descriptions, and none so polite as that." Michael tried to keep his voice light; this counting of days was wearing on them all. Syrenya, picking up on her new friend's tone, began to chide him unmercifully.

"Michael, thou art staring at me yet again. Honestly, are all men everywhere so impossibly besotted with sex?"

"Thou knowest it to be true, Syrenya. We cannot keep our eyes off a beautiful woman. It is only because all thy court are so used to thee, that it is not a daily occurrence in this keep."

"It is a daily occurrence, Michael. We have simply learned not to be so overt about it. Indeed, Syrenya has been my bride for twenty-three years now, and I still cannot help myself. Fortunately, I may claim the right."

"My liege, please. My blushes."

"Blushes make a beautiful woman more so, Syrenya. And I fear I am smitten; even in the very presence of thy husband, I cannot keep mine eyes off thee."

"Thou art a gallant swain, Michael. As long as men do nought but look, we women have become so vain as to accept it as our due. We would be hurt if we did not note the occasional roving eye." While she bantered thus with the Spectator, Syrenya had her hand in her king's, resting on the table. She suddenly winced, and whirled in Ballizar's direction. His grip had become that of a vice; now his head lolled forward, and in another moment the king's body went rigid. "Michael! The sentry! It's time!"

CHAPTER 20

Exorcism

As it happened, Darien was in conversation with Father Benedic when the hue and cry set up by the sentry alerted them both to what was happening. Darien started immediately for the king's rooms; Father Benedic took only enough time to gather up The Book, as it had now become known, and was then moving at a speed otherwise unknown to a man of his years and condition. So fast was he moving, in fact, that Darien arrived only seconds before the Father himself. What they found was the king, now unclad, lying on his bed, and Syrenya lying atop him. But unlike the situation when Darien first witnessed the possession of his father, Syrenya was attempting to do two things at once: she was trying to help Michael secure the king to the bed with her arms, while she kept whispering in the king's ear. Both Darien and Benedic joined in securing the king, and among the four of them, they were able to get the his legs tied down. This, however, left the man's arms free, and inexplicably he was beating Syrenya with his fists. Darien, without even realizing it, began to fight the king in an attempt to protect his mother; from the sounds those fists were making, Syrenya was in peril. Fortunateley, John Paul and Sebastian arrived next, and the two of them joined in the fray. Darien was thrust aside, and as he fell backwards, he stumbled over something on the floor. He discovered what had been the Shepherd's Cross; now lying discarded on the floor, it was a glowing cinder, which due to extreme heat had been fused to the stone of the floor. He did not take the time to ponder this; he merely noted it for future reference. He retreated from the bed, which was now surrounded by clergy, and took up a posiiton near Michael, who had also been relieved of his duties. Both men were out of breath, but Michael had his hammer in his right hand; he had taken an instant to return to Syrenya's room and recover it. The circle of priests succeeded in securing the king, but he still heaved his body upwards, causing Syrenya to be thrice thrown off the bed. One of the clergy was lighting every candle; another came and handed Darien a crucifix before returning to his place among the men ringing the bed. Once the priest finished lighting candles, he opened all the windows; a blast of winter wind flooded the room. Then he, too, joined the ring of priests, who were now all chanting in unison. Syrenya was again atop the king, trying to occupy Ballizar with the sex act that had succeeded in routing this fiend before, but she was having far less success, apparently, than previously. Darien had expected to hear words similar to what she had spoken when last he found her thus, but instead she was speaking in a tongue that sounded to Darien very much like Latin, which the Father was intoning nearby. He had taken up a place near the head of the bed, on Syrenya's right, and he had a crucifix in one hand and a vial of Holy Water in the other. With each phrase he spoke, he splashed the king with the vial, but only partially succeeded, as Syrenya caught as much of the water as did the king. The room was deafening; in addition to the chanting of the priests and the prayers of Syrenya and Benedic, the roars from the throat of the king were savage and thundering. His face was contorted, and he rained down curses on all around him; Darien had not been apprised of any such action by the king before today.

As had been the case while Darien had fought the rebels, everything seemed to be going in slow motion to him. Despite the windows being open, the room was increasing in temperature; the flames of the candles, those still not blown out by the wind, seemed to slowly dance rather than flicker, and the intoning of the priests was deeper and slower than it had been only a moment before. Darien lit a taper and began relighting the candles; this he did not only because it had been previously discussed; he used the process as a reason to look away from the spectacle of the king. The room was getting hotter; Darien's focus was drawn back to the bed, which was beginning to smolder. He realized that the reason for the increase in temperature was directly due to the state of the king's body, which was a deep scarlet. His face was still contorted, but his eyes glowed with an unholy light, and his grey hair seemed to be smoking. Every single priest was sweating heavily, especially Father Benedic, who had paused briefly to obtain another vial of water. Darien watched the father closely; he was not at all used to seeing the unassuming old gent in such command as he was now. His voice was even and confident; he had learned his lessons well. The water that he was splashing on the king seemed to steam up from Ballizar's body, and Syrenya was fighting valiantly to remain in constant contact with her husband. The temperature continued to rise; Darien realized that he, too, was sweating badly, and a glance at Michael showed his garment drenched as water slid down his face. The noise in the room seemed to rise with the temperature; Darien identified the sound of thunder, and looked out to find a blackened sky cascading sheets of water through fierce wind.

With a scream, Syrenya flung herself from the bed to the floor. She immediately attempted to regain her position atop the king, but she was prevented from doing so by two of the priests. It was evident that the king's body temperature was now far too hot; Syrenya, however, struggled against the two men and succeeded in freeing herself. Still, the point had been made. She did not again try to mount her husband, but stood now opposite the Father, trying vainly to stem the thrashing the king continued to maintain. Throughout all of these events, the chanting and intoning kept up nonstop; Syrenya continued to speak what Darien thought was Latin, in an entirely different phrasing than that of the father, who was now on his third vial of Rome's holy water. But now, when the water struck the body of the king, is seemed to burn him; his reaction was of intense pain. Still, the din within the room continued to mount; Darien barely had time to note the increasing ferocity of the storm when a thunderous crash reached them from within the courtyard. Darien was drawn momentarily to the window; lightning had struck the chapel tower, which was now no more than a gaping hole. Fire seemed to burn brightly from it, despite the fact that it was a stone edifice; the fire seemed far too substantial for the amount of fuel that would have been available to it. The roaring of the fire added to the din, and the noise became almost unbearable.

Father Benedic then did something that seemed highly unorthodox to Darien; prying the king's clenched teeth apart with the crucifix in his left hand, he emptied the vial in his right down the king's throat. This caused a violent reaction within the king; his head flung itself back and a scream to wake the dead poured out of him. Then two things happened simultaneously; the king's body went completely limp, and a ball of fire shot out from somewhere within the king's chest. It rose nearly to the ceiling, where it hovered and began to spin. The ball began to increase in size as it spun faster and faster, and then, without warning, it darted downward, and entered Darien's body. Darien was flung back against the wall and he felt himself consumed by fire; without realizing it he screamed out one word within his mind.

Mother! Immediately he felt her within him. She was screaming at the demon in Latin, but she was also addressing him, as well.

Darien! Fight him! Thou art strong! Demand him begone!

With a will he did not know he possessed, he focused his mind on the creature and began to attack it with every fiber of his being. He fought valiantly, and his mother joined in the fray. After what seemed eons, Darien suddenly felt wet—the result of Michael's having picked up a bowl of holy water and pouring it over the prince. The demon fled, and again assumed the fireball overhead. It again began to spin, but it would not again try to overtake Darien; instead, it attempted to reenter the king. But by this time Syrenya had again covered the king with her body, and now Michael fought his way through the ring of priests, pressed his left hand down upon Syrenya's back, and with his right hand thrust the hammer at the fireball. This dual protection kept the beast at bay and, thwarted from again gaining control of Ballizar, the ball again began to spin, faster and faster, spitting bits of flame and emitting that same deafening roar. Again it dove for the bed, but this time, rebuffed by the hammer, it caromed off at breakneck speed, and caught the Father full in the chest before again arcing across the room. Without pausing, it shattered the window and was gone. Father Benedic was violently thrown clear of the bed, and struck the wall with the sickening sound of breaking bone. He never knew what hit him.

Suddenly, Darien realized two things. Time again regained its normal passage, and the noise in the room dropped dramatically. Syrenya was still lying face-down on top of Ballizar; she was weeping softly. Michael had released her and gone to see to Father Benedic; it was several more seconds before the priests broke their self-induced trancelike state and stopped chanting. It was another minute still before they realized what had happened. The exorcism had been successful; the demon was routed and gone. Darien picked himself up and went to his mother; he rocked her against his chest and began to speak to her softly. After a moment, she reached for him and spoke to him silently.

My son! My darling boy; thou art well!

Yes, Mother, thanks to thee. Is Ballizar…

He is unconscious, but he lives. And he is free; at last he is free from that monster.

Michael moved out of the way of the Father's brethren, who had all come and gathered around his limp form. He went to Syrenya and Darien; his words were soft, but they confirmed the worst. The Father was dead; he had given his very life to save the life of his king. The beast was gone. But it had exacted a terrible revenge upon the keep before it fled.

Outside, the storm continued, but it had abated drastically. The rain was now assisting the men below, who were attempting to douse the fire. Shortly, both the fire and the rain subsided. Within the hour, the sky was blue again. The long night that had covered Tabit's Keep for so long was at an end.

"Good God, Darien! That is a horrowing account, indeed. It makes the hair on my neck stand up. Thou wert thyself possessed?"

"Yes, Sire, but only momentarily. I fought with everything I had, and my mother aided me. And, of course, there was the dousing I received. I cannot fully understand what happened; but I think it was the sum total of all of it that finally routed the beast."

"And a good thing, too! It would have served thee nought if the demon was sent from the king's body, only to possess the prince."

"As I mentioned earlier, it was due principally to the alacrity and demanding presence of Father Benedic. He was masterful. I would not have believed it had I not seen it with mine own eyes. And once outside the king's body, the demon had nowhere else to go. Michael saw to that. His ascertaining exactly what was necessary perhaps saved the king's life. Had the beast reentered him, I could not say if he would have survived."

"And the good Father lost his life as a result of it. I doubt that could have been forseen. I have been privy to a number of accounts of cases of exorcism, but none that claimed the life of the priest."

"It was a blow, Sire, to all the court, to lose such a friend as Father Benedic. He devoted his life to seeing to the king's release, from that very first meeting with my mother until he routed the monster himself. I suspect he was welcomed into heaven with open arms, for such a life as he gave King Ballizar."

"So I should think, Darien, so I should think. And this was 1141, ye said? Tis only 1147, now. How much longer did the king have on this earth?"

"It was only five years from his release to his death, Sire. But Ballizar was already old and gray, even before his final ordeal with his demon. That is not the question that troubles me so. What I find so astonishing, what I cannot explain, is that the queen, robust and healthy as she was, died on the very same night. It was a blow to us all, Sire, but to me, especially."

CHAPTER 21

Denouement

The people of the keep were oblivious to the event that had taken place in the king's chambers. They were intent upon the chapel tower and the resulting fire; it occupied the men of the keep for some time. Such a storm was itself scarcely heard of; its sudden appearance and ferocity was beyond the memory of anyone, even those as advanced in years as the king himself.

Had it not been for the fact that Father Benedic has lost his life, there was a question whether the court would have ever even heard of the exorcism. As far as any of them knew, the king was blessed with a talisman. It would have been far simpler to have left it at that. But Darien and Syrenya felt that the court had to know; it would be easier for them to understand that the priest had lost his life in service to the king, than to try and explain it any other way. The priests had joined together to carry the Father's body from the chamber; they spent the next day preparing to bury their friend and leader. Father Benedic lay in state in the chapel for two days, so the court could pay him proper goodbyes; many would have private rituals to perform, in losing so devoted a shepherd. On the third day, John Paul held a ceremony celebrating the life and ultimate sacrifice of his long-time friend. As were the Father's wishes, he was cremated the next day, and his ashes were scattered through the fields and hills surrounding the keep, for which he'd had a fondness since childhood.

The king, on the other hand, was soon recovered from his own ordeal, and it was never again necessary for Darien and Stephanie to hold court because of his absence. Indeed, the king took to riding in the countryside, Syrenya beside him, to relearn the realm he had found it necessary to neglect while in the throes of his possession. The pair would leave the castle and not return for days; but this was a much happier excuse to let the children rule than the sudden attacks that had been the norm for most of his days. The king was a beloved figure to most of the populace, twenty-five years after the end of First Night; now, with his frequent trips to various locales of his kingdom, he had become even more endeared to his subjects.

The remaining five years of the king's reign were also a happy time for Darien and his family. Young Prince Randall was married at age fifteen to a lovely girl he had chosen from the court. This was the preferred means of betrothal for both his parents; they had frowned on court intrigue as a means of marrying off their only son. The plottings of many a couple at court were thwarted when Randall announced his betrothal to Lady Edna, daughter of Lord and Lady Simon. Syrenya, Stephanie, Darien, and the Simons spent many a happy hour planning the nuptials, and the wedding night, of the young man and his bride; it brought back fond memories of the night Darien and Stephanie had had, after their own nuptials.

Young Lylanya had also entered her teen years, and many a young swain had his eye upon marrying the daughter of the crown prince. It was all Darien could do to keep track of them all, but it gave him a good excuse to sit each one down and have a long chat about the duties of a husband with them. Not just any member of court was to have the hand of his precious daughter; there would be many a crestfallen swain—not to mention his parents—who heard a father's refusal as Lylanya blossomed at court. Stephanie was becoming worried; it would never do to have an old maid for a daughter, she chided her husband, simply because there was not a man at court good enough for her father's approval.

Darien also marveled at the king and queen, as well. He would never have thought it possible, but the two seemed even closer now that the spectre of devils had been dispelled. There was barely a cross word between them, before; now, they seemed to have fallen in love all over again. It did Darien's heart good to see it. Ballizar was so devoted, in fact, that he had barely a stern word for even the most outre requests of his citizenry; court during these blessed days was a happy event, rather than a responsibility merely to be gotten through. But never again was it necessary to try to decifer so entangled a web, either, as had been Syrenya's handling of Alderon and his Maritha. The populace itself seemed happy; those who brought their woes to court seemed to number less and less, as these five years progressed.

It was early in the year 1146 that the first signs of deterioration of the king manifested themselves; shortly after the Feast of the Epiphany, King Ballizar seemed to lose a touch of his old confidence. He would often find himself searching for the proper word he sought, or else he would lose the train of thought at court on occasion. Darien was not the first to notice; it was Ariadne that first mentioned it to Syrenya. The queen, of course, was fully aware of it; she merely did not see the point of discussing so small a thing with the family. But once Darien was made aware, it seemed that it was the case more and more with Ballizar; and that wizened old head of his was white, now; not even the gray it had been merely a few years earlier. Syrenya, in times she was alone with her son, would mark it as unfortunate, but that was the most drastic term she ever gave to the king's condition. By the onset of spring, however, the king required a cane when he walked; and by the beginning of August, it was clear even to his bride that the end was not far removed.

Many a family meeting was held as the king's health declined. It was Darien's notion that the queen should assume the duties of sovereign, but Syrenya was adamant; the crown would pass to the king's son, as tradition demanded. Darien argued that his mother was far more beloved by the people of Tabithia than was he, but Syrenya brushed that aside. It was expected and proper that the king's son assume the crown; she cautioned Darien that it was a duty that should be placed squarely on his shoulders. And the king agreed; Darien had been groomed for just this eventuality since his tenth birthday. It was now his right and his responsibility to accept the crown. Had he not fought Lord Farraman for this very right?

Darien did not voice his reservations to his parents, but he and his princess had many a late night, as Darien discussed his misgivings with his bride. Stephanie did her best to encourage him, however, and it seemed inevitable that, ill-prepared as he felt, he would ascend to the throne upon the king's passing. He had resigned himself to it, in fact. But the mysterious circumstances the night the king did indeed leave this world were so troubling to Darien that, even with the chants of "The king is dead; long live the king" ringing in his ears, he found himself rebelling at the notion of ruling in the absence of both Ballizar and Syrenya.

Alissa and Ariadne, both of whom were approaching their own half-century mark, seemed to have little patience with their new king; and Stephanie, though she did not voice such to her husband while her in-laws lived, was eager to assume her new duties as Queen. But her husband was adamant; the circumstances surrounding the dual deaths of the king and queen were highly suspect. Darien put off any decisions until after his parents' funeral, but the reservations remained. It would make for many a heated discussion behind the doors of the royal chambers; everyone was ready for Darien to rule except Darien. And as far as he was concerned, that's all there was to that.

A week before the celebration of Michaelmas was to be held, the king took to his bed. There was not anyone, from the physicians to the priests, to even Syrenya herself, who believed that he would rise from it again. The queen spent a good bit of time seeing to the events that should take place once the king did, indeed, pass; but she did not spend so much time that she was often from her husband's bedside. And every night, despite the cautions of the doctors, Syrenya shared the king's bed. Dying he may be, but he was not dead yet; and Syrenya wished to be as close to her king as possible. She would do this every night for a solid week. The evening of Michaelmas Eve, she and her king fell asleep in each other's arms. That was exactly the way that the servants found them the next morning.

The shock to the court came, not so much from the king's passing, as from the inexplicable fact that his bride died on exactly the same night. This despite the fact that she had been robust in her efforts to see to the coming coronation of her son as the new king, just the day prior. Ariadne and Alissa were inconsolable; there has been no indication at all that the queen was anywhere near death. How could this have happened? The physicians were all for having an autopsy, but Darien, using an authority he did not feel was his own, denied the request. He was sure that the doctors would not have found any physical reason for the queen's death. He felt that, close as the two were, once Syrenya ascertained that her king had died, she simply willed herself to do the same. He had no reason to believe she was not capable of it; he had learned long ago that any feat that the queen put her mind to, she was quite capable of accomplishing. No, the questions that scarred King Darien's mind were of a far more reaching kind. Was this the intention all along? Did she always plan to ascend along with her beloved? For Darien scarce believed anything else could be true; if there were any two individuals who better deserved entry into the kingdom of Heaven, Darien certainly did not know them. But he felt deserted; now facing the biggest decision of his life—to rule Tabithia as was planned for him, or to abdicate—he was now bereft of the one individual whose counsel he would have most sought. True, she had already made her feelings on this subject plain; and there was a whole host of other people who would proffer the same advice as had she; but Darien could not escape this dreadful feeling of *doubt*. He wryly recalled a passage he had learned, early in the teachings of his aunts, about greatness: "some have greatness thrust upon them." He certainly felt himself firmly ensconced in that category.

All through the elaborate preparations and the stirring pomp and glory of the king and queen's final rites; through the last act, of loading the two side by side upon their pyre, to be floated down the canal to the river, and thus out to sea; before the final torch was lit and their bodies set in flame; before he must say his final goodbyes, he had reached a decision. It was not one that would make any of his family happy, especially Stephanie; but there was no other way. Under any other sircumstances, he would have had a private—mental—conversation with his mother, and together they would have worked out what to do. Now that the option was no longer a possibility, he would have to make these decisions himself. Get all the counsel available, but the decision was yours, my fine friend; yours and yours alone; and it would be so, now and hence. He needed answers, and for the nonce, all he had were questions. Until those answers were found, there would be no King Darien, of Tabithia or any other realm.

Darien sat his family down that evening; the smoke from the king's pyre was still a black smudge in the distance. Before laying out his plan, he made sure that everyone knew this was a temporary arrangement; but his decision was this: Queen Stephanie was to assume the role, with all rights and responsibilities, of the Queen Mother; Randall would assume the role of King Regaent, with his bride as queen; Ariadne and Alissa would remain as counselors for the three. In this manner, rule would be maintained; in fact, rule would differ very little from what it had been before the king's passing. With the aid of his mother, his bride, and his two advisors, and with the abundant support of the priests under John Paul, Randall would have every support he could want. It seemed to Darien that this temporary arrangement would allow him the time he would need to seek out the answers he had to have. He would begin with a pilgrimage to Rome; the counsel of the Pontiff should most certainly be sought. If his answers lay not in Rome—and he suspected they did not—then he would continue his pilgrimage; seek out other kings, other realms; tell his unusual story and see if any other regal mind could make sense of it for him. He would allow himself a year; if, by the end of that time, he did not have what he sought, he would return to Tabithia and abdicate. Only in the event that he could put these myriad queries to rest, would he return to rule as King of Tabithia.

He put these several facts to the family in as calm and reasonable a fashion as he could; nevertheless, when he had finished, Stephanie fled the room in tears. Darien could not have expected less; Stephanie's dream of their sharing the thrones of Ballizar and Syrenya was dashed. And unless he could find some answers of his own, she would never be in a position to rule. So her reaction to this pronouncement was understandable. Alissa and Ariadne were an easier pair to deal with; if it meant postponing the coronation a year, they could handle that. But they expected him back ready to rule. They made no bones about that. His son looked, to him, to be a mass of conflicting emotions. The mantle he was passing to Randall was a heavy one, for all it's being a temporary arrangement; he looked to Darian to feel as unprepared for the job as Darien had felt, himself. Darien felt that maybe it was true of any man who must prepare to rule; that until he got in and felt his way around and got comfortable in his new robes, anxiety was the letter of the day. Still, the court and the country expected a coronation, and a coronation they would receive. Simply not the one they expected.

What with one thing and another, it was yet another week before Darien was able to make his departure from Tabit's Keep. Stephanie, by this time, had accepted Darien's decision, but she was still unhappy about his being gone for an entire year. She spent half an hour in the courtyard with Darien, making sure he knew she loved him, would miss him terribly, and expected him back the soonest he could. Darien loved her more in that half an hour than he had done at any time previously, and that was immeasurable, already. But he had decided to leave only on horseback; a coach was too fine an object for thieves to ignore. A man on horseback was merely a traveler; nothing more. It would be a faster trip to Rome, that way; and he would draw little attention to himself. His missive to the Vatican placed his arrival in Rome at three weeks; if the Pope were unable to see him immediately, Rome would provide plenty of distraction until he could. But Darien did not place much stock in the answers he might receive from the Pontiff; if the priests at the keep were any indication, Darien could already imagine the answer he would get. "The Lord works in mysterious ways," and "it is God's will." Hardly the answers he sought. But there was always the possibility that the Pope would surprise him. Darien promised himself he would not prejudge the Pope's words before they were even spoken.

The trip south, though a long and arduous one, was marked more by the continuously increasing temperature than it was by anything else. Travel from the northern reaches of the globe down to the equator tended to be such. To Darien, who had spent his life in temperatures more suited to a Swede than a Roman, felt at times he was wading through a Turkish bath. The humidity in the Mediterranian was almost more than a man could bear. Despite the fact that Darien was able to reach Rome a day earlier than he was expected gave Darien the chance to bathe, change, and rest. Even so, Rome was sticky this time of year, and though he traveled by coach to Vatican City, rather than by horse or on foot, he still arrived bathed in sweat. While he felt this was not any way to meet the Pope, there was no reason to believe that the Pontiff was not himself undermined by the weather. The man he met upon entry knew his name; he immediately sent a boy running with the news of his arrival. He then looked at Darien and, scowling down at the parchment before him, asked hesitantly if there were not others in Darien's company.

"And, uh, who else might be joining Your Highness?"

"No one, Sir. I am quite alone."

The attendant brightened at this, and quickly shuffled a sheaf of papers on his desk.

"That is very good indeed, Your Highness, though I must say that it is a rarity that a visiting monarch arrives without even one manservant. We have in the past found it necessary to entertain as much as an entire contingent of associates during a royal visit."

"I should imagine," replied Darien, and smiled. "I should think I just cleared up several people's dockets for this afternoon."

"You have indeed, Sire, you have indeed. May I offer you refreshment while you wait?"

"If you can supply anything cool to drink, it would be much appreciated."

"Of course, Sire. If you would care to retire to the sitting room, I shall see to it."

The "sitting room" the attendent referred to would have made a fine substitute for the Throne Room back at the keep. It was amazingly long and nearly two stories high; windows faced an interior court and sunlight flooded the room, making it warmer than Darien had hoped. It was filled with sculpture and paintings, including portraits of many of the Pontiffs who had held the seat prior to the present Pope, Eugene III. As Darien understood it, this pope was not the one who had so spectacularly come to their aid five years ago; in fact, yet a third Pope had ruled between this one and Pope Celestine II, who had sent the Spectator to Tabithia.

Darien knew that the Vatican was always a busy place; nevertheless, he did not expect to wait for over an hour before he was met by a man in a scarlet robe, who beckoned graciously and led Darien down a long and exquisitely-appointed hall. Though the trip was of several minutes, his guide never spoke, but merely kept the same vacuous smile upon his lips. Finally, he came to a door, pulled it open, and bowed Darien in. The door shut smartly behind him, and Darien found himself in another richly-appointed but, this time, much smaller room. Rising from a mammoth desk, another scarlet-clad figure approached him, in tandem with a second gentleman who merely smiled at him. Darien was immediately aware of the man's purpose; as soon as the Cardinal began to speak, this gentleman spoke to Darien in Norwegian. This was to be Darien's interpreter while he was here.

"Welcome to the Vatican, Your Highness. We are honored by your visit."

"I am honored that you had the foresight to provide me with an interpreter, but it is quite unnecessary. I speak fluent Italian."

"Then that is the second surprise you have brought us, Your Highness. The fact that you arrived without staff of any kind is frankly astonishing." The Cardinal spoke softly and briefly to the interprester, who bowed and left.

"So I understand. But my audience with the Pope is one that may contain many troubling aspects, and having a platoon of support personnel would simply complicate the issue."

"Ah, a man of military stripe, I see. But I fear I must disappoint thee, Your Highness. The Pope is not going to be able to meet with thee this day." Darien frowned.

"I see. Was three weeks not enough notice, then?"

"Three months, alas, would not have been enough. There are those who have waited as much as a year to have an audience with the Pope. But let me finish. I must tell thee that Pope Eugene has only been Pope for a few months. And the Pope he succeeded was only here himself less than two years. Your missive referenced the passing of thy father, King Ballizar. We remember, very clearly, the first time that name crossed our path, and why. The exorcism that freed thy father, and cost us the life of one of our own, as well, is not soon forgotten. I have been working in the Vatican for over two decades, and I was one of the cardinals who sat on the counsel that sent the Spectator to thy keep. Further, when Michael returned here from Tabithia, it was I who took from him the full report of what took place there. So I am hoping that, in lieu of the Pope himself, I might be of assistance to you."

Darien relaxed. This thin Italian cleric might be just what he needed, indeed. The Pope would be constrained by politics and reticence. This Cardinal, he hoped, might not be so constrained.

"I am grateful, Your Eminence, for thy honesty and thy memory. It is possible that thou may be the better man to speak with, under the circumstances. Michael made a whole host of friends before he left us, all of the Royal Family included. Did he tell thee that it was his quick thinking that may have saved me from being possessed that night?" It was the Cardinal's turn to frown.

"He, ah, failed to mention it."

"As I thought he might. Michael intimated to me that his report to the Pope would center on Father Benedic's role in the exorcism, both his success, and his demise. He told me that any mention of himself or his hammer would not make it into the final record, in any case. But I should be pleased to tell thee all about it, should ye wish."

The meeting with Cardinal Vincenzio lasted more than two hours. Darien thought he might have spoken far too long, but Vincenzio reassured him.

"Nay, Your Highness, that is not what troubles me. It is that the tale of thy most unique queen strikes me as one similar to other tales that have been brought to our attention. In every case, the person who figures prominently in these tales is possessed of powers only dreamt of by us mere mortals. Her ability to communicate with thee silently, her ability to detect the presence of a metaphysical being, and thy final report of her passing, all qualify her as being like unto the individuals who weild such powers. I feel I would be remiss if I did not tell thee of these folk; for though we cannot openly acknowledge them, nonetheless we are aware of their existence. There are simply too many of these tales extant to be ignored.

"If I am correct, and she is indeed one of these individuals, I can only tell thee that we feel she was sent to thy country by God Himself. Despite the holy stance we maintain as to miracles, please understand: anyone who brings us tale of a miracle is closely and thoroughly vetted. Any acknowledgement of an actual miracle is made only if we can prove to ourselves that the tale is not a hoax. But, that being said, tales such as I describe, which cover years, or even decades, as does thine, rather than single events, convince us that such individuals do indeed exist. They are as much a part of the Heavenly Host as the angels."

"And it is thy belief that Syrenya might well be one of these individuals?"

"I cannot state it as fact, Your Highness, but she certainly fits the mold."

"And if she were one of these beings, that would certainly go a long way in explaining her sudden and unexpected demise on the very night we lost the king."

"And as to that, Your Highness, let me say this. If indeed she had been sent to save thy king, and she was, as thou hast said, able to accomplish such, then she might very well feel that her final act must be to carry his soul back to God, from whence it came."

Darien rose, and Cardinal Vincenzio rose with him.

"As I said before, Your Eminence, thou hast given me much to ponder. I thank thee, most humbly, for agreeing to meet with me."

"It is the reason we are here, Your Highness. I hope I have been able to be of help."

The same bespectacled, ever-smiling and ever-silent clergyman that brought Darien to this office now led him back out again. There was a carriage waiting for him when he made it to the street. It carried him back to his lodgings, where he packed his bags and reclaimed his horse. Rome had revealed all the secrets it had to tell, and he was beyond the gates and away before nightfall.

CHAPTER 22

In King Arthur's Court

"I traveled north out of Italy into Austria, west into Switzerland and France, then I doubled back into Germany, and finally up into Denmark. I was received by some of the greatest minds in Europe, but none could offer me any more information, nor even an approximation, of what I had witnessed or why. When I reached Copenhagen, I had to make a decision; I was low on funds and very close to home. I must decide, then, to continue my quest or go back into Tabithia. I sold my horse and took passage on a ship bound for Britain. I have walked from the coast to thy castle, Sire, and now I have laid all my tale before thee. I now ask thee, most humbly, is there anything thou canst glean from what I have told thee, as to why I am burdened with these questions?"

"Darien, there are a number of things I can tell thee, but I fear none of it will be of much aid to thee. First, I tend to agree with that Cardinal that ye spoke with in Rome. It is the only explanation that even begins to cover all thy facts. Second, thy kingdom is in thy son's hands, and I tell thee truly, that gives me pause. Finally, thy tale is one I shall ponder for many a day, and not soon forget. We have spent the day at it, and I fear we are no further toward any answers for thee than we were at dawn. I am sorry, Darien, but I am afraid I must offer thee the same answer ye received in every other country. Thy tale presents a host of questions, but offers no answers for any of them. At least, I fear, not to me."

"Then I have one further request of thee, Sire. When I was told, by thy Lady in the Lake, to speak with thee, she added yet another aspect which we have not touched upon. She told me that, if indeed thou couldst not offer any aid, I was to ask to speak with the mage."

"The mage? What, Merlin? Of course! If there is any man in this world who will have insight into this conundrum, it is he! I should have thought of this myself; dashed that I did not! Let us go and seek him out this instant!"

Getting to Merlin was no small feat; it meant journeying out of the castle, into the surrounding wood, and a trip into the darkening night. When, finally, they arrived at their desination, Merlin was sitting upon the stoop of his dwelling, lantern by his side, and a finger on a passage in a weighty volume. When Arthur hailed him, he looked up sharply.

"Ah, Darius! Thou art here at last. We have been waiting for thee!"

"Now, wait a minute, Merlin, hold hard. Knowest this man?"

"Indeed I do, Arthur, indeed I do! Oh, we have not yet been introduced, but I have heard many a glowing report of thine exploits. I would have been happier if thou hadst skipped Germany, Darius, and come straight here from France. The Kizer was a waste of time. It would have saved thee well over a fortnight. But, tut, thou art here now. That is what matters."

"I am afraid thou hast mistaken me, good Sir. My name is Darien."

"Darien is the name given thee by Syrenya, Darius. It was necessary, my boy. But Darius thou wert born, and Darius ye shall be, hence. King Darius of Tabithia! It hath a noble ring, eh, Arthur?"

"Merlin, if my head is spinning with all thy spoutings, then poor Darien here must be…"

"Nay, Arthur, I tell thee: this man's name is Darius. Has been, since his mother gave him life. I was sorry to hear of Ballizar's passing, m'boy. He was a good man, and beset on many sides. I hope thy reign goes much more smoothly than did Ballizar's, Arthur. He will be remembered."

"Merlin, I have spent the day in conference with our guest, only to find out that thou art as familiar with his tale as I. Pray put the man's fears to rest, and explain thyself."

"Arthur, thou dost know, for I have told thee often enow, that I am privy to sources of information that thou, and most everyone else, are not. Is this not so?"

"Of course it is, Merlin, but in the name of all that's holy…"

"Well, that doth enter into it, does it not, Arthur? Darius, pray walk a bit in the direction of that firepit, yonder. There is someone who is waiting to speak with thee." Darien, who could make neither head nor tale of anything the mage was saying, did as he was told, if only to clear his head. But a moment later, he was stunned to hear a familiar voice.

My son, thou art here. It is well! We have so much to discuss.

Mother! Praise be! I thought thou wert gone from this earth, for good and all.

Alas, my son, tis true. But I could not go without a long farewell; and, too, I have the answers ye seek. But it were necessary that ye come to this place, before I could explain. Now that ye have arrived, at long last, I can explain all those things I have found ye questioning till now. Well, speak, my son. Art thou not pleased to hear my voice?

Beyond measure, Mother! But where art thou? Why can I not see thy face?

Well, my only son, thou hast rightly ascertained that I am in heaven. At least, that is the name given this place by all the many inhabitants of that planet thou dost stand upon.

Thou art not in heaven?

Yes and no, my son. I have returned to the place from whence I came, and 'heaven' is the best description I can give that thou wouldst understand. But, my son, 'heaven' is a description that has many discrepancies from the actual truth of where I am. Let me try to explain. Dost remember thy lessons from Ariadne about geometry?

Of course.

Good. The earthy conception of heaven is a place amongst the stars, where God and angels dwell and where all good souls return. But that is incredibly inaccurate. This place is not even remotely close to earth. Recall the discussion of various planes, and how it was not necessary that two distinct items exist on the same plane?

I do, Mother. So where thou art is on a different plane from the cosmos?

Exactly, my son. That is why thou cannot bring up my face; we here are not beings like unto human beings. Here, our 'bodies' are made up of light.

Light? I do not understand.

We are creatures of energy here, my son. We do not have corporeal shape.

That is… incredible, Mother. But let me understand. Thou art with God there, art thou not?

Yes. Of course.

Then thou art an angel?

Nay, Darien. The angels are a very special form of life, the closest there is to God himself. I am not of that ilk. Remember what Cardinal Vincenzio told thee about his belief that I was indeed sent by God?

Certainly.

I firmly doubt that he himself believes what he told thee, my son, but he is essentially correct. Not that he would ever tell thee such. I believe he told thee that tale in order to have anything to tell thee at all. I am an emissary from God. I am a part of a group called the Peacemakers. Dost remember how we told thee of my explanation to thy aunts of the Peacemakers? In order to restore peace to Tabithia, I was sent to Ballizar. But it was not until I discovered the true cause of First Night that I realized just how long I might be at my task. God knew; but until I came face to face with that demon, I did not.

Mother, I am all agog at thy words. My mind swims. Can we not speak face-to-face? I needs must see thy face. May I not?

Of course, my son. Syrenya's face and form swam into Darien's view. It was a welcome sight, indeed.

Mother, I am so very heartened to find thee! But I am full of questions! Why doth this Merlin call me Darius? Surely I have been called Darien all my days.

Not quite all, my son. Before ye came to us, thou wert Darius. Think back, my son. Dost thou remember the story Alissa told thee, of Lady Berneice and her son Darius? Remember how he brought me my tiara?

Of course I do, Mother. Allissa made sure I would not forget.

With good reason, my son. But before we contunue, I have a gift for thee.

Darien was suddenly flooded with memories that he had never had before, of a time when he was very young, in the court at Tabit's Keep. His mother and father were with him constantly, and their love was staggeringly wonderful. He then felt a desperate loss at his father's death in the field of battle; and shortly thereafter, at his mother's passing after a long illness. He suffered a savage feeling of abandonment, and recalled being shunted about in the court's nursery, where he felt vasty unloved. These feelings passed, but his memories remained. One crystal clear image was of his mother as she watched him march determinedly across the Throne Room floor, carrying a velvet pillow and a diamond tiara. Then of how his next few hours were spent, in the lap of the Queen, as people came and went. The queen spoke softly to him, telling him all that was happening around them. He felt a great love from her, for both him and his mother. Next, his mother's funeral stung his eyes. His next memory was that of sitting opposite Alissa, who winked at him, and the decision that the Queen and her ladies would be his teachers from that point on.

By this time he answered to Darien. But it was now clear to him that this was not his given name.

My son, thou hast necessarily suffered under a need for us to teach thee all of the story thou hast so nobly relayed to King Arthur. But for us to do so, we needed thy mind to be a clean slate. So thine own memories, we saved for thee; now I am pleased to be able to restore them to thee. Thou art Darius Sauvage, son of Nicholas and Berneice Sauvage. Thy father was a Lord, a Colonel in Ballizar's army, and a brilliant tactician. Remember I told thee thou wert a warrior born, my son? It is his brilliant mind thou dost possess. It is that mind that did so often bring so learned a counsel, when it was sorely needed. We have, Ballizar and I, been most grateful for all that ye have done for us. But I regret having to steal these memories from thee, Darius. I am greatly relieved to be able to restore them to thee.

'Darius' still sounds strange to me, coming as it does from thy lips, Mother. But, indeed, I do remember. I remember all, as clear as if all these events had only just happened.

And thou shalt continue to remember, Darius, as thou shalt reign in Tabithia. Knowest now these several answers to thy questions? Canst recall them as I have given them to thee?

Yes, Mother, yes! Clearly and well. Thou hast lifted a great weight from my mind! I see it all with crystal clarity. Oh, Mother, this is such a gift! Now I may return to Stephanie and rule as thou didst mean for me to rule.

And not a minute to lose, Darius. The kingdom is in peril. Sweden doth pressure poor Randall with annexation; if they do not receive an answer from Tabithia soon, they intend invasion. Thy wife needs thee sorely, Darius. Ye must leave for the castle tonight.

Mother? Wilt thou go now? Am I to lose thee again so soon?

Nay, Darius. Thou wilt see me again, and soon. At least, soon as we here tell time. In fact, thy reign should be a long and illustrious one, King Darius of Tabithia. Songs shall be sung of thy gallantry, thy wisdom, and thy valor in the field. And when it is time for thee to join me here, and Ballizar and Benedic, I shall tell thee many another tale, and thou wilt have much good work to do. So hie thee home, King Darius. And dream of our future reunion.

Goodbye, Mother! Thank thee for all thou hast done for me. I will carry thy words in my heart always.

Goodbye, my darling son. Be well. Syrenya's image shimmered and disappeared. Darien stood one moment longer, to cement their goodbyes. The he turned and swiftly covered the distance between him and his hosts.

"Merlin, would thou hadst whispered in mine ear those many weeks ago, and I would have been here sooner! King Arthur, ye have my devoted thanks! Thou hast brought to me all the answers that I sought. Darius is indeed my name, and my heritage, as ye didst think it so. But, Sire, I have received word from home, and I must hie myself away, posthaste! May I ask of thee the boon of a horse?"

"Darius, my boy, we have been waiting for thee for days. All is ready for thee," inserted Merlin, before Arthur could speak. "We have a carriage waiting for thee, and a boat waits at the coast to take thee over into France. A horse waits for thee there. It would never do to set thee upon thy journey home with anything less, after thou hast traveled so long and hard to reach us. Canst thou make it back to the castle by yon path, O King? They await thy return, with food and drink to attend thee. Go, and be well. I needs must keep Arthur here with me for the nonce."

"Merlin, my eternal gratitude! O king, I must fly! Fare thee well, and peace rule thy reign!"

"And thine, King Darius. Godspeed!" He spoke these words to his new friend's back. Darius was away and gone a moment later.

"Well, Arthur, we have done well today. Word shall reach our ears often of our new friend, though our paths will not cross again. Now, my young friend, thou art full of questions. Speak, and I will tell thee all."

EPILOGUE

Merlin and Arthur

"Merlin, what just happened here? One minute I think I can help my new friend Darien, and the next he is not Darien at all. What the duece is going on?"

"Arthur, Darius—thy friend, Darien—is the true and rightful king of Tabithia. Far earlier than Syrenya appeared at Tabit's Keep, shortly after Nicholas's death in a skirmish over Tabithia's borders, King Ballizar spoke at length with Nicholas's widow, Berneice. Ballizar had been named godfather to young Darius, at his birth. Now, with Nicholas gone, with his godson in need of care, and with no wife of his own, Ballizar arranged for Darius to be looked after, even after Ballizar was gone. How was he to do this? Ballizar hoped to accomplish two things together. He had no heir; Darius had no father. The king solved both problems with a stroke. He made Darius his sole heir, provided he did not at some future point produce an heir of his own. This act was one of amazing prescience; for even after his possession and the coming of Syrenya, Darius—who had now become known as Darien—would still ascend to the throne at Ballizar's passing.

This is why Ballizar found it unnecessary to adopt Darien when Syrenya wished him to do so. Darien was already the king's heir."

"Merlin, I am astonished! How came ye by this knowledge? And further, what was happening while Darien stared off into space, there by the firepit? He seemed transfixed."

"Arthur, I sometimes despair of your retaining anything I tell thee. Have I not explained that everything on earth is connected?"

"Of course. But how…?"

"Syrenya contacted me long before Darius—Darien—arrived at our doors, Arthur. She did so because everything is connected. Just now, while Darien seemed so transfixed, it was because he was communing with the dead. His dead mother, to be exact."

"He was speaking with Syrenya?"

"Yes! Arthur, thou hast finally caught up. Syrenya told me everything, long before Darien arrived. It was necessary that he come here, because he had a message to bring thee. One that is even more important than the tale he spent all of this day relaying to thee. So those doubts that plagued Darien were the impetus to draw him here."

"And what was this message? Darien conveyed to me no message."

"Well, he did and he didn't. He told thee the circumstances; but the conclusion is one I see I shall have to impress upon thee. Think back, now. Remember Darien explaining how Lady Sarah held off the Rebels of Pine? How Gerhard was kidnapped and held as the future king of Tabithia?"

"I do."

"Alright. Now, remember, too, how we have discussed alternate histories? That infinite possibilites stretch both ahead of, and behind, this moment in time, in order to account for individual decisions and alternatives?"

"Of course; thou hast stressed it often enough. But I fail to see the connection between the two."

"Of course ye do. Let us return to Pine, then. Sarah, along with Darien and the King's Knights, disarmed that rascal Zander and disbanded the mob that accompanied him. Recall?"

Arthur sighed. Would he never be able to dispel Merlin's penchant for speaking to him like he was a boy? "Yes, Merlin, I recall."

"Good. Now, I am going to explain to thee one of those alternative histories. It begins as we know history does not, with Gerhard—not Darius—being ascendant after the death of Ballizar. Now, such an event would never have taken place had not Syrenya done exactly what she did. Here is why. Syrenya sent Darien out to find Gerhard. Had she not done so, and had he not been successful, these two factions—those pro-Queen Syrenya and those anti-Queen Syrenya—would eventually do battle. In the history I wish to relate to thee, the Anti-Syrenya forces are victorious. Gerhard is the new King of Tabithia. This is the fact I wish to stress to thee, for it is the beginning of events that will effect places far from Tabithia's shores. In this history, Zander becomes Gerhard's chief advisor, specifically his Commander of the Army. Both Gerhard and Zander are ambitious men, Arthur. Tabithia is soon found to be far too small for either of them. They decide it is time that Tabithia have a larger stake in the world. They begin with lands to the north, in Norway. As they are successful, their army grows, and their appetites grow with it. Soon they wish for all of Scandinavia. And once they have that, they wish for more still. The armies of Scandinavia, under the command of this Zander fellow, begin a march south. The Frozen Horde—which is what they become known as—are frightfully successful, and they begin a campaign that will soon take over most of Europe. Finally, Zander and his king set eyes on Britain. Their ships cross the channel, and they are soon at the castle gates of a new and inexperienced king known as Arthur. Art thou with me still?"

"Yes, Merlin, I am with thee. This Frozen Horde has come to our gates. I assume we do battle?"

"Correct. And thou art in the field, Arthur. This Zander, who now leads this gigantic army, and thee, Arthur, fight a battle to the death. And I fear it does not end well. In a hand-to-hand fight between Zander and thyself, Arthur, Zander proves victorious. Thy rule, alas, ends before it ever gets truly started."

"I see. And when is all this to have taken place?"

"It has already taken place, Arthur. In that reality, thou art no more."

"Alright, Merlin. Thou hast my full attention. Let me understand something. Because Darien and his company are successful in disbanding the rebels on that road outside, what, Pine, was it? Because they defeat Zander there in Pine, then Zander and his Horde do not rule Tabithia."

"Yes, Arthur. Thou hast grasped the idea splendidly."

"So, the only reason I am standing here today is because of a little skirmish in a Scandinavian country, half a world away?"

"That is the way of it, Arthur. Because the Rebels of Pine were disbanded before ever they could muster enough force to win the crown away from Ballizar, thou art still, and will long be, King of Britain." King Arthur seemed to focus on a point somewhere near the horizon for a long, silent moment. Then he sat down with a thud. His brow wrinkled, the corners of his mouth drooped, and he stared at Merlin in disbelief.

"Darien told me he brought this tale here for my edification. I doubt he understood just how exactly right he was."

"Indeed, Arthur. So, Darien hath played an important role in the rule of King Arthur of Britain. And King Arthur hath played an important role in the rule of King Darius of Tabithia. The two of thee will not meet again, Arthur, but thy fates are inextricably linked. Always remember. Everything—*everything*—is connected."

Editor's Notes

When I discovereded the original manuscript in the home of a friend of mine overseas, it was in a terrible condition. The entirety of the tale had been tied with a cord, wrapped in something akin to burlap, and then stored. The parcel was discovered in the basement of a home in Göteborg, which is in Southern Sweden on the southwest coast. This locale would have been within the boundaries of Tabithia, if indeed the country ever did exist. Exactly where the parcel spent its time prior to its storage in Göteborg is anyone's guess.

The title on the original manuscript was simply "An Arthurian Legend." There was no mention of either this being a *tangential* legend to that of Arthur, nor was there any mention of a Naked Queen in the title. These are my additions alone.

Attempts to authenticate this manuscript have met with mixed results, at best. The language is indeed Swedish, although it is an early version of the language that was prevelent from around 1200-1600 A.D. Analysis of the paper and ink suggest that it is paper that was used in Sweden around the year 1500. The ink is a permanent concoction of dyes from plants mixed with common soot as a binder.

My first question was, "why Arthur?" This particular tale, with very little work at all, would stand alone without any mention of the British king whatsoever. One may assume that the author included Arthur in the original text possibly as a means of widening his audience. Or, possibly, surrounding the central text with a dialogue between his main character and King Arthur is a way of broadening the implications of his work, as laid down by Merlin in the epilogue, and the final sentence of the text, which literally translates as "everything connects."

My best guess as to the actual location of Tabithia is as the Southern tip of Sweden. This conclusion is drawn from the location of Crevice and its bridge to Norway; the location of the huge lake in the River Quadrant, which very much resembles the current "Marlestad," and the ease with which, it is often noted, one might have passed from Tabithia directly into Sweden. The one thing that gives me pause about such a locale is the suggestion that the Tabithian language was a derivative of Norwegian, rather than Swedish. The one concrete reference to Tabithia being part of modern Sweden, and its having been annexed by Sweden, is the statement by Darien to Arthur that he was very close to home while in Denmark. A short boat trip from anywhere along Denmark's eastern shores would have taken him to Tabithia.

Historically, there are literally thousands of references to a King Darius, the first dating back to 550 B.C. Included here is what I believe to be the best locatable image of King Darius of Tabithia. King Darius ruled an uncommonly long time for a king in the 1100's. Already in his thirties when he ascends the throne in 1147, Darius reigned in Tabithia for forty-three years. His son Randall would have been into his fifties by the time his father died.

King Randall was by no means his father. All of those individuals who impacted King Darius's reign, from his father and mother to his wife and his 'aunts,' were long since dead. Randall would have his own ministers, advisers, and counsel. None of them, apparently, were any match for Sweden's appetites. Sweden succeeded in forcing Tabithia into annexation a mere dozen years into Randall's reign, in 1202. By agreement, absorbtion was total. Randall's rule ended on September 11, 1202.

Historically, Sweden was very much in the business of Scandinavian unification during the time period from 1400-1600. In fact, Sweden was able to bring Norway, Sweden, and Denmark together under a single crown during that time. In order to do this, it would first have been necessary to "handle" such small fiefdoms as Tabithia before any of this could have been brought about. When Syrenya intimates to Darius, in the final chapter, that Tabithia is threatened by just such a move from Sweden, this tends to lend credence to the actual location of Tabithia as being inside Sweden's current borders.

As to any reference of Tabithia in the history books, there simply isn't one, at least not by any reference I have been able to find. It is entirely possible that the author simply created Tabithia as a place to tell his legend, making it as "real," and just as "unreal," as Camelot.

It would be interesting to examine some of the lower extremities of Sweden with an eye toward locating any possible artifacts of Tabithian culture. There are many ruins of castles dotting the southern Swedish landscape, and one of these might well be Tabit's Keep. It was located near a mill, which would require a water source, and possibly yeild up some ancient machine parts. There is also the existence of the canal, presumably built from the western river to the keep as a means of supplying water for the moat and, depending on the quality that could be maintained, a fresh water source. If a castle located in the same vicinity of Sweden as then-Tabithia's Coastal (southeast) Quadrant could be examined, a couple of quick, readily-ascertained signs exist as a means of identification. The high, wide window that was located in the royal quarters, looking out over the keep itself, is one. The other is that very distinctive relic that fused itself to the chamber floor: a stone Shepherd's Cross. Either of these discoveries in a still-standing castle ruin would go a long way toward identifying a concrete structure that would verify the country's existence.

Alan R. Hall
Chapel Hill
July 30, 2018

CPSIA information can be obtained
at www.ICGtesting.com
Printed in the USA
FSHW020753190719
60140FS